"THE ONLY THING WE
HAVE TO FEAR IS FEAR
ITSELF" FDR'S FIRST
INAUGURAL ADDRESS

FEAR ITSELF

JAY FITZPATRICK

To my wife Patricia, my daughter Kelly and to all those who survived Vietnam. One way or the other.

Disclaimer:
The characters and events in this book are factious. Any similarity to real persons, living or dead, is coincidental and not intended by the author.

CHAPTER 1

MANHATTAN

On Monday November 10th., six 14-foot U-Haul and Budget rental trucks rolled into Manhattan from Connecticut, Long Island, Staten Island and New Jersey. Entering Manhattan through three tunnels – the Midtown, Holland and Lincoln – and across three bridges – the George Washington, Tri Borough and the Brooklyn. Six trucks, six different means of ingress. They hoped that three would make it through unsearched. Even if they were searched, not to worry, all were empty, and the drivers were all legitimate drivers who got the well-paying driving gigs from Craigslist. Each driver was given cash and told to rent a truck locally and drive it to a designated location in Manhattan. There they would be met, loaded and sent on their way to their delivery location, near to where they rented the trucks thus saving a drop off charge. No loading, just driving, and for this they were paid extremely well – half up front and the balance when they arrived in Manhattan.

Three of the trucks – designated for the West Side, Soho and Midtown – were randomly stopped by Port Authority cops, searched, and given the green light to proceed. When they arrived at their destinations, they were loaded with some furniture, the drivers were paid and sent back to from whence they came, to deliver the goods and return the trucks. These three trucks would be written off as "the cost of doing business." Of the three unsearched trucks, one headed for the Upper East Side, one to Harlem, and one for Lower Manhattan.

1

The drivers of these trucks were amazed and pleased to see that red cones were placed in the street, in front of their pick-up locations, and that someone was actually there to remove the cones and help them park.

Tim Baker, the driver of the Upper East Side truck, got out and was cordially met by a young man wearing a Yankees cap who introduced himself as Aaron. Aaron gave Tim his balance in cash plus twenty bucks for lunch. It seemed that the building had approved two apartment moves on the same day and our furniture was held up but would be down soon. Tim thought Aaron polite and in a hard spot so agreed to have lunch, but as Tim was walking away, Aaron asked another favor. Could Tim, for another twenty, help him move a couple of furniture pieces, onto the truck, that did manage to get down? A small desk and chair. Tim agreed, and he and Aaron got the desk loaded. While Tim went back for the chair, Aaron grabbed a tool bag and shopping cart full of moving blankets.

With both men, chair, desk and tool bag all inside the truck Aaron tossed the additional twenty on the desk. When Tim turned to reach for it, Aaron reached inside his tool bag and came out with a white rag, grabbed Tim from behind, and held the rag tightly to Tim's face. Tim was completely taken off guard and although he tried to react, Aaron, a much younger and stronger man prevailed. Tim went limp in a matter of seconds as the chloroform soaked rag produced a head rush, giddiness and eventually unconsciousness. Aaron caught him and set him in the chair. He would be out for about thirty minutes, more than enough time for Aaron to set up the truck control office. First he closed the truck door then went to work bolting the metal desk to the truck deck. With that complete he pushed the chair, with Tim in it, over to the desk and bolted the chair to the deck and duck taped Tim's body and feet securely to the chair legs and his forearms to the chair arms so Tim's hands rested on the desk. Although Tim's head was dropped, it appeared as though he was asleep at his desk.

Aaron exited the truck and proceeded to gather, then load a bunch of the boxed and equipment. When he had three 50-gallon barrels, coils, wooden crates, batteries, computer, cell phones, clocks and assorted pipes, wires and timers loaded, unboxed and staged, it resembled a Rube Goldberg version of a Kentucky still. One barrel contained a small amount of fuel oil and diesel fuel;

the other two contained lawn mulch, topped off with ammonium nitrate fertilizer, all readily available from most hardware and garden stores in New Jersey and Long Island. Just one small bag of ammonium nitrate fertilizer, ANF, was purchased, as not to draw attention. Aaron then lined the truck bed, roof and deck with the lead blankets from the shopping cart. He set up the pipes, coils and wires, that went this way and that and connected the batteries to the timer, the timer to the fuse, the fuse to the shock tube and the shock tube to the barrels. Small amounts of Cesium 137, a radioactive material used in hospitals to treat cancer patients, was also present. It looked like a real ammonium nitrate/fuel oil bomb – an ANFO bomb. But with the Cesium 137, it smelled like a dirty bomb. There was a live, though sedated, person at a desk with his computer on. The illusion was complete. Aaron set up a procedural sedative IV, containing Midazolam, to keep Tim awake but in a fog. Aaron then turned everything on, exited, and locked the truck bed and cab. But at the end of the day it was all smoke and mirrors and would never explode. That was the point. They had two other trucks in Manhattan, five in Los Angeles, and three in Chicago. The whole operation had cost under $15,000 and raised no suspicion. The whole production went undetected. They long ago realized they could not bring nuclear weapons into the United States or try to build them here. The materials necessary were prohibitive and would arouse the suspicion of the FBI, CIA and Homeland Security. Flying a commercial plane into a building again just wasn't going to happen. This was about them becoming more creative but for less. What they proposed was not destroying the cities but scaring the cities to death. And that is exactly what was about to happen.

CHAPTER 2

MANHATTAN

They were the American Muslim Brotherhood and Aaron was really Amid Al-Adel, aka Aaron Adel, a 25-year-old leader of Cell 13 and a U.S. citizen. Amid's area of operation, his AO, was the Upper East Side location, and he communicated with fellow cell members, Saif in Harlem and Mohammed in Lower Manhattan, with toss-away cell phones. Amid received his orders from his leader Samir Khan, who was responsible for the entire U.S. operation. Two years earlier, when Samir Khan was given approval for U.S. operations, he immediately started to develop a two-phase attack starting with "Operation Fear" and the soon-to-be unveiled "Operation Burn." Amid received calls from Saif and Mohammed that they were both set and now Amid waited for the go ahead from Samir. The call from Samir came at 12 noon EST, to allow the Chicago and L.A. cells, joint participation. Amid and the two other cell leaders knew exactly what to do. At exactly 12:15 p.m. EST, all three cells, New York, Chicago and L.A. placed their calls.

In Manhattan, Amid called Mayor Bloomfield's office. The cells in Chicago and L.A. called in similar messages to their city's mayors. The message was the basically the same; Amid specifically stated: "Listen carefully. I represent the American Muslim Brotherhood. There are three rental trucks parked at Lenox Avenue & 125th, 72nd & 3rd, and Broadway & Canal. Each contains a dirty bomb capable of destroying entire neighborhoods and rendering them uninhabitable for the next twenty years. Our struggle is with the government of America, not the American people. Therefore, the bombs will detonate exactly twelve hours from now at exactly 12:15 a.m., giving the people of this city time to evacuate. Any attempt to enter the trucks or dismantle the bombs in any way, will force us to prematurely detonate the bombs and kill tens of thousands of people. You have been warned. Allahu Akbar"

CHAPTER 3

Bronx, NY

Tommy Burk was a very successful international design consultant, based in New York City, who was now down on his luck. In his prime he designed hundreds of international award winning commercial projects. He designed stores and shopping centers for the retail princes of the world. Tommy may not have been a prince himself, but he knew them. That was then and this was now. Tommy was now 66 and his new mantra was "When you have nothing, you have nothing to lose." He was at rock bottom. His business was doing lousy before 9/11 and like the towers, imploded immediately thereafter. He owed everyone including the IRS. His bookkeeper neglected to pay employee taxes amounting to over $100,000 plus fines and late fees and that was the reason for this meeting. Mr. Skinner of the IRS was due at his apartment any minute. Tommy knew, from the phone conversation with Mr. Skinner that Skinner was dirty and was coming to meet with him privately, to propose a payoff. The IRS reduced the amount owed to $40,000, but Skinner was coming to make an even sweeter deal.

Tommy was a tough kid who grew up in Southwest Philly. He stood 6' tall and about 200 lbs. Not fat, not muscle. He was just a big guy. He had blue eyes, dirty blond hair, and an infectious smile that let you in but not for long. In other words, you had to earn his respect, then his friendship. Tommy didn't suffer fools and didn't take shit from anyone. He never started anything but when he felt in the right, he went in with his left.

Tommy now lived in a tired Bronx high-rise. As he looked out his window to the parking lot below, he saw a black Ford sedan, similar to his own car, pull in the open space next to his. A man in a suit got out. It had to be Skinner. Tommy's apartment buzzer rang, and he pushed the access button and waited. Skinner took the slow moving, noisy elevator and arrived a few minutes later. He got out, found Tommy's apartment, knocked, came in and got right down to business. Skinner, a scrawny, balding man with thin lips and the pallor of a mortician, said that upon a more careful examination of the record, the entire $40,000 IRS debt has been forgiven. The only caveat was that a $10,000 stipend had to be wired into Skinner's account by noon tomorrow. If it wasn't, he would reverse his decision, and the $40,000 plus late fees and penalties would be due immediately. It seemed like a good deal, and Tommy accepted. Skinner gave him the particulars and left.

Tommy thought Skinner was scum. He knew where the money was going, as he was sure Skinner pulled this scam off on others. Tommy was pissed off that he had to deal with this shithead. He heard the elevator arrive for Skinner, heard Skinner enter, and the elevator door close. Tommy then left his apartment, walked down the hall to the window by the elevator that looked down into the parking lot 13 stories below. Tommy looked down and saw three young black men sitting on the hood of his car. He opened the window, stuck his head out slightly and yelled, "Get the fuck off my car you black motherfucking niggers, or I will come down and kick your ass" He closed the window, returned to his apartment, sat on the couch and waited. This wasn't the first time Tommy saw them sitting on his car, but it was the first time he said something. Next time he would follow through with his threat. Tommy soon forgot about Skinner.

Skinner's slow, noisy elevator eventually reached the ground level lobby, and he exited toward the parking lot and his car. As he got closer to the car, he saw three black guys sitting on his car hood. Not one to be intimidated, Skinner put his right hand in his pocket and removed his key and with his left hand motioned for the guys to move away from the car.

It seemed to work because all three immediately jumped off the car. Skinner, only a yard or so away now, pointed his keyless remote at the car. He pushed the button, and his car horn sounded, and the car lights blinked on. That was the last thing Skinner saw before his lights blinked out.

CHAPTER 4

BRONX, NY

The police arrived quickly and Tommy soon began hearing the sirens and seeing strobe light reflection in his ceiling. He looked out his window to see what was up. He knew it was bad, as well as near where his car was parked, so he headed down to see if his car was ok and to find out what was going on.

Just as Tommy arrived near his car, he was stopped by a cop, but not before he saw the body of a badly beaten Skinner, being now covered by a sheet. Tommy knew it would soon all lead back to him, so he told the cop he may have some information. When questioned, Tommy admitted the man he saw laying there before he was covered, resembled a Mr. Skinner who had been had been to see him in his apartment. But that the business had been successfully concluded and Mr. Skinner left. Tommy said that after Mr. Skinner left, he heard some yelling from down the hall by the elevator, but that that was not unusual in this building. Another witness collaborated the yelling from the window and elaborated the essence of what was yelled. The detective asked Tommy if he would identify the body, and he agreed. The sheet was now blood-soaked and when removed revealed a terribly battered face, but there was no doubt it was Mr. Skinner. Remarkably, Skinner now seemed to have some color, and his lips were a bit fuller. Tommy made a positive ID, and as the Skinner's wallet was still on his person, robbery was ruled out, and it became a race crime instead.

From all witness accounts, Skinner, a racist, threatened and said the "N" word to the wrong guys and paid for that mistake with his life. No one could identify any suspects. Since Skinner was a federal employee, his agency would be notified. But as far as NYPD'S finest were concerned, the case was closed, though they would keep an eye out for suspects. Tommy was free to go and thanked for his assistance.

Later, around 1:30 a.m. with the police, Skinner and the voyeurs all gone, only the blood, chalk line and yellow tape remained. Tommy walked towards the crime scene, guided by dimly lighted overhead pole lights. Passed the graffiti covered trash dumpsters, passed the basketball backboard with its rusted net-less rim. He walked to his car and saw the same three young black guys sitting on his car hood. Tommy, also not one to be intimidated, put his right hand in his pocket, removed his key, and with his left hand motioned for the guys to move away from the car.

As before, all three immediately jumped off the car. Tommy, only a yard or so away now, pointed his keyless remote, pushed the button, and the horn sounded and the lights blinked on. Tommy then reached his hand toward the leader and tossed him an envelope. The leader, Abdul Azim Williams, opened the envelope, counted ten $100 bills, nodded, and then he and his two fellow gangbangers walked away.

Tommy got in his car and thought that although Mr. Skinner's suggested caveat was good, the deal that he'd made with Abdul was better. Besides, Skinner would not be around to reverse his decision at noon. Abdul, walking away, stopped, turned and said to Tommy, "Hey white motherfucking honky, you need anyone else do the Houdini let me know, I am always out here in the parking lot."

"I will but only if your black motherfucking ass ain't be sitting on my car."

Tommy felt his luck was finally changing. He started his car and backed out past the gangbangers. Tommy drove to the 7-11 to buy some lottery tickets. Then his cell rang.

CHAPTER 5

ONE CENTER PLAZA

Manhattan

Within a minute of NYC Police Commissioner Riley receiving the threat flash from the mayor's office, he made three phone calls. The first went to his precinct commanders of each threat district, to have them verify the threat. Riley instructed all three commanders to send patrol cars to each location; Lenox Avenue & 125th, 72nd & 3rd, and Broadway & Canal, to see if there is, in fact, a rental truck parked in each location. Rental trucks in Manhattan are not unusual at all, with so many people moving in and out. But it would be unusual for three rental truck to be at these three locations at the same time. The second call was to his Deputy Commissioner Turner, to be prepared to shut down all; "bridge, tunnel, air and train" traffic to and from the city. In other words "Button up Manhattan" and to be prepared to circulate and activate the threat flash if the threat is verified. The third call, the commissioner made, was to Tommy Burk.

In less than five minutes, all thee precinct commanders reported back "Threat Verified." Riley called the mayor, and the decision was made to "Button up Manhattan." The mayor directed all key personnel immediately to the Office of Emergency Management Headquarters at Water Street in Brooklyn.

Not since 9-11 had NYC had a threat this big or this real. The mayor didn't want to scare the city but something like this could not be ignored. He also knew that something this big could not be contained for long.

CHAPTER 6

I Corps

Vietnam, 1967

Tommy was eighteen and attending Villanova University, outside Philadelphia, for engineering, when he received his draft notice. His cumulative grades had dropped below 3.2 and he became draft eligible. He really didn't care because he hated engineering and besides, Uncle Walter told him, every night during the evening news, that an adventure awaited him in a far off exotic place. Four of his boyhood friends also received draft notices and he and two of them decided instead, to see if they could join the Marines. At the USMC recruiting station, the recruiting sergeant said there would be no problem getting Tommy and his two friends out of the army draft and into the Marines. They just needed to come back the next morning at 8 a.m. to sign some forms and be sworn in. All three friends agreed to meet at the schoolyard at 7:30 the next morning and walk to the recruiter's station together. The next morning Tommy was on time but his two friends never showed. Tommy walked into the Marine Recruiting Station alone, signed the forms and was sworn in. The two no-shows and his two other boy-hood friends all went in the Army and spent their tours in Europe. Tommy now knew that if he couldn't trust his friends he would learn to trust only himself. After basic and advanced training, Tommy left for that far off exotic place.

Tommy Burk served under Commissioner Riley in Vietnam with Golf Company, 2nd Battalion, 7th Marines, in 1966-67. Burk was a sergeant and second platoon weapons leader. Riley was captain and company commander. Riley and Burk started out like oil and water but slowly gained respect for each other. Captain Riley took care of his men; Burk took care of business. Golf Company was constantly thrown out as bait, and that bait was constantly eaten. Literally. The enemy was smart, and when they took the bait they did so from many Marine companies, simultaneously, leaving regimental with limited reserve resources. Regimental had to decide which companies to reinforce and support and which companies would be left hanging in the wind.

In other words, whose ass gets pulled out of the fire and whose doesn't. "Give a Huss" Golf usually got burned. Riley and Burk figured this out pretty fast, so when they went out on an operation, they went out strong. Burk was good with demolitions and always carried a half dozen blocks of C-4 explosives, blasting caps and fuse. He used it for everything from clearing an LZ and blowing tunnels to cooking fuel for c-rations. Riley and Burk spent the entire tour together. Twelve major operations against the Viet Cong and North Vietnamese Army in twelve months. Most operations lasting on average twenty five days. Their tour, as it was nicely called, was almost entirely in the bush and entirely in contact. Riley was a team player and a natural leader. Burk was a one off. Marines like Riley and Burk were good in combat, but when it came to taking or defending a hill, that's where they really excelled.

While men in front of and behind Burk were killed or wounded Burk never got hurt bad. Oh he bled, he hurt, but he never left the bush. A corpsman once wanted to put him up for a purple heart after a rocket sent some shrapnel into his face but Tommy declined because it was nothing and not deserving of the award. Burk was street smart, and somehow that translated to bush smart. Golf Company gave as good as it received and if you asked 2nd Platoon, they would tell you Burk was the main reason many of them survived. Golf saw a lot of action, and Burk carried many dead and wounded to the choppers for evacuation. But when the choppers left and the rotor noise died out, it became very quiet. Burk and the other survivors picked up the dead and wounded's gear, added it to their kit and continued the mission. They didn't give out medals to survivors.

When he came home from the war in '67, people avoided or ridiculed him. The first thing people would ask him was "Did you kill anyone?" and "Were you wounded?" He would lie about the first and answer no to both questions. People lost interest if you if you weren't a killer or didn't have a wound, so they would soon leave him alone. Survivors got no respect. Burk didn't talk about the war with anyone but other vets, and most of his veteran friends were dead.

Toward the late Seventies, when finally he thought the country was ready to forgive and forget, a certain Vietnam veteran, who championed himself their spokesman, testified before Congress. This veteran testified that soldiers and marines in Vietnam had killed, raped, cut off ears, cut off heads, blown up bodies, randomly shot at civilians, razed villages in fashion reminiscent of Genghis Khan, shot cattle and dogs for fun, poisoned food stocks, and generally ravaged the countryside of South Vietnam. Burk would not forget this veteran or his depiction of combat soldiers and marines. Later, movies like "The Deer Hunter" in '78 and "Apocalypse Now" in '79 came out. The madness portrayed in the veteran's congressional testimony and these films reinforced the stereotype crazy killer veteran image, and Burk and other veterans went back into their shells. Finally by the mid-Eighties, moms began allowing their children near the vets, and dads allowed them to date their daughters. Then "Platoon" and "Full Metal Jacket" came out, and Burk and the vets went back in.

CHAPTER 7

PRESENT

Office of Emergency Management Headquarters at Water Street in Brooklyn.
10 hours and 25 minutes before detonation.

The four-level Office of Emergency Management building sits almost directly under the Brooklyn Bridge. It contains the most advanced technology and features available for OEM's emergency response and planning personnel. Conference rooms facilitate interagency training and coordination. Redundant electromechanical systems ensured continuous operation during a power outage. A fully equipped media briefing room leverages the resources of the city's Emergency Alert System and provided a venue for instantaneously transmitting emergency information to the public. Access from Manhattan was by car, chopper, boat, or you could just walk over the bridge. This building also served as the NYC headquarters for Homeland Security.

Over fifty Emergency Management staff were assembled in the main conference room when the mayor and the police commissioner arrived. The main oval conference table seated twenty. It included the mayor and police commissioner, commissioners, and liaisons or agents in charge of the Fire Department, Emergencies Services, Utilities, Transportation, Homeland Security, FBI, CIA,

NYC Public Relations, and the Governor's office. Several large monitors covered the walls, three dedicated to the three threat zones and several large electronic maps showing the city's transportation, and utilities. The mayor began by asking Commissioner Riley for a threat situation update. Police Commissioner Riley confirmed the three threats appeared real, and local residents and businesses were being evacuated. NYPD had cordoned off a four-block grid and bomb disposal unites were on site.

"We are waiting for their report," Riley said.

As that was happening, the door open and in walked Tommy Burk, and without so much as a 'by your leave' he walked right over to the seat next to Riley's and sat down. He and Riley quietly conversed for a few minutes then Burk said aloud, "OK, what have I missed?" All heads turned from their phones and iPads to see who this stranger was, sitting next to the police commissioner. Before anyone could say anything, Burk whispered into Riley's ear, then Riley introduced Burk as someone he has worked with before.

"Burk is the best demolition and intuitive person I have ever worked with," Riley said. "I want Burk with me on this."

With that came a few nods of acceptance, as no one would second guess Police Commissioner Riley. If Riley wanted Burk in, then so did they. Riley had earlier dispatched Burk to the threat sites so he could get a first-hand report. Then Riley's phone went to his ear and everyone, and everything stopped. He finished listing and ended the call.

Riley told the group, "Based on Burk's assessment and my72nd street field commander's call, just now, the threats are indeed real. The trucks' interiors are lined with some sort of lead blankets that are impeding X-rays. But our field guys got enough of a look to determine that there are three 50-gallon barrels, containing some sort of liquid. Additionally, car batteries, cables and wires. Their sniffer equipment registered strong doses of ammonium nitrate and cesium 137, a radioactive material. If that's not bad enough, infrared detected a live person inside, seemingly sitting at a working computer.

In the opinion of my onsite field commanders and bomb disposal team leaders, this has all the markings of an ANF bomb. That's an Ammonium Nitrate Fertilizer bomb, similar to but larger in size to the McVeigh Oklahoma City bomb. But the addition of Cesium 137 takes it to an entirely new level. Ladies and Gentlemen, everything the American Muslim Brotherhood said in their phone call to the mayor has been verified. I am still waiting for similar verification from the other two threat locations but I have a feeling we are going to hear the same thing."

The people around the conference table, dropped their pens, looked around at each other and shook their heads in disbelief at what they just heard. This was not a threat anymore, it was real. They all had a job to do, but now they were scared – not for themselves, but for their families and loved ones.

The mayor broke the silence. "Gentlemen, as I see it we have two options. The first is to immediately evacuate the city. If the bombs go off, we did the right thing. However, if we are able to defuse the bombs or they are duds, then we erred on the side of caution. Option two, is we don't evacuate the city, just the immediate threat zones. If we are able to defuse the bombs or they are duds, we end up heroes. If on the other hand the bombs go off, as it appears they will, we had all better be standing next to them because I don't want to be around for the fallout. And I don't mean the radioactive kind."

Cell phones and iPads around the room started vibrating as flash threat messages were coming through. They were all getting the same Federal DOHS threat updates. Both Chicago and L.A. had also been targeted.

CHAPTER 8

ALL ACROSS AMERICA

While Operation Fear was about to go viral, Operation Burn was just getting under way. Samir Khan fancied himself as the American Muslim Brotherhood CEO and Creative Director. He used the American talking point of "*Doing more with less.*" He truly believed his shows in New York, Chicago and L.A. would be well received internationally, but now it was time for Operation Burn. It was a simple, yet creative concept. "We will burn America down," he had told his followers. There are ten national forest and grasslands zones and fifty state forest and grasslands zones. Close to a quarter billion acres of fuel. Twenty American Muslim Brotherhood camping families in assorted vehicles from SUVs, RVs to camping trailers and from as many different starting places had set off for a week of fun and camping. They would camp in several different campsites every day and hike out some two miles distance. While hiking back, they would set as many as five different fires, using an incendiary, like Duraflame or Red Hot Fire starter, commonly available in supermarkets and 7-11s. In just a couple of days, more than 180 forest and grassland fires erupted in every state across the country, from the Pine Barrens of Long Island and New Jersey to the Florida Everglades, from the White Mountain Forest in New Hampshire to the Allegheny Forest in Pennsylvania, from the White River Forest in Colorado to the Shasta Forest in

California and every forest and grassland in every state in-between. "You would be surprised what twenty enterprising, motivated camping families can accomplish in a few days," he joked.

Samir originally considered fewer campers with more time but realized that three days was about all he could stretch it before Homeland Security would figure it out. By then, America would be in flames, and Americans would become "illegal aliens" evacuating into Canada and Mexico.

CHAPTER 9

Office of Emergency Management Headquarters at Water Street in Brooklyn
10 hours before detonation.

The mayor looked around the table for reactions to his options. The FBI and CIA liaisons were busy tracking down who rented the trucks and where the cesium 137 came from.

The fact that both organizations completely missed this attack did not escape those present.

The mayor asked NYC Homeland Security Director Patricia Santos for her recommendation. Santos said, "Absolutely Option One and do it immediately. Evacuate the city now!"

Most of those around the table nodded approval. Riley said that the Bomb Disposal Unit will attempt to ascertain the bomb structure and their ability to defuse.

Santos added, "If there is a 100% chance of containment or 100% chance we can defuse the bombs, we can slow down or reverse the evacuation."

The mayor asked his deputy to give everyone the short version evacuation timeline. Deputy Frank Stein said "We have over 2.5 million residents, workers, and tourists in Manhattan. If we give the mandatory evacuation order immediately, we can safely have the three threat zones completely cleared in a 20-block radius each. In addition, we could have over half of Manhattan cleared out to Brooklyn, Queens, Staten Island, the Bronx, Riverdale, Jersey City, Weehawken and Fort Lee."

The mayor asked for a show of hands from those around the table for ordering immediate evacuation and of the twenty seated at the table seventeen raised their hands. Only Police Commissioner Riley and Burk didn't have their hands up. Ignoring Burk, the mayor said "Commissioner Riley, you don't agree?"

Commissioner Riley said, "I would like you to hear what Burk has to say first."

Ignoring the commissioner's request, the mayor said. "Commissioner Riley, you are on record as being against evacuation."

Deputy Mayor Stein turned to the mayor. "Mr. Mayor, the clock is running. Shall I give the evacuation order?"

The mayor turned to his deputy. "Give the order to begin the evacuation."

Just then a loud irritating squelch sound emanated from Riley's area, a sound similar to what you would hear when you got the question wrong on a quiz show. Everyone turned to the source including Riley.

"Wrong answer," said Burk. In describing Burk to the assembled group, Riley forgot to add "irreverent."

Burk looked directly at NYC Homeland Security Director Patricia Santos, and keeping with the mayor's political incorrectness said, "Gentlemen, you're not going to evacuate the city. And besides, you would never get half the people off this island as Frank Stein suggested." The way Burk pronounced Frank Stein's name, it sounded more like "Frankenstein." Turning to Stein he continued, "This thing is a monster, and it's trying to scare us." The double entendre was not lost on the group, and a few snickers were muffled. "This whole threat is just that. A threat, a hoax. That's exactly what they want us to do. They want us to run scared. So every time we get a phone call there will be a federal mandate to evacuate the city. Life in Manhattan will be like living in Kennedy Airport. Take our shoes and belts, but turbans are persona non grata. Don't evacuate. Let's see what happens next. I believe these guys wear two sandals."

CHAPTER 10

NYC

The first citizens to know something big was up were the 30 or so Manhattan garage attendants who received frantic calls from moms, dads, drivers and assistants to have their vehicles brought up immediately.

These callers were wives, husbands or in the employ of the city's movers and shakers, and many garage attendants got several calls at the same time. The second group to quickly become aware that something big was happening were the principals of Christ Church, Convent of the Sacred Heart, Dalton, Dwight, Chapin, The Blue School and all the other top private schools in Manhattan, who received calls to have little Johnny and Susie accompanied by their teacher, at the school pick-up area immediately. Most, but not all had received quick, muted tip-off phone calls and texts from someone inside the Emergency Management Headquarters. Although instructed to keep it quiet, it is impossible not to want to get your love ones out of Dodge. After the school pickup, many of these before warned drivers, faced traffic jams and closed tunnels and bridges. A few had prearranged get out of jail cards or received courtesy police escorts out of town to up-state New York, New Jersey, or the Hamptons. The others named names or made frantic phone calls to their sponsors for assistance.

The word that something big was happening was starting to spread from the garage attendants, school principals and teachers to the average cop on the beat, and before long everyone seemed to know a catastrophe was this way cometh.

CHAPTER 11

Office of Emergency Management Headquarters at Water Street in Brooklyn
Time left before the bombs are set to explode: 9 hours and 25 minutes.

First word about the massive forest fires blazing in numerous locations through the country appeared as a crawler on *CNN* and quickly came live with several correspondents at different locations. At first, the consensus around the room was similar to what everyone felt when the first plane hit the World Trade Center – total disbelief and an inability to connect the dots. Everyone was commiserating about the bad timing of having forest fires occurring while they were in the midst of a major terrorist action.

Everyone except Riley and Burk. Burk just stood up and said, "Gentleman, the other sandal has just dropped." It took Riley and Burk a few minutes to connect the dots for everyone but soon heads were shaking in agreement. Then Burk said, "We are dealing with a very creative mind here, and he is way ahead of us. Don't know exactly what his game is yet, but I have some ideas where this is going."

The mayor asked if Burk would be so kind as to enlighten the group. Burk leaned forward, gazed around the table stopping at the NYC FBI director and said. "I can only tell you what my gut is telling me, and that is that the brotherhood is behind the truck bombs and the fires. I believe they want to cause so much confusion, panic and fear that we implode ourselves. We attempt to evacuate the city, panic sets in, and hundreds if not thousands die. We play their game and evacuate everyone from Manhattan, Chicago and Los Angeles out of the metropolitan areas and into the fires that are real. In their minds, we are the beast, and it will be fear that kills the beast. I can tell you this, if we play their game, it will destroy us as a country. It will destroy our economy, it will break down our social system, and it will leave us vulnerable to rising superpowers who will see our weakness and strike. Let's not go there."

The mayor's secretary entered and informed the mayor that the president was on the line and wants to conference with the group. A second later, the President of the United States, from the Cabinet Room, appeared with her cabinet and security directors.

On the screen, Mayor Bloomfield and his team could see President Hilton and her federal team. If one was anticipating pleasantries, they didn't come. The president looked at the assembled and said, "Mr. Mayor, Chicago and Los Angeles have ordered evacuation. What are you waiting for or what do you know that we don't?"

The mayor replied, "Madam President, not everyone here believes we should evacuate."

"And that is because?"

Before the mayor could respond, Burk stood and said, "You're the President; order us to evacuate. But before you do, consider this: We didn't get any hits to these trucks bringing anything dangerous or dirty into the city. They could not purchase working bomb ingredients and components in this city, and if they tried we would have known about it."

The mayor and Riley tensed in their seats – not because Burk spoke out but because they knew the president's demeanor.

The president looked at the man who just spoke, then turned to look at her advisors, who all shrugged, then she looked back at the man who just interrupted the President of the United States, the most powerful human on earth, and said, "Who the fuck are you, and why are you talking?"

Burk was about to answer when Riley grabbed him and pulled him down and said, "Madam President, this is Tommy Burk, and he's with me."

The President said, "Do you agree with his assessment, Police Commissioner Riley?"

"Yes Madam President, I do," said Riley.

"Do you Mr. Mayor?"

The mayor answered, "Madam President, I stand with Riley but I am waiting to be convinced."

"Well" said the president, "trust and verify. That's a good position, Mr. Mayor, but every great mind here in Washington, Chicago and Los Angeles thinks the bombs are going to explode in less than 9 hours and have started to evacuate. Any second now, *CNN* and *FOX* and everyone else will be going live to tell the world that three U.S. cities are about to blow up, and you are waiting to be convinced? Looking at Riley and Burk, she continued. "How can you be so sure they won't go off?"

Burk pulled away from Riley and stood. "They told us they won't."

Everyone looked at Burk with the universal 'did I miss a meeting' look.

Burk said again, "They told us. They said 'Their struggle was with the American government not the American people.' That's bullshit! If the bombs were real they would have blown them by now. They hate the American people and would have gone for the proverbial 1-2 punch. If the bombs were real they would have gone for a knockout. A body count, and a destroyed city. Not just a destroyed city. The fires outside the cities are real; the bombs are not."

"Well Mr. Burk," said the President, "what would you have us do then?"

Before Burk could reply, Riley squeezed his arm and at the same time whispered, "Respect." Burk stood again and said, "Madam President, the fires are real, the bombs are fake. What we should do Madam President, is the four F's."

"If my memory serves me correctly…" said the president, turning to look at her Homeland Security Director Debra Wines. "…cover your ears Ms. Wines; in high school, that was guy slang for certain girls. Find them, feel them, fuck them, and forget them."

"That's a bingo, Madam President" said Burk. "And that's exactly what we high school guys are going to do to these girls as soon as we stop yapping about it and go after them. So let me 'Find' these girls. Let me 'Feel' them for a while, then I will 'Fuck' them. Then we can 'Forget' about all this bullshit." He looked down at Riley, then to Santos then back to the president and added, "And that is with all due respect Madam President."

"So Mr. Mayor, you're not going to evacuate the city?" asked the president.

The mayor looked round the table, then to Riley, who nodded agreement, then focused on Burk and said, "Madam President, we are going to call their bluff. But if Commissioner Riley and Burk are wrong, there will be two more girls added to the four F club."

The president smiled and looked directly at the mayor and said. "Make that three." The president disconnected and was gone.

The mayor said, "That went well." The drones around the table all nodded in agreement. "It did not go well, you idiots. My ass, your asses, the city and all its citizens are on the line." The mayor looked towards Riley and Burk he said, "Find them."

The mayor's secretary came into the room and whispered something to the mayor. The mayor listened, became irritated, and said to the others around the table, "Phone, text, email or twitter your loved ones that you leaked the threat to, and get them back here. No more passes are to be issued. I don't want to see a *FOX* reporter with video of your kids, wives, husbands and significant others on Main Street in Southampton when all the other citizens are just finding out what we have known for hours.

CHAPTER 12

NYC

Amid called *The New York Times*, Mohammed called *CNN*, and Saif called *FOX*. They gave the three media outlets the same message Amid had earlier given the mayor's office. To stir up more trouble, they added that they had informed the mayor's office about the bombs more than three hours ago. Although the media all knew something big was up, through their beat cop contacts and scanners, their usual mid-level sources were out of the loop, and the mayor, police commissioner, and all the other big wigs were unavailable. So they did what any good media outlet would do: They went live. Anchors or whatever talking heads happened to be in the studio got in front of the camera and after the boiler plate alert said "We interrupt this program….This just into *FOX*. New York City mayor's office was notified at 12:15 p.m. today, over three hours ago, that dirty bombs have been planted in three Manhattan locations – Harlem, the Upper East Side and Downtown. The American Muslim Brotherhood has claimed responsibility. They said the bombs will explode at 12:15 a.m. tomorrow morning, giving the citizens of Manhattan time to evacuate. No evacuation order has yet to be issued from the mayor's office or from the police commissioner. If fact, we have been trying to get through to either the mayor's or the commissioner's office, but they are not available. We can confirm that all bridges and tunnels into and out of Manhattan are closed. There have been reports that the NYPD have escorted several private vehicles out of the city. More as it comes in."

Riley and Burk, during their initial phone call and touch base, set into motion activities to keep things moving while they were in the Brooklyn OEM meeting. In fact, that's why Burk was late. First and foremost of their initiatives was to jam all cell phone operation within all three threat areas. The police and other agencies were on the new Inter-Operable Communication System, unaffected by cell phone jam.

Riley and Burk then left Brooklyn for Central Park. Sheep's Head Meadow was their command post, which now looked like a war zone – choppers, Humvees, SWAT teams, cops and a lot of brass. A command tent was up and wired. The first report they wanted was from Team A/V. The best audio/visual techs got great pictures and sounds from inside the truck. The military had provided advanced X-ray and Thermal Imaging Red Scanners that could pretty much pass through the lead blankets so they could see the basic forms of bomb-like equipment, and a live person at the desk with a computer. The only thing was that the person behind the computer was still. Very still. His head bobbed up and down a bit, but other than that he remained almost catatonic. There was no sound except the hum of a laptop computer. Burk asked them to put a transmitter/speaker in and ask him who he was and what he wants. They attempted to communicate in several languages, including several Arab languages. They heard a grunt, and there was some movement of the head, but that was it. No audible response.

The next team to report was Team Smell. Everything they suspected was there: fuel, ANF, and Cesium 137. Also a slight scent of HMX/aluminum explosive, water, sweat, plastic, dirt, grease and urine. There was one unexpected smell, though – a sweet burning sugar smell, called Trichloromethane. When Burk heard this, he burst out laughing and shaking his head. "No shit you stupid motherfuckers." The Smell team knew where Burk was going, but Riley had the "what?" look on his face. Burk said, "Trichloromethane is chloroform. The guy behind the desk is not moving because he was chloroformed and is probably sedated. He is probably duct taped to the chair and desk. He is a patsy."

The third team was Team Cocoon. Three 40'x40' Kevlar bomb blankets were in the air, over the three threat areas, waiting drop orders from Riley. Burk nodded and said, "Let's do it. Then I am going in." Riley gave the order to drop the blankets. Three Sikorsky CH 54 twin engine heavy lift helicopters hovered over the rental trucks. Below, sidewalk trees and telephone poles tumbled. Park workers and utility workers cleared the trees and poles with precision timing. Cars were towed away. The helicopters swooped in, dropping the bomb blankets dead on. Dozens of workers secured the blankets with steel beams then railroad track spikes right into the asphalt. This all happened in less than 20 minutes. This entire procedure was beamed live to Chicago and LA as a primer, should they decide to follow New York's lead. Snipers scanned all the surrounding buildings searching for a "looker" – someone who remained behind and was overly interested in what was happening. The snipers found two.

CHAPTER 13

WASHINGTON, DC

The White House.
6 hours left till the bombs are due to explode.

President Hilton, back in the Oval Office after the three separate video calls to NYC, Chicago and Los Angeles, dropped down to her chair exhausted. Chicago and L.A. were evacuating, fires were burning across America, and NYC was in denial. Governors, senators and representatives were calling her to let her know they have been inundated with calls from their frightened citizens. Americans were scared that they were going to be blown up or burned to death. They were seeing their country destroyed and were scared to death.

This is not the second term President Hilton envisioned. Her Iran attack on Memorial Day was a political and strategic success, but this could be a disaster.

"I can't believe what a jerk that guy is," said the President. "What do we know about this Burk? Get the FBI and IRS directors on it, and let's find out who he is and what his game is. It seems he has Riley, the mayor, and everyone else there snookered. For all we know, he could be behind the bombs and the fires."

"Madam President," said Vice President Joe Denning, "I think you are on to something, and we could use this to our advantage.

"And what exactly is that?" asked the President.

"Madam President, you influenced and directed the evacuation of Chicago and L.A. but Mr. Big shot NYC cares more about the city's real estate than its people. When the bombs go off, and they will, you will be the president who saved Chicago and L.A. while Bloomfield, Riley and this Burk jerk will be the ones who destroyed New York."

Secretary of the Interior Sally Jewel interjected, "We are making progress containing some of the fires, and FBI Director Miller has arrested some of the arsonists."

"Madam President, continued Vice President Denning, we could also prepare a retaliatory military strike against these terrorists."

"That's a good idea, Joe," said the President. "They are the American Muslim Brotherhood, are you're suggesting we attack ourselves?"

"Good point," said the vice president. But not one to let the attention slip from him, and taking the president's rebuke as encouragement, continued. "Then we should strike their parent company, The Muslim Brotherhood in Egypt, Syria, Israel, or one of those other sand countries."

The president turned to the vice president and put her hand to her mouth contemplating the VP's suggestion. "Joe, why don't you narrow it down a bit and take it up with the deputy secretary of defense."

The Vice President, now beaming because his contribution was accepted, grinned and winked at the president. "I'm on it chief." He left the room in search of the deputy secretary of defense.

After the door closed the President turned to a few of the present cabinet members and said. "Sometimes I think Joe is retarded – excuse me, mentally challenged. You know he wants to run for president. Can you imagine that? He could run for President of the American Idiot Brotherhood but I seriously doubt he'd win."

CHAPTER 14

ACROSS AMERICA

While the White House, *CNN, FOX*, New York, Chicago and L.A. were fixated on the bombs and evacuation, the rest of America was looking out their windows and seeing the countryside burning. In neighborhoods many miles from the fires, skies were black, and breathing was becoming difficult. One could only imagine what it was like near, or god forbid, in the fire. Currently there were 90 active forest fires through the United States. It was estimated that it could cost almost $2 billion attempting to contain them. Three thousand homes had been destroyed so far, hundreds were dead, and thousands were missing. A quarter million people had been evacuated. Some evacuees, in New York State, Illinois and California were being evacuated toward New York City, Chicago, and L.A. – a real cluster fuck in the making.

Between the bombs and the fires, America had come to a halt. The stock market had dropped 10%, and the president earlier ordered the exchange closed. No one was working, as everyone watched TV or looked out the window. More and more people went outside to talk with neighbors because the smoke was blocking out most of the sky and had severely limited satellite reception. Most cable providers were now down. If that was not bad enough, America's enemies and detractors – which seemed to be most of the world – were sensing blood and jumping on the bandwagon. China, Russia and our good friend Japan bought and sold as much oil as possible using the Chinese Yuan instead of standard dollar reserves currency, sending the value of the dollar even lower, if that were possible. North Korea demonstrated a huge military presence on the DMZ. China moved warships into the strait of Taiwan. Russia began demonstrations on the Ukraine border. The Syrian Cyber Army hacked into America's electric grid and water supply. Egypt, Lebanon and the other surrounding countries made noise about the final destruction of Israel. Iran's new president, Hassan Rouhani, scheduled to lunch with President Hilton, decided instead to launch a new test nuclear warhead missile capable of striking the United States. The only bright side was, at least for the Republicans, tens of thousands illegal immigrants (potential Democratic voters) were fleeing back across the border to Mexico.

Basically what these little towhead bastards have done, with their bombs and fires, smoke and mirrors, is bring America to its knees.

Lights flickered off, water was not being pumped, and gas stations were seeing huge lines. Food stores were facing huge shortages, and banks were closing to avoid runs.

Burk summed it up by saying, "We can send our hot shots to fight the fires and bomb disposal units to dispose of the bombs but Americans are fighters and need someone real to fight. Fear is invisible and right now it is spreading across America. President Roosevelt could not have said it bette: *"The only thing to fear is fear itself."* And that was exactly what is happening. To put it another way, Americans are scared shitless."

CHAPTER 15

NYC

5 hours left till the bombs are due to explode.

The lookers that the NYPD sniper spotted at the East Side location, were seven blocks away in a hotel. The NYPD sniper got Burk on the horn. Burk arrived a second later and confirmed two lookers on the 15th Floor. Amid and his boss, Samir, had an unobstructed view of the U-Haul truck. Amid didn't know that the man with him was his boss Samir. He just thought he was a messenger. They had the window closed and were behind curtains. The hotel was far enough away to be excluded from mandatory immediate area evacuation. The lookers had binoculars and were extremely keen on what was happening. They thought themselves well hidden. To himself, Amid was almost giddy with all the disruption he has caused.

Helicopters, blanket drops, evacuations, battalions of cops, military troops and all the news coverage…what a masterful production Samir had achieved. They had the hotel TV tuned to *CNN* and were enjoying all the panic caused by the bombs and fires.

The media talking heads couldn't be more inwardly excited and appreciative by this godsend of events, while showing respect, and sorrow in their head movements and facial expressions.

Samir's only setback was that the mayor had not, unlike Chicago and L.A., ordered a full mandatory city evacuation. But he consoled himself, knowing that all the major news agencies were now reporting that wives, kids, lovers and friends of the city's bourgeoisie all got the word early and got out of Manhattan. They all seemed to make it to the Hamptons and Upstate New York, while the bridges and tunnels were closed to the proletariat. Samir knew that it would come back and haunt the mayor and his cronies to such a point that they would be forced from office at the least, lynched in Central Park at the best.

Unfortunately for Amid, the sniper spotter knew what to look for and had the equipment to zero in on the window through the curtain and was taking close up pictures of Amid's all-American face under his Yankee cap. The NYPD spotter noticed that the other looker must have left the room. Almost simultaneously, the Harlem and Downtown spotters, linked into what the Upper East Side spotter was seeing, went to work looking for their lookers. It didn't take long. Their lookers were also in similar high-floor locations.

After a quick stop at a corner hardware store, Riley, Burk and Riley's security, high-tailed it over to Amid's hotel room. The SWAT team, upon Riley's orders, had surrounded the hotel and moved in for an easy capture. Amid didn't hear them coming. The door just flew open, and a flash bang was tossed in. But there was only one looker. The other face in the window, seen by both the spotter and Burk, had disappeared. When Amid came to, his hands were tied behind his back, a vice clamp was holding his jaw apart and someone had their fingers in his mouth. When his mouth passed inspection for hidden poison or cyanide pills, a photographer came in and started photographing Amid, especially his face. Amid was told to smile, as his photo would undoubtedly end up on the cover of Rolling Stone. After they got some good shots, the plastic restraints were cut, and all his clothes were stripped off and a complete body search was done. He was now totally nude. Except for the hair on his head, Amid was hairless, not a hair on his body, a good sign that he intended to visit Allah's brothel sometime in the very near future. That wasn't going to happen. Riley and Burk needed answers and fast. Burk wanted Amid nude for the interview, and Riley could only imagine why. Amid's laptop and cell phone were confiscated and rushed to the NYPD computer forensics. In the living room outside the bedroom where Amis was being held, Burk gave final instructions to the photographer. The photographer went into the bedroom to get the shots. Riley long ago gave up trying to understand Burk's methods, but there was always a method to his madness, so Riley would have to wait and see.

The photographer came out of the bedroom, had a quick conference with Burk, and then left the hotel room. Riley told the SWAT team leader to escort the prisoner into the living room and sit him at the table and restrain his hands in front of him.

Riley and Burk sat at the other end of the table while the SWAT team leader and his men waited just outside in the hallway. Amid was scared and looked at the two faces staring at him and felt a chill sweep over him. Amid knew he was in the presence of the Satan and his assistant but was not sure yet, which one was the devil Satan.

Then one of the men spoke, and Amid was sure he now knew. Burk leaned forward and very near to Amid and said softly, "You are not going to have your big date tonight. I see you have already taken a bath and shaved for the occasion, but it ain't going to happen until I make it so. You must be very proud of yourself for what you and your cell members accomplished today. You have brought this city and the country to a standstill.

Our government was blindsided. Our people are scared to death, and our economy is in a tailspin, and you did it with nothing more than smoke and mirrors. You are going to be a hero to your people and people around the world unless you fuck up in the next few minutes and do something stupid." Burk then pulled out the bag from the hardware store and removed the item that was inside. It was a garden pruner. It was strapped to a cardboard description/instruction collar describing and showing pictures of it use. One small picture illustrated how one could snip off branches an inch or so in diameter. First praise then this threat was not lost on Amid, as he knew exactly whose branches would be pruned.

Burk continued. "I am going to ask you a few questions and you are going to answer them. What do I call you?"

"Amid Al-Adel"

"Where do you live Amid?" asked Burk.

Amid gave his Brooklyn address, and the SWAT team outside, monitoring the interrogation, relayed the name and address to the search teams currently cruising all the cities different neighborhoods. Within the next hour Amids apartment would be completely tossed and anyone and anything Amid ever knew, saw, and met or even thought about would be swarmed upon, collected, photographed, printed, interview, and arrested, held as a person of interest or released.

"My last question to you, Amid, is 'Are the bombs in the trucks real or fake?'"

Amid looked at the pruner then back to devil. "The bombs here in New York are an illusion, smoke and mirrors as you say, but I cannot answer for Chicago and L.A."

With that, Burk excused himself, and Riley continued the interrogation. Outside, Burk got on the horn and told the east side location to get ready to open it up and he would be there in a minute.

Upon Burk's arrival at the bomb scene, he was met by the chemical abatement team wearing orange Hazmat, hazardous material, suits consisting of an impermeable whole-body garment worn as protection against hazardous materials, a clear Lexan visor with a self-contained breathing apparatus (SCBA). A suite was handed to Burk and he was helped into it. The Kevlar blanket was zippered, and there sat the rental truck rear, all under a completely contained, white chemical entrapment tent which enclosed the entire truck, Kevlar blanket and small prep space. The Kevlar blanket was unzipped, the lock on the bed door was cut. The active truck door was opened and the abatement team, led by Burk, entered. While Burk looked with amazement at the entire stage set, the abatement team collected and remove the cesium 137. With the cesium 137 secured in a lead container, huge blowers were positioned and engaged to disperse any remaining chemicals and gases. When Burk received the all-clear from the abatement team, the tent came down and his orange Hazmat suit came off.

The smell hit him first. Diesel fuel, oil, urine, and just plain stale heat. A smell from the past. It reminded him of Viet Nam. The man, who Burk now knew to be an innocent driver, Tim Baker, from Hicksville Long Island, was secured to the chair and desk and was still alive. Burk checked Tim for any trip wires or IED's then he was unbound. The Bomb Detection Unit, came in as a double check but found it just as Burk said it would be, smoke and mirrors. On the all-clear, paramedics came in and assessed the situation, stabilized then transported Tim to Lenox Hill Hospital. Burk stood there and was amazed at the realistic effect Amid had created. Burk got on the horn to have the other two sites similarly invested. He then got a ride back to the hotel but first got on the horn with Riley. He confirmed with Riley their hoax was just that and said he would be with him in a few minutes. Riley called the mayor and gave him the good news – and the mayor got on the phone to the White House and the president.

Burk next made a quick stop at the photographer's studio. Several photos were laid on the table, and Burk choose two. Photoshop was amazing, and the photographer knew how to use it. The first photo had Amid, sitting on a stool, nude with a 12-year-old dark skin Arab boy sitting on his lap, both with big smiles and both nude. The second photo had them in an embrace and kissing. That they were both hairless was quite obvious, but it seemed that Amid journey as a martyr to be with 72 virgins would have a slight gender change. Amid seemed to be excited by virgin boys not virgin girls. Also in the photo, a copy of the Koran were conveniently placed on the bedside table. Burk put both photos in an envelope and headed off back to the hotel.

CHAPTER 16

WASHINGTON, DC

The White House
3 hours left until the bombs are due to explode.

It was getting late but the president and her advisers continued to monitor the bombs, fires, evacuations, economy, international events and cyber-attacks. She moved from the couch to her desk and sat in her chair with an appropriated back pillow embroidered with the saying "It ain't easy being queen."

After a knock on the door, FBI Director Miller entered.

"What have you got, Bob?" asked the president.

"I have some interesting information on our Mr. Burk. Seems he has run afoul with the IRS and his back taxes and fines exceeded $100,000. They were reduced to $40,000 as a settlement offer, then reduced down to $0."

"That's a bit strange."

"There's more, and it gets stranger. I have a *CNN* reporter in New York that doesn't miss a beat. When I asked her if she knew anything about Riley and this guy Tommy Burk, I hit a gold mine. She didn't know about Riley and Burk working together but she would dig into that. What she did know, as she was the one who broke the story, was that an IRS agent, who was on the job, was murdered outside the apartment of Tommy Burk. The police have no suspects, and they are calling it a hate crime."

"Isn't that a coincidence" said the president. "And you know, I don't believe in coincidences. The plot thickens. See how it all ties together and why Burk and Riley are so chummy. Who is the reporter?"

"Kelly Sullivan."

"Ah, very nice. Ask her if she wouldn't mind coming down to see me, will you Bob?"

After the FBI director left and the secretary of the interior knocked and entered. "What have you got, Sally?" asked the president.

"Madam President, the fires are disastrous, but we are containing them. We believe we have arrested most, if not all, of the terrorist arsons."

"What's their story?"

"They are all part of the same American Muslim Brotherhood. They are all American citizens, and several are starting to sing to save their asses. We are talking complete families here. Going from forest to forest in campers. Even their kids, as young as 8, admitted to lighting the fires. And the singing birds are pushing it back to New York and to the American Muslim Brotherhood. We are working with the CIA, and Homeland and are getting close. We also have some good weather reports coming our way. It seems a great deal of moisture is coming down from Canada and warm air up from the Gulf are, with God's help, about to collide and saturate most of the country for the next few days."

The president seemed to take this all in. "I don't think God has anything to do with this mess we are in. I think it is Allah who got us into this mess, and he damn sure better get us out it."

The president's private secretary, Paula White, knocked and stuck her head in and informed the president that Mayor Bloomfield was on the phone and it was urgent. The president picked up the phone. "Yes, Mr. Mayor?"

"Madam President," said the mayor, "Good news. The New York City bombs are all fakes. Smoke and mirrors, just like Burk said they would be. Not evacuating the city was the right decision. We have the terrorist cell leader, and his cell under arrest, and they can't seem to stop talking. We are working with NYPD, DHS and the FBI to get the mastermind's name."

"That's great news Mr. Mayor, did your prisoners say anything about the Chicago and L.A. bombs?"

"Madam President, they said they do not know if they are real or smoke and mirrors as are ours. Completely different cell. Only the mastermind would know, and we are close to getting his name, and then we will find him."

"Thank you, Mr. Mayor, keep me posted."

The president opened her door and asked her secretary to get her cabinet members and security chiefs to the Cabinet Room in five minutes.

The vice president walked in. "Did Mayor Bloomfield blow up his city prematurely?"

"No such luck," said the president.

"I have got a preliminary strike plan for you, Madam President."

"Hold that thought Joe, we are meeting in the cabinet in five."

CHAPTER 17

WASHINGTON, DC

The White House, Cabinet Room.

When the secretaries, directors, aides and military brass or their assistants were seated, the president entered the room and they all stood. She sat and motioned them all to be seated. It was like a Keystone Cop routine.

The president looked around the room and made eye contact with all the top people and then began. "Mayor Bloomfield just called to say all the NYC bombs were duds. Just like that jerk Burk said. And that not evacuating was the correct move. Let's not forget we all told him to err on the side of caution and assume the threat was real and evacuate. And as you are all aware, I went live on TV, to tell the American public, based upon all our collective intelligence, the mayor of NYC disregarded the advice of the president and all her top advisers and security agencies by not taking this threat seriously. And that the mayors of Chicago and L.A. were following our advice to the letter. Now gentlemen, if the bombs in both Chicago and L.A. prove to be duds, we are all going to look like idiots and we all will be out of a job. You just better hope something goes boom in a few hours.

"Debra, call Chicago and L.A. and fill them in on what New York City found out. They better hear it from Homeland Security before *CNN* and *FOX* release it.

"How did we miss this? What were you guys doing? What do we have? The CIA, FBI, DIA, DISA, NSA, NSC, NGIA, Naval Intelligence, Homeland Security? Who have I forgotten? Maybe we should just fire all you idiots and hire Burk to be a one-man Intelligence Czar. He seems to be the only person who knows what's going on."

The vice president said, "Do you want to hear my retaliation attack plan now Madam President?"

The president stood, the keystone cops stood, then the president looked at the vice president, turned and walked out.

CHAPTER 18

UPPER EAST SIDE

Back in the hotel, Riley was finishing up the interrogation. Burk saw that Riley had allowed Amid to dress and had given him a Coke. Riley had been playing the good guy and got more info out of Amid but not who Amid's leader was. Amid would tell the obvious and what little he knew but would not betray his faith and would not give up his leader. He would die first. His eyes went cold when Burk entered but he felt a bit more in control now and felt he could stand up to the devil.

Riley had texted Burk his progress, so Burk was up to speed. Burk sat down, leaned forward and close to Amid, and said, "Amid, I am going to ask you a few more questions, and you need to answer them honestly." He took the garden pruner out, now liberated from its packaging, and put it on the table along with the envelope containing the photos. Riley had already shared with Burk, Amid's cell and laptop info and contacts. NYPD, DHS and FBI teams were currently out on the hunt. There were hundreds of contacts, but Burk only wanted one. The right one and right now. Burk said. "Amid who was the other man here in the room with you and was he your leader?"

Amid stared into the devil's eyes but did not answer.

Burk grabbed Amid's left hand, isolated his index finger and with lighting speed pruned the finger off at just below the first joint. It happened so fast that even Riley couldn't react. Amid screamed as blood spurted across the table, some onto Burk's face. Riley got up and pulled out a handkerchief and wrapped it around the bloody hand and finger stump.

Riley, looking back to Burk as if to say, *what the fuck?*

Burk grabbed and flattened Amid's right hand and asked the question again. "Amid, who is your leader?" Nothing but sniffles and a look of contempt came from Amid. The right hand was flattened, and the pruner was around his right index finger with the same lighting speed, but this time Riley was ready and put his hand roughly on Burk's. "Burk, let's think about this for a minute, shall we? I don't have any more handkerchiefs."

Burk ignored Riley. "Amid, I can tell you are a religious man. You know you are going to spend the rest of your life in an American prison, but if you coop-erate with me, you'll be respected and revered at home for what you have done today. Do you want Allah to welcome you and be proud of you? Or do you want to spend the rest of your life in an American prison and be detested and rejected at home. Your family will be embarrassed and persecuted. Allah will be shamed by you and shun you. Which do you prefer, Amid?"

Amid looked at the devil Satan and said "I may go to your prison, but my family, my people, my god, will be pleased with me and proud of me. I will be a martyr walking until I find the chance to kill myself."

With that, Burk took out the photos of Amid and his young boy friend and pushed them in front of Amid. The pained expression from the pruning accident paled compared to the shock and outrage he now exhibited. "You are the devil, Burk," seethed Amin. "This is not me and you know it."

"True" said Burk, "but as we said, 'smoke and mirrors,' and I can make the world see you as a boy lover, and here are the photos to prove it. If you like, I can release these to the media today including posting them on your Facebook page, YouTube and Al Jazeera. Is this what you want your family to see? Tell me your leader's name, and the photos will disappear."

New tears began to form and trickle down Amid's cheeks. From his earlier bomb success to now, seemed like an eternity. This devil is going to put him in prison for the rest of his life, has taken his finger and now is going to take his honor-his glory. Amid look at Riley for some support or sympathy but saw only a hard stare. Riley had become the little Satan. Amid spit on the photos and said "Samir."

"Does Samir have a last name?"

"Kahn."

"Where does Samir Kahn live and how do you contact him?" asked Riley.

"Brooklyn and by cell phone but we have never met."

"Where in Brooklyn does Samir live and what is the cell number?" asked Riley.

Exasperated and reluctantly, Amid gave up his leader.

"You said you never met Samir. So who was that in the room with you here?"

"He's a nobody. Just a messenger. His name is Shihab. I only met him that once."

Burk and Riley turned Amid over to the SWAT team leader and started to leave the room. Burk turned and grabbed the pruner and photos and looked intently into Amid's eyes and said. "If you lied to me, Amid, I will come back and snip your little dick off. But don't worry, you and your Muslim friends will be able to see what your dick used to look like, because these photos will be pasted on your Facebook wall."

CHAPTER 19

THE MAYOR'S OFFICE, NEW YORK'S - CITY HALL

The mayor's press secretary, James Marr, stuck his head in the door to inform him that the press conference was ready to start at the mayor's pleasure. The mayor, Police Commissioner Riley, and a large entourage of security and agency heads filed out of the mayor's office, down the hall to the outside press conference lodge and podium. With Mayor Bloomfield and the Police Commissioner Riley forward, the entourage filling in behind. The only obvious missing person, but not yet obvious to most of the media, Tommy Burk, stood way off to the side. He, despite Riley's objection, was not invited. He was not officially part of the team.

The mayor took, as expected, the lead and told the story of how he and the police commissioner decided, despite the urging of the president and her Homeland Security director, not to evacuate the city because from the beginning they strongly suspected the threat was a hoax. He told how they eventually tracked all six trucks into the city, and about the three trucks that stayed, and the three trucks that left the city. The mayor explained how the FBI determined the three trucks that left the city did so because they were stopped and searched while entering the city. We would know they came in empty. While the three trucks that stayed and perpetrated the threat, did so because they were not searched and could have brought the bombs in. That's what the terrorist wanted us to believe. That the bombs could have gotten past bridge and tunnel security.

He told how they found the three drivers of the searched trucks and started to piece together what exactly they were seeing and what they were not. He took them through the immediate area evacuation, the blanketing of the trucks, and the capture of the terrorist. Finally, he told them how the chemical abatement team and bomb disposal team entered the truck and determined the Cesium 137 was not a lethal dose and that the bombs could not detonate.

The roar from the media with questions was deafening, but as *CNN's* top NYC correspondent learned from hundreds of previous press conferences, it's not the loudest but whoever is last heard over the gaggle of reporters that gets to ask the question. She was and did. Kelly Sullivan was an anomaly among NY's female reporters. She was a brunette among blondes, attractive, investigative, politically and street smart. Born and raised in Manhattan, at 29, to say she knew her way around the city would be an understatement.

The mayor pointed at Kelly.

"Thank you Mr. Mayor; Kelly Sullivan, *CNN*. When this threat was first verified almost 12 hours ago, the police commissioner closed all the bridges and tunnels and buttoned up the city, while you decided whether to evacuate Manhattan or not. You held back notifying the media and your citizens. Yet many wives, kids and significant others of you cabinet and other top officials managed to get passes out of the city."

The Mayor, not one to not share glory, stepped back and said, "Commissioner Riley would be able to answer this better than me. Commissioner?"

Riley stepped to the mike. "Ms. Sullivan, we tried to put a cap on it from the beginning, but something this big can't be 100% contained."

"Yes, Commissioner, I understand that," said Kelly, "but who okays passes for them to get through the bridges and tunnels that you closed?"

"I don't know for a fact that occurred, but I will certainly check it out and get back to you. I will tell you for certain, my wife and family were here in the city the entire time."

"One more question commissioner... *And this was a plant question from FBI Director Miller.* "...who is Tommy Burk and what was his role in all this?"

48

CHAPTER 20

BROOKLYN, NY

Samir Kahn, like his NYC cell leader Amid, felt good about what he had accomplished in one day and without spending a lot of money. He felt that no matter what happened next, he would be viewed as the greatest thing since Osama Bin Laden. It wouldn't be long before the mayors of Chicago and L.A. joined New York to announce that their bombs were also duds. But regardless, they took the bait, unlike New York, and evacuated their cities. Thousands were killed or injured while looters, who stayed behind, infiltrated deserted neighborhoods and stole whatever they wanted from homes and businesses.

The fires did their job and were still burning. No one would ever feel safe again in an American forest. Hell, the forests around Mt. Rushmore were burning, and the videos of fire hoses washing down America's great presidents was priceless. One YouTube video, that was going viral, showed George Washington with what appeared to be tears cascading down his checks. The end game of Samir's great productions, is that there will now be more security and delays coming into and out of the city. And not just New York, Chicago and Los Angeles but all cities. Just like after New York was hit on 9-11, every city from Podunk Nebraska to Looneyville Texas got Homeland Security *color*-coded terror *alerts* and FEMA assistance and FEMA cash. There will be more threats real or imagined and just plain more harassment of anyone not lily white. Samir's Operation Fear and Operation Burn will make future: ingress, egress, and regress to our cities and parks a living hell. The bombs and burns may be over by the night-mare is just beginning.

Samir Kahn was born and raised in the United States and educated at MIT on the American tax payer's dime. Life is good when you have nothing in America. It only sucks when you have a family and job, pay your taxes and ask for nothing. Samir had an apartment in Brooklyn and there quietly, in his spare time and while not working at his day job, started the American Muslim Brotherhood. He was Muslim for sure, but he didn't really hate America. It's just that while reaching for a crescent moon, one might fall on a star. He wanted to be a star. But first they had to know it was he who planned this amazing production, and he had no doubt that that pussy Amid would spill his guts. He actually counted on it. How else would Samir become famous? But Samir would not make it easy, and he was still a bit bothered by Bloomfield's not taking the bait and evacuating. He watched the press conference and thoroughly enjoyed the mayors and other big wigs being questioned about issuing friends and family bridge and tunnel passes, then getting busted with photos of some of them having brunch on Main Street in Southampton while the rest of the Manhattan was purposely kept ignorant. He knew that would happen. Either way he had a win-win situation. As he was watching the mayor's press conference, he couldn't help but wonder why the smoke and mirror performance didn't work in New York as it did in Chicago and L.A. And who is this Tommy Burk?

CHAPTER 21

THE MAYOR'S PRESS CONFERENCE OUTSIDE NEW YORK'S - CITY HALL

Burk, hearing his name, leaned deeper into his corner but not before he made eye contact with Riley.

Kelly caught the eye contact and followed it back to Burk. *"So that's Burk,"* she thought. Then he was gone.

Riley, not dumb enough ever to lie, yet smart enough to know how to hold just enough back, said, "Mr. Burk is a private citizen and terrorist consultant whom I have worked with on numerous successful operations. He has assisted me and NYPD during this threat and we are very grateful for his insight and advice. For obvious reasons, he prefers to remain anonymous and I trust you will respect his privacy."

Other media correspondents now felt it ok for them to again yell out in hopes they would be called on, but Kelly again outlasted them and when they heard her next question they knew it was all over for them and a new ballgame.

"What's Mr. Burk's relationship to the murdered IRS agent found outside Burk's Bronx apartment yesterday?" she asked.

Everyone, including Bloomfield, Riley and all of the other correspondents and cameras, turned toward and focused on Kelly. Everyone became immediately quiet. Riley turned to where Burk was standing, but Burk was gone. He was – as was everyone else, except Sullivan, Burk, the President of the United States and FBI Director Miller – completely blindsided by the question. He was aware of the incident but not of Burk's proximity to it. After what seemed like a minute, he regained his composure and responded, "I am aware of the incident but have no direct knowledge of Mr. Burk's apartment proximity to same." He knew this was not going to satisfy the correspondents who now looked like wolves after the gate has been opened. He added, "I will see if there is any connection and get back to you."

As the roar of the wolves grew, the Mayor and Riley decided simultaneously that the press conference would only go downhill from here and that retreat is the better part of valor. The mayor said, "No further questions. We will let you know when we will have more information and when the next press conference will be." With that, he, Riley and the gaggle turned and rushed off the loge before Kelly and the wolves could get another clear audible question heard let alone acknowledged.

CHAPTER 22

WASHINGTON, DC

The White House, Oval Room.

"Ha!" said the president, slapping the FBI director's back. "We got him. Well done, Bob."

The vice president added, "Bob you're the best."

The president looked at the vice president knowing full well he had no clue what Miller had pulled off by outing Burk and said. "Joe, why don't you go and implement your Arab attack plan."

"You really mean it, Madam President? I've narrowed it down to a single strike."

"Of course I do, Joe. But don't tell me so I can have plausible deniability. Get on it."

"You can count on me, Madam President," and he was off, as only as a man with a mission could be.

After the door closed, FBI Director Robert Miller and the Secretary of State John Kearney both looked questionably at the president, who said "What?"

"You just gave the vice president a green light to attack the Mideast," Kearney said.

"Is that what I did?" replied the president. "I just wanted to get rid of him. Anyway, let's see how far he gets. When the media finds out what he is up to, we will deny it. They know Joe is a nut, and this will push him over the cliff. It will be a distraction and get the media away from us and the fact that our 'eye on the ball' intelligent agencies missed this entire terrorist threat and attack, while we try get the country back on track. Trust me. I won't let him bomb Israel."

The vice president navigated the hallway to his office, his Secret Service detail in tow. He instructed his secretary to have the Deputy Secretary of Defense, Tom Dempsey, and the Vice Chairman of the Joint Chief of Staff, Air Force General Carter LeMay, in his office immediately. This had been what the vice president has been waiting for. *"They think I am dimwit,"* he whispered under his breath. *"Well watch out, my friends, this bulb is going to shine."*

Ten minutes later, both LeMay and Dempsey were in the vice president's office. The vice president let them stew for a while then smiled and said, "We just got the green light to strike. The president wants us to move on it. I have decided on, and the president has approved, a single target, Saudi Arabia. We are going to implement Operation Payback. Fifteen of the nineteen 9-11 hijackers were from Saudi Arabia, and we did nothing. Now we are going to even the score.

"Gentlemen, we are going to implode the tallest building in the world. The Kingdom Tower in Jeddah, Saudi Arabia, 5282 feet high. A tad over a mile high. We are going to blow the Kingdom Tower to Kingdom Come."

"Mr. vice president," said General LeMay, "If I am not mistaken isn't that still under construction and won't be finished until late 2017?"

"Correctomondo, General LeMay. And we will hit the tower tomorrow at 8:46 a.m. on the 93rd floor. Do you see the symbolism?" asked the vice president.

"Not really," replied both General Lemay and Assistant Director Dempsey.

The vice president focused his eyes upward and said "Gentlemen, that's when and where they hit the World Trade Center, North Tower and we are going to return the favor.

"Mr. vice president," said Assistant Director Dempsey, "Don't we need congressional approval?"

"Hell no "said the vice president. "We got the president's authorization to act. And she has the War Powers Act, which allows her limited engagement authorization without notifying Congress.

"Gentleman, we have just received a direct order from our Commander-in-Chief to retaliate against those who have done us harm. I don't mean to sound like a racist, but a towel head is a towel head. We have the green light, so I want this to happen tomorrow morning. The message we will send will be loud and clear. You knock down two of ours and well knock down one of yours."

The vice president went on to say, "The president wants this done fast and quiet. She can't handle it personally because of the current bomb-fire mess but has entrusted it to this small can –do group. Gentlemen, to: the president, success, glory and kingdom come."

CHAPTER 23

The mayors of Chicago and L.A., Manny Rohm and Tony Anthony, were getting their lunches handed to them from the media and the voters, for issuing mandatory evacuation orders because of the bombs. Their defense was, "We didn't know they were fake, and we could not take the chance. The president and Homeland Security strongly recommended we do so." Both, big supporters of the president, couldn't pass too much of the buck back to the White House. The problem with this defense was that NYC's Mayor Bloomfield didn't fall for the hoax, didn't listen to the president, and New York was the hero while Chicago and L.A. were now being looked at as clowns. New York had zero loss of life with a few minor injuries and no looting. The clowns had over a hundred killed and thousands more injured. The loss to residential and commercial property due looting and arson was in the billions and counting.

The only good news was the rains had come and most of the country was soaked and the fires were somewhat more contained. The bad news for millions of Chicagoans and Angelinos walking back to the cities, from as far away as Elmhurst and Santa Monica, was that most of their neighborhoods were now cordoned off as crime scenes. So not only were they homeless, they were wet and homeless. It seemed that Chicago's and L.A.'s gangs and other criminal elements didn't get the evacuation memo or at least choose to ignore it. What happened in New Orleans after Katrina was now going to happen in Chicago and L.A., but only a hundred times worse.

All in all, there were close to 2.5 million residences and businesses in each city.

Five million wet and pissed off people with nowhere to go and another 5 million trying to keep them out of their suburban neighborhoods. They had the makings of a Katrina Tsunami. Allah help us.

CHAPTER 24

BROOKLYN, NY

Samir knew it would be only a matter of time before the ring closed in on him. Amid, although a good soldier, was young and except for this production, untested. He would not hold up under Guantanamo Bay-type interrogation. Samir knew he would eventually get caught but had no intentions of becoming a martyr. He wanted to be famous, and he no doubt would be after what he pulled off. After all, the Boston Bomber got his picture on the cover of Rolling Stone, didn't he? But Samir still had some things to take care of and it was time to go deep undercover where they would never ever find him, until he was ready to be found.

Samir removed the hard drive from his computer and smashed it with a hammer. He then started to destroy the rest of the computer, so if found, no one would consider rebuilding it. He deposited the different parts of the computer in trash bags, filled with his cat's dirty litter, as a further deterrent, into dumpsters throughout Brooklyn. He would bring out later his sanitized computer, which he would leave for the authorities when they came. It had current emails and a lot of good clean misdirection. He packed up most everything else left in his apartment, which wasn't much, tossed it all and called a small ServePro-like company to sanitize the apartment. Afterwards, he went to a homeless shelter and picked up: clothes, toilet kit, towels, etc. and invited some friends for a small party. Samir wore thin latex gloves, which he explained away as a germ phobia. Later that night, after his few friends left, he didn't bother to clean up; he just hooked up his safe computer, grabbed his suitcase, closed the door and left. The few friends he invited to his little going away party would be hunted through their fingerprints and harassed by the feds but eventually dismissed. They would hate him but he didn't care. They were unwitting bit players in this scene and should be happy to have played a small part in his big production. When the Feds came, and they would, they would spend weeks on misdirected evidence and worthless computer DNA. Samir walked to the train station and took the train to 59th Street then to 42nd Street and walked to Penn Station. He got a ticket on the 2 a.m. metro liner to Washington DC. Samir was going to hide where no one would think to look for him – in plain sight.

CHAPTER 25

WASHINGTON, DC

The White House, Oval Room.

The president was taking a great deal of heat over the bombings, fires, evacuations, deaths, looting, and most of all over the fact that all this happened under the noses of Homeland Security and all alphabet intelligent agencies. Pundits, Senate and House leaders were calling for the president's impeachment and the removal of all the agency directors. *FOX, CNN*, and even the always loyal AARP networks – *ABC, CBS* and *NBC*, we're pounding the White House for answers. If that wasn't bad enough, Aljazeera America was calling for her head.

The *NY Post* front page headline for Tuesday the 11th, read "NYC Bombs Bomb".

With the president were Secretary of State John Kearney and FBI Director Miller. For some unknown reason, the president was giving the FBI a pass for missing the bombs and fires. Kearney was about to find out why.

"Director Miller, something is going on that I don't get," asked the president. "How did all this just happen, and why did New York not fall for it?

Somehow this Burk is behind it. What did you find out about the IRS Agents murder?"

"Madam President," said Miller, "the FBI has been working this through its New York field office and we have some interesting developments. Remember the reporter Kelly Sullivan? Well, she has been snooping and reporting back here to FBI Special Agent-in-Charge Michael Hoar. She has been getting the run around from Riley and the NYPD, but she has a contact who was the detective handling the original murder call. It seems Burk and the murdered IRS Agent Skinner had some sort of under-the-table deal going on. The bottom line is that Burk owed the IRS $100,000, got it reduced to $40,000, and then got it reduced to $0. Then Skinner is killed. Special Agent Hoar and the reporter think Burk is up to his eyeballs in this. And Riley is protecting him."

"Director Miller," said the president, "if Burk is a murderer and Riley is protecting him, then it is not too much of a stretch to imagine Burk and Riley setting up other scams including this whole bomb thing to divert attention away from the IRS murder."

"Madam President," said Kearney, "you think Riley and Burk set up the NYC, Chicago and L.A. bomb threat and set the country on fire to cover up a Bronx murder?"

"Exactly," said the president.

Secretary of State Kearney looked at the president, as though she were crazy.

The President continued, "I knew you would figure it out, John. You know I am going to drop Vice President Denning and was considering you to replace him. Is that something you would like, John?" Without waiting for an answer she continued. "You know, John, you are a highly decorated war hero, for Christ sake, and the Republicans have no one to run against you next election. You will be a shoe in."

"Of course Madam President, I would be honored," said the secretary of state.

"Well then, Mr. Vice President, let's get to work outing Burk and put this whole murder-bomb-fire mess back where it belongs – in Burk's lap. I will get my writers to draft something up. I will call a press conference for today at 5 p.m. I will start it off, then you blow the lid off it. The media will go into a feeding frenzy with it. NYC, Burk, Skinner, Riley and Bloomfield will be the top and only prime time news story. Goodbye Washington, hello New York."

The president's intercom phone buzzed. Her personal secretary said that the *CNN* reporter, Kelly Sullivan, was on her private line. The president whispered, "Hold it while I move everyone here out the side door."

CHAPTER 26

WASHINGTON, DC

Samir Kahn arrived in Washington Union Station a little after 4 a.m. He took the Metrorail to Foggy Banks, George Washington University stop, got out, and walked around the corner to his apartment.

He was only gone a couple of days and had to be back at work in a few hours. He carefully checked his door and found undisturbed, all three fine threads he set two days before. The apartment had not been entered, at least not through the front door. When inside, he checked his motion detector, and it had "0" incidences occurring. He checked his email and phone messages and had seen or heard that all were from safe friends. He returned emails, but would return phone calls the next day, he decided. He then went to his bedroom and stood by the window. He looked out at the street to see if anything looked out of place or if anyone seemed interested in his building. Nothing out of the ordinary. It was close to 4:30 a.m. when he set his alarm for 6 a.m. and took a cat nap.

He awoke at 5:55 a.m. and turned the alarm off. He never needed the alarm, but he never took unnecessary chances. He got up and placed his prayer rug on the floor facing Mecca. After his morning prayers, he slipped on his running outfit and "Made in America" New Balance 890 ve's and proceeded out the door. Once outside, he began his sit ups and upper body work and stretches. Once he felt warmed up he took off for his usual 10K run. He loved Washington as a fabulous running city almost on the level of Paris—but not quite. New York's

Central Park was right up there, but only if you didn't have to run many city blocks to get to the park.

He ran to Washington Circle and then down 23rd Street to Independence Avenue. He ran an 8-minute mile and felt very good. He continued east over the Kotz Bridge and down to the Capitol reflecting pool then north to Madison Drive than west back to his apartment.

He walked the last hundred yards to cool down and completed the run in less than an hour.

Inside the apartment, he showered and shaved, then got dressed. He wore a dark grey traditional two-button suit with split vents, a white shirt with a spread collar, blue tie and cordovan wing tips. Safe yet stylish. His hair was short, and he was clean shaven. A real company man. After a Diet Coke, he grabbed his briefcase and headed out the door to work. He took the bus to Pennsylvania Avenue and 11th Street. The building resembling a giant waffle with a coffee table on top. It was the FBI Building, also known as the J Edgar Hoover Building. He presented his credentials to the guard and was greeted in typical informal fashion – "Good morning, Sammy." It seemed as though Samir had changed back to his day job name to compliment his daytime wardrobe.

Taking the lift down to level 1BG, Sammy aka Samir, exited and walked down the narrow white corridor toward his bull pen open landscape work area. Passing the department secretary, he was handed a note that almost froze him in his tracks. Almost but not quite. Sammy was a very cool character and had good trade craft for an FBI non-operative. He wasn't an agent but a chemical engineer assigned to the Forensic Response Division for chemical, biological, radiological and nuclear sciences. The note was from Assistant FBI Director Johns requesting his presence immediately upon receipt of this notice. Sammy took the note to his desk and sat down. They could not have connected the dots that fast, he thought, and if they did, they would have swooped down on him the moment he entered his apartment earlier this morning. No, it had to be something else. He put his briefcase aside and took the lift to level 4. He had never been above the ground level let alone level 4. His security clearance ID must have been reprogramed for the meeting, because he had no difficulty arriving onto level 4.

He walked into a huge reception area with windows looking toward the mall and stopped in front of the receptionist.

"Mr. Kahn, Mr. John's assistant is on his way out to get you," she said.

This really was the FBI, he thought. She knew who he was without asking. The ID card swipe in the elevator must have alerted her.

A man identifying himself as Agent Hoar appeared and escorted Sammy to the assistant director's office. "Have a seat, Kahn" said Assistant Director Johns. "Do you have any idea why I have asked you here?"

Staring directly into Assistant Director John's eyes, to see if he could pick up a hint of where this was heading, Sammy said "I would imagine it is about the terrorist attacks, over the last couple of days."

"That's correct, Mr. Kahn, and I am assigning you to assist Special Agent Hoar, for your expertise and assistance in tracking down connections between a person of interest and the Ammonium Nitrate Fertilizer and the Cesium 137 dirty bombs. Until further notice, you are assigned to Special Agent Hoar. Do exactly as he says, and we won't have a problem. Is that clear Mr. Kahn?"

Not a trace of anything in John's eyes or face flection gave up anything. *"I can't believe of all people to assign to this case, they would pick me. It is too much of a coincidence, and I don't believe in coincidences,"* thought Sammy. Searching for a reply, he couldn't help to think that Tom Cruises response to Jack Nicholson would be appropriate in this situation. "Crystal," he said but then added, "Sir."

After Sammy and Special Agent Hoar left and the door buzzed closed, Assistant FBI Director Johns, picked up the secure in-house phone and pushed 1 for his boss, FBI Director Miller. Miller pick up immediately and Johns said, "It's done" Miller hung up without saying a word and dialed Secretary of State Kearney's cell. The secretary was with the president in the Oval Office. When Miller heard the connection he repeated to Secretary of State Kearney the same message he received from Johns. Secretary of State Kearney listened, then hung up without saying a word.

CHAPTER 27

WASHINGTON, DC

The White House, Oval Room.

The president and Secretary of State John Kearney were alone. Kearney motioned for the president to turn off the proprietary voice recording system.

"The plan is in motion," said Kearney. "Miller has his 'A' team, led by Agent Michael Hoar, planting the evidence in Burk's apartment, as we speak. We will then have that reporter, Kelly Sullivan, let slip that Burk as a person of interest in the IRS the murder, which she will do an hour before the six o'clock news. Miller will then have his court order in hand to toss Burk's apartment. His Forensic 'B' team, specifically Agent Sammy Kahn, will find evidence linking Burk to the murder and surprise-surprise, as Gomer Pyle used to say, they will also find traces of ammonium nitrate fertilizer and Cesium 137."

"Can't Burk claim he brought traces of it home with him after he touched things in the truck?" asked the president.

"He can," said Kearney, "but he had a Hazmat containment suit on and was completely hosed down after he left the truck. And besides, he hasn't been back to his apartment since the threat. He has been staying at the Carlyle Hotel on the city's dime."

The President smiled and rang for the steward. When he entered, he was asked to pour two neat glasses of Maker's Mark. He positioned the silver tray first in front of the president, then the secretary. Both sniffed and gently swirled the whiskey as they patiently waited for the steward to leave the room. When the door closed, the president proposed a toast. "To a successful mission, to Burk becoming the main attraction, and to the next President of the United States." Both took a sip and enjoyed the slight burning sensation going down their throats. The president finished hers, then said, "Now John, get Miller to have that reporter slip the story."

"Yes, Madam President, we will let it slip. As Shakespeare's Anthony said after murdering Julius Caesar, 'Cry havoc and let slip the dogs of war.'"

"I like that, John; you certainly do have a way with words, and you know your history. Didn't you once, in a Senate hearing, compare our military in Viet Nam to being as ruthless as Genghis Khan?" asked the president.

The secretary considered that a very sore point, and was about to respond, but then the president stopped him for a second and said. "Is that a coincidence or what? Miller's 'B' team forensic guy, who is going to make our case is Sammy Kahn. Wonder if he is related to Genghis?"

"Madam President, I hope the FBI vets its employees better than Riley and the NYPD did with Burk."

While they were both having a laugh, the door opened and in walked the vice president. "Madam President, Mr. Secretary. Chief, have you a minute?" asked the vice president.

"Joe, you can speak freely in front of John, he knows what you're up to," said the president.

Secretary of State Kearney cringed at the thought. He had a premonition that this knowledge would come back to haunt him.

"Chief, I know you want to be kept under the radar on this retaliation strike—plausible deniability and all that—but we are launching tomorrow morning from King Fahd Air Base," the vice president said.

"Stop, Joe, I don't want to know," said the president. "This a second tier operation of your making and with your second tier team. Let's see what you guys can do. You get the credit or you fall on the sword. Do it or don't do it, but make sure it doesn't come back to us. And I mean the little us and the big U.S.. They can suspect we were involved, but can't be sure and can't prove it."

That was as good as a go from the president as he could have ever hoped for. The vice president said. "Got it, Chief, and God bless the America," and walked out of the Oval Office.

"Madam President, you're going to let him go through with this strike?" asked Secretary of State Kearney.

"John, I might be under the radar, but I am not off it. I have a little bird inside the vice president's team, and the plan is to fly some sort of cargo plane into an uninhabited building. It will be piloted by a Royal Saudi captain who has decided to martyr himself to show solidarity with America. The story will come out that he did it because he loves America and because he wants Muslims everywhere to have sympathy for Americans, especially during the recent attacks on us."

"Madam President," said Kearney, "with all due respect, that is the stupidest fucking story I have ever heard. No one will buy it."

"Exactly," said the president. "It's so unbelievable, so stupid, that everyone will have to buy it. Who could make up something like that? Well, we know who, but… Listen, John, This will be big news and a big distraction for us. The plane attack and the Burk revelations will make our problems go away. They will be on the front cover, and we will be on the back. Muslim-on-Muslim terrorism. An American murderer and traitor. A mayor and police commissioner part of a conspiracy! We are going to have the biggest RICO bust in history. The world has gone crazy but you and I John, will grab hold of this insanity and pull America back to reality. Then we leak the vice presidents rouge involvement in this Jeddah thing. He's out, you're in and you are on the fast track as the Democratic Presidential Nominee. Now, let's go John. It's show time."

CHAPTER 28

EAST WING OF THE WHITE HOUSE

President's Emergency Operations Center – PEOC.

The vice president was in charge, there was no doubt about it. He had the entire second tier assembled in the PEOC, the President's Emergency Operations Center. The assistants and deputy directors of the all alphabet agencies and the Joint Chiefs, the assistant press secretary and deputy advisers – the second string, if you will. This second string was about to show the world that they could step in and fill their boss's shoes without missing a beat.

The vice president stood at the head of the long operations table. "Ladies and Gentlemen, this is our finest hour. I just left the president and secretary of state, and I was given the green light.

"Tomorrow morning at 1:25 a.m. EST, 8:25 a.m. in Saudi Arabia, we will launch our retaliation strike from King Abdul Aziz Air Base in Jeddah, against those who have done the US harm. The exact impact of the C-130 Hercules into the 93 floor of the Kingdom Tower, also in Jeddah, will be 1:46 a.m. our time and 8:46 a.m. their time. The exact time, on 9/11, when American Flight 11 crashed into the World Trade Center, North Tower, 93rd floor.

"The C-130 is 80 tons including 10,000 gallons of fuel. The pilot, Waleed Al Suqami, is the younger brother of Satam Al Suqami, one of five American Airlines Flight 11 hijackers."

The facts that the Kingdom Tower was designed by an American firm, that it would be the world's tallest structure, when complete in 2017, at a hair over a mile high, that none of these people in Saudi Arabia had done America any harm, and that the American Muslim Brotherhood caused the recent US attacks, not Saudi Arabia, was not lost by any of those present.

But for these seconds in command, an opportunity to be part of something this big and exciting was too powerful not to want to be part of. Besides, the American Muslim Brotherhood was an unknown entity at the moment, whereas the Kingdom Tower was a known entity. So, as armies have always done through history, when you can't find your enemy's army, you attract your enemy's fort. Kingdom Tower would certainly qualify as a fort.

The vice president continued, "You all know your jobs. You all know what to do. Make me and America proud."

The vice president exited the PEOC with General LeMay and Deputy Director of Defense Dempsey and headed across the White House grounds to his offices in the Eisenhower Executive Office Building, located next to the West Wing on the White House premises.

When situated behind closed doors, the vice president asked Dempsey how he was able to find and recruit this Waleed Al Suqami to fly the plane and become a martyr.

Deputy Director of Defense Dempsey replied, "We have been watching him and his family for a while now, and one would think, because of his brother Satam, they would be heroes in the Muslim community. Actually they are, but not within the house of Saud. Most, not all, of the royal family were taken off guard by 9/11. Besides their loosing face, they lost a ton of money. So the hijacker families of which most were Saudi, are persona non grata. Waleed Al Suqami and several of his junior officers in similar situations, have agreed with our Saudi agents' premise that the royal family was selfish not to embrace the Al Suqami family as heroes. Everyone feels Waleed Al Suqami is well within his rights to take revenge. The Kingdom Tower is King Abdulla's baby, and tomorrow it will suffer."

The Vice President asked LeMay to pour some Maker's Mark into three fine Waterford Chrystal tumblers. "That's an amazing, patriotic, heartwarming story, but cut the crap, general, and tell me what it took to get Waleed to martyr himself," asked the vice president.

"His immediate family will be relocated to a sandy desert town in Arizona with $10 million in a Phoenix bank."

The vice president smiled and said, "To the successful abortion tomorrow morning of King Abdulla's baby. Oh, it tastes so good going down."

CHAPTER 29

NYC

At the mayor's earlier press conference, Burk tried to slip away when he heard his name mentioned by that *CNN* reporter. He waited in the shadows and after the press conference broke followed her back to the *CNN* truck to get a better look at her. Slim, attractive, and diffidently dangerous.

Kelly felt she was being stalked; it happened often. She had good trade craft and circled the truck so she would loop right around into Burk. Burk was startled but knew he had been busted. They just stared at each other for what seemed minutes.

"What's your game?" Burk finally asked.

"I don't play games. Mr. Burk. Why don't you tell me your story and we can go from there?"

"Ms. Sullivan, I think someone has fed you some bad information about me. I told the cops what I knew, and they cleared me. Who's saying it ain't so?"

"Mr. Burk, why so defensive? I just asked the commissioner about your proximity to the murder. You know you have been in the limelight, so to speak, for the last couple of days. Doing all kinds of hero stuff, then your name came up on the Skinner murder report. I put two and two together and asked the question. That's all."

"Why don't I believe you, Ms. Sullivan?"

"When you get to know me better you will know I don't lie and I don't play games."

"Everybody plays games, Ms. Sullivan. It's just that some play fair and some cheat. Which do you play?"

Kelly didn't take the bait.

Burk had no immediate desire to know her better so he turned and walked away.

Kelly thought him attractive, but cold and dangerous.

When Burk finally caught up with Riley, he knew he would have a lot of explaining to do. The commissioner stuck his neck out for him, and now it would be hacked off. Sure, Burk had performed and because of him, NYC, unlike Chicago and L.A., didn't evacuate. His city survived without all the baggage that Chicago and L.A. now have to deal with. But instead of the mayor and commissioner being heroes, the media is now after their heads, all because of him. How did that happen? Burk smelled a rat and knew where to find it. By the time Burk got a hold of Riley, Riley was back at One Police Plaza.

Riley told Burk, "Get your ass here now, get your story together and it better be good."

Burk complied and was met in the lobby by the commissioner's aide and bodyguard, Captain Bounty. After Burk passed through the metal detectors, X-ray scanners and a trace portal machine (aka-puffers that detect explosives and illegal drugs) he was escorted into the express elevator up to the 14th floor and into Riley's office.

"Sit," said Riley. Riley had his back to Burk, and was looking out the window at the Brooklyn Bridge. As if by magic the door automatically closed. After a minute of silence, Riley said, "What the fuck were you thinking Tommy? Why didn't you tell me? Christ, Tommy, you know better than that."

"You're right, Captain," said Burk, "but just hear me out."

"It better be good, and keep it simple."

"Captain, I just didn't have a chance to tell you because the bombs and everything were happening so fast. Besides, I didn't do anything wrong and wasn't charged. This IRS scum Skinner, came to see me and tried to shake me down, but I didn't go for it. He left pissed and must have said something bad to the wrong people in the parking lot and got himself killed. That's it."

"Tommy," said Riley, "I know you better than that. I know that's not it. There is more and you're holding back."

"Right, Captain, I am holding back. Holding back from smacking that *CNN* reporter and whoever is pulling her chain."

"Where are you going with this Tommy?"

"Captain, this Sullivan broad might have picked up on the IRS agent's murder, and my named might have popped up, but who tipped her off that I was in on this bomb threat team with you and the mayor? I was under the radar, and my name was never mentioned. Only your and the mayor's inner circle and the president's team knew I was involved, and the mayor put a tight lid on the former. Sullivan was tipped off and for a reason. That reason was to make the mayor, you and me look bad."

"But why, Tommy? Why was she tipped and who tipped her off?"

Burk looked his captain in the eyes. "I just don't know for sure who or why, but I have my suspicions and need your help to sort it out and fast."

"What do you want to do?"

Just then there was a knock on the commissioner's door and in came his deputy commissioner, Captain Turner. "Boss, said Turner, I just got off the horn with Lt. Scrubs, our State Police liaison guy. Seems Trope K out of Brewster is running interference for the Feds and are, as we speak, hitting Burk's apartment in the Bronx."

Riley looked at Burk. "I think we now know who. Let's go find out the why."

CHAPTER 30

BRONX, NY

FBI Special Agent-in-Charge Hoar pulled up to Burk's Bronx apartment in a big black Suburban with two additional team members in the back seats. Two other FBI Suburban's were already there along with an FBI forensic equipment truck and two NY State Trooper Cars. Kelly Sullivan was there with her *CNN* camera crew. Not a low-key operation. Sullivan had just, 15 minutes previously, let slip live the incriminating evidence of Burk's involvement with the IRS murder. She had dug deep enough and found someone who heard a story. One of the three guys who turned Skinner's lights out supposedly bragged about it to an undercover cop. One thing lead to another, and after some deals granting complete immunity and a good amount of cash, gums began to flap, and she had the beginnings of a great story. Not one to be suckered, Kelly got three different sources before she broke the story and Special Agent Hoar got his warrant.

With the State Police cars light bar flashing and the Suburban's LED takedown lights flashing, Burk's apartment parking lot resembled a Christmas light show. There hadn't been this many cops and flashing lights in the neighborhood since, well, since last night. The apartment manager was rousted, keys produced, and doors unlocked, all in a matter of minutes. Special Agent Hoar, first in the door, to check for improvised explosive devices, was outfitted with a Hazmat encapsulated suit and a self-contained breathing apparatus. He had one of the techs air lock seal the open doorway and stationed a trooper to block anyone else entering, until he said differently.

Hoar, knew there would not be any booby traps, as they used to be called before the term IED's became politically correct. Hoar guessed *it was because boobies would be offended*. Hoar went directly to the computer and inserted a 32GB flash drive in the USB port. He turned the computer on and the flash drive started to download. He then went to the bathroom and sprinkled some powder near the toilet base, and another substance down the bathtub drain and ran a little water. He went back to the living room and put a glass on the table, some material in the ceiling then removed the flash.

In the hallway, Kelly in front of her camera crew, went live again.

"Breaking news," the anchor said. "*CNN* interrupts our regularly scheduled program to bring you the following breaking news. We are going live to Kelly Sullivan in the Bronx."

"Good Evening, Kelly Sullivan *CNN*. I am standing outside the Bronx apartment of FBI person of interest in the murder of IRS Agent William Skinner, New York bomb scare consultant, Mr. Thomas Burk. As you remember, I asked the mayor and commissioner about, during the mayor's press conference – I asked of Burk's relationship to the dead IRS agent found outside his apartment. As you will recall, the police commissioner said at the time, that he was aware of the incident but had no direct knowledge of Mr. Burk's apartment proximity to same. And the commissioner added that he would see if there is any connection and get back to me. He didn't, and that's why I, along with the FBI and NY State Police, are here looking for the truth. What are the mayor, police commissioner, and the police commissioner's 'private citizen/terrorist consultant,' Mr. Tommy Burk, hiding?

"FBI Special Agent Hoar, with warrant in hand, is now in Tommy Burks apartment, single handedly searching for IEDs, which may have been planted to destroy evidence. Earlier today, I reported that I uncovered new evidence connecting Mr. Burk with Abdul Azim Williams. Mr. Azim, the leader of a fanatic group in the Bronx, has admitted killing Federal Agent Skinner outside Mr. Burk's apartment Monday, November 10th. Mr. Azim has also admitted that he received a cash payment from Mr. Burk shortly after the murder and that they had some sort of special agreement. Speculation has it that IRS Agent

Skinner was closing in on Burk and Azim and their 'special agreement'. That was enough cause for a federal judge to issue a warrant to Special Agent Hoar to have Mr. Burk's apartment searched. We are about to go in now to Burk's apartment to see if that 'special Agreement' had anything to do with Monday's truck bombs in New York City.

"Here comes Special Agent Hoar with the all-clear for his forensic team and my exclusive *CNN* live crew, to enter the apartment to see if there can possibly be more, to Mr. Burk, than meets the eye."

Kelly and her crew along with a four-person forensic team, comprised of a computer tech, a print tech, a concealment tech– someone who looks in side-walls, and under floors and Sammy Kahn, who specializes in hazardous chemicals and toxic materials, entered the apartment. All similarly dressed in Hazmat suits as Hoar. Special Agent Hoar, after giving instructions to his photographer, told Kelly to stick with Sammy. The computer tech went to the computer, the concealment tech started looking in the ceilings, the print tech picked up the glass in the living room, and Sammy, Kelly, with her visor now down and her camera crew headed to the bathroom. With the *CNN* camera feeding a live report, Kelly began describing the search using her internal microphone. Sammy's laser detection systems, and radiation equipment could pick up minute traces of what they were looking for. As if on cue, Sammy turned the equipment on and bells and whistles started to go off just as they entered the bathroom. It was CSI meets reality TV, live.

This would become the perfect storm of live TV, what all other stations and media would die for. The world was all watching *CNN* live, and no one was watching anything or anyone else.

Live and simultaneously on: TV, radio, social media, and the internet, the world was about to learn of the unsung hero of NYC truck bombing scare. And that that hero, Tommy Burk was in fact a killer and the terrorist leader himself. That Burk had a federal agent, who was closing in on his bombing plot, killed. That Burk and a Muslim accomplice Abdul Azim Williams plotted to create the entire truck bombing scheme including Chicago and L.A. A story like this only comes along once in a life time, and Kelly had it and was going to take it over the top. This was her ticket to success in the 'Big Apple.'

CHAPTER 31

NYC-the Bronx

With front and rear security, three NYPD black Chevy Tahoe's, electronic sirens chirping, and LED takedown lights flashing, sped up FDR Drive, over the Triborough Bridge, to 287 North into the Bronx and to Burk's apartment.

Riley and Burk sitting in the rear seats of the middle Tahoe, were watching the live broadcast from the Burks apartment. Riley was shaking his head and looking back and forth between the LED screen and Burk. "Tommy, tell me this is all bullshit," said Riley.

Burk, ignoring Riley's question said, "This is good. They're good. It's all over; it's done."

"Burk, what the fuck are you talking about?" said Riley.

"It doesn't matter; they put the whole thing on me, on us."

"It does matter," said Riley. "For the record, Burk."

"For the record, Captain, it's mostly bullshit."

"Mostly? Mostly? What part is not bullshit, Sargent?"

"It is my apartment. Skinner was in my apartment—at his encouragement, I might add—but for no other reason than to shake me down. After he left my apartment, I saw, from my window, three gangbangers in the parking lot sitting on the hood of my car. I yelled down for them to get off my car. I went back to my apartment and did not see these gangbangers or anyone else for that matter attack or murder Skinner. Later when I heard sirens and lights in the parking lot,

I went down and saw the body and volunteered what information I had to the detective and ID the body. I was not charged, and went back to my apartment. I later went out to go to the store and bumped into the three guys that looked very much like the guys I saw from my window. As I went to my car, they approached me, and they were packing. They threatened me, so I bought them off. Yes, stupid, but I have to live with these guys, and if a thousand bucks makes life livable, it's my money. We did not have an agreement; we had an understanding. And that understanding was that for the cash they would leave me alone and stay off my car. Worth every penny as far as I was concerned.

"He told me his name was Abdul Azim Williams, and if it's now politically correct to call a gangbanger a fanatic group leader, then I am a primate's parent's brother."

Riley looked at Burk; looked him straight in the eye and saw it. Burk had told the truth. Pretty much, that is.

Soon they saw all the lights and action coming from Burk's apartment parking lot and were about to make the turnoff from the ramp when they heard *CNN's* Sullivan go live again.

CHAPTER 32

WASHINGTON, DC

The White House, Oval Office.

It was late for the president—almost 1:20 a.m. She and the secretary of state were on the last glass of Maker's Mark and had been watching the *CNN* exclusive. "John, said the president, it could not have gone better for us."

They had watched Kelly Sullivan's live exposé of the FBI forensic team's finding traces of Cesium 137 and ammonia nitrate in Burk's apartment. The pictures and sound were incredible. Now the Hazmat suits were off, and dozens of agents were hauling computers, trash, clothes and everything not nailed down, out of the apartment.

Secretary of State Kearney turned to the president. "This guy Burk is going away for a long time."

After they were done congratulating one another, the president picked up the phone to call FBI Director Miller to tell him he was now forgiven for missing the original threat. Just then, *CNN* broke onto the screen with a talking head announcing to stand by for a major breaking news out of Saudi Arabia.

The live Kelly broadcast, the most watched news program ever, was being bumped by a bigger story in Saudi Arabia. Could that be possible?

CNN reporter Dianne Kampar, came up live with a horrible building fire raging in the background and was looking around when her producer told her she was live.

"Good morning. This is *CNN* live from Jeddah, Saudi Arabia. Dianne Kampar reporting. But I don't think the morning will end well. Just about 20 minutes ago, at 8:46 a.m. Saudi time, a C-130 Hercules turbo prop crashed into the 93rd floor of the still under construction Kingdom Tower skyscraper here in Jeddah. Information is sketchy, but we have some initial reports that it took off from King Abdul Aziz International Airport around 8:30 a.m. this morning, piloted by a crew of Royal Saudi airmen out of the 4th Transport Squadron. It looped around the city and came straight for the Kingdom Tower."

Just then, film of the huge aircraft coming over the city at an extremely low altitude came up on the screen. The video with sound showed the Hercules getting lower and seemingly slower but louder and heading directly toward the middle of a huge building. Closer and closer, as if in slow motion, with the engines roaring, it smashed into the side of the building with a tremendous explosion of noise and fire and kept going almost out the other side. You could actually see the building shaking. Fire erupting from both penetrations and fuel and fire was spilling through the floors and cascading like napalm down the building skin. The nose was sticking out the back side of the building, and the tail was sticking out the front where the plane entered. The camera panned closer to the disaster and zoomed in at the tail sticking out of the fiery inferno. There it was, big as life, and for all the world to see. Right on the vertical stabilizer was an American flag decal. What the world would soon know as the "Joe Show" had just eclipsed the "Burk Show" as the most watched event in the history of the world. *CNN* was back on top.

The president and Secretary Kearney both remained staring at the screen. Secretary Kearney broke the silence. "I distinctly heard you tell the vice president to 'make sure it doesn't come back to us,' but the fucking idiot vice president of yours takes out a building with a plane with an American flag on it. No matter who flew the fucking plane, the world and the Muslim lunatics are going to blame us."

A knock on the door and the vice president sheepishly put his head in. The president waved him in and had him stand in front of the desk while she went around and sat down.

Secretary of State Kearney stood to the side waiting to be dismissed but instead the president laid into Vice President Joe Denning. "Joe, you fucked up big time. What were you thinking? Why the fuck didn't you have him fly a Saudi plane?

"Madam President, this is not what it looks like."

Excuse me, Mr. Vice President, but this is exactly what it looks like. The entire world knows we make the C-130s, but you had to advertise it by a plastering an American flag on stabilizer."

"Madam President, the pilot and crew were Saudi and sympathetic to the Unites States, but they stole one of our planes. The Saudi Air Force has its own fleet of C-130s with their flag plastered all over them, and he was supposed to fly one of those."

"Joe," said the president, "this morning at 9a.m., we are going to have a press conference in the Rose Garden. "Secretary of State Kearney, FBI Director Miller, and I are going to skewer Burk, the NYC mayor and the police commissioner and become heroes doing so. But now all everyone will want to talk about is why we, the United States of America, crashed the biggest fucking plane in the world into the biggest fucking building the world. When those questions come up, and I am sure they will, I am going to defer to you, Mr. Vice President, and you better calm everyone's fears and get them rooting for our team. Joe, you remember what I said to you last time we spoke?"

"Yes, Madam President, you said if it works I get the credit, and if it doesn't I fall on the sword."

"That's right, Joe, you get the credit or you fall on your sword. So at this morning's press conference you will stand in front of the press corps and convince them that we had nothing to do with this tragedy, but that you are going to find out who did and hold them responsible. But just in case the press doesn't buy your story – and I don't believe they will Joe – bring that sword you have hanging over your fireplace mantel. You must convince them that you're president and your country had nothing do with that big plane crashing into that big building. But if you can't, I want to see you fall on your sword in front of the entire fucking press corps on live TV.

"And Joe, don't fuck it up. I want to see it go all the way through with just the sword grip showing out the front of your bloody jacket. And on the pommel I want to see a tiny decal of the American flag."

The vice president knew the president wasn't kidding when she picked up the phone, got connected to his Secret Service director, and informed her that Celtic – the Secret Service handle for the vice president – would be bringing his sword to this morning's press conference.

CHAPTER 33

NYC-the Bronx

Just as the police commissioner's caravan turned into the parking lot, Riley and Burk watched both live out their window and on the LED screen, as Special Agent Hoar stood next to and in camera, as *CNN's* Kelly Sullivan reported that they had found traces of Cesium 137 and ammonia nitrate in Burk's apartment and that a federal judge had just issued an arrest warrant for Burk.

Just then, the caravan of New York's finest screamed into the parking lot only to be stopped dead by a State Police barricade and Feds in blue jackets with a big yellow FBI on the back. Vehicles with flashing lights and chirping sirens, guns drawn, badges flashed and words exchanged. It was a near run thing. Police Commissioner Riley got out and went right through the barricade, followed be his bodyguard, Captain Bounty and Burk. The State Police captain and FBI agents all rushed to head him off.

Riley walked directly up to Special Agent Hoar.

Special Agent Hoar said, "Thank you, commissioner, for delivering Burk. I have a warrant here for his arrest."

Police Commissioner Riley looked at Hoar and said, "How did you get the arrest warrant so fast, Agent Hoar? Did you just happen to know what you would find?" Hoar smiled, and held the arrest warrant up and started waving it in Riley's face and said, "This is for you, Police Commissioner Riley." Riley raised his hand up, as if to accept the warrant and said "And this is for you, Special Agent Hoar" 'Pow,' sucker punched Hoar right in the face.

Hoar dropped like a sack. Kelly Sullivan and *CNN* were of course filming this encounter, so Burk refrained from stomping Hoar. The State Police Captain and other agents looked on in complete shock. They all knew they should come to Hoar's aid but….

Before they could react, Riley took a step back and said, "You all know me and you know this is my city. You don't come into my city and pull bullshit like this. What you just attempted to pull off is unlawful and criminal. This whole thing is a setup, all the evidence was planted, and you're all accessories."

Just then twenty of NYC's finest patrol cars swooped into and surrounded the parking lot. Now the NYC Police outnumbered the Troopers and FBI by 3 to 1. The NYPD quickly took control. Riley asked the state police captain which SUV belonged to Hoar, and the captain pointed to the middle black Suburban. Riley directed one of his newly arrived lieutenants, to secure the vehicle and did the unprecedented: he placed all the FBI agents and their forensic team under arrest and directed the State Police Captain to remove his troopers immediately and head north out of the city.

Hoar slowly rose to his feet and screamed at the commissioner, "Riley, I have direct authorization from my director and the president to be here. You're obstructing an FBI investigation and have assaulted a federal officer. Riley, you're going down."

Riley looked at Agent Hoar and his bloody nose. "It looks like you're the one who went down, Special Agent-in-Charge Hoar. Take them away lieutenant." To one of his commanders, Captain Squire, Riley said, "Take charge of the apartment and all the collected evidence. Get our own forensic team here now and go through Special Agent Hoar's Suburban and the apartment; you know what to look for."

As the State Police began pulling out and the FBI agents and techs were being escorted to a newly arrived NYPD transportation cruisers, Burk made eye contact with one of the FBI agent as he was being led by. Burk keep staring and thinking until Riley interrupted his thoughts.

"Burk, follow me," said Riley and started off toward the apartment. When Riley turned back and saw Burk had not moved, he said "Burk." When Burk still didn't respond, he headed back to see what held Burks complete attention. Right into Burk's ear he said "Seen a ghost have you, Tommy?"

"As a matter of fact Captain, I have. Remember we had two lookers at the East Side location? Amid and someone he said was a nobody, just a messenger. Someone called Shihab?"

"Yeah, so what" answered Riley.

"Well," said Burk, "that nobody, that messenger, is now an FBI agent, and he's sitting in the back of that police cruiser."

"Sergeant, come with us and bring two men," said Riley.

The five of them, with the *CNN* team in tow, walked directly to the cruiser Burk had pointed out. Standing behind the car as not to be seen. Burk pointed out, through the rear glass window the man known to him as Shihab. Riley directed his sergeant to text the officer inside the car to release the door lock and be prepared to be boarded. Riley then directed to sergeant to be prepared to do an immediate oral exam of the man. The sergeant pulled on some latex gloves, and his corporal with a baton in hand pulled open the door, released the seatbelt restraint, and pulled the cuffed FBI agent out of the car and into the parking lot ground. The corporal had the man's mouth open, and the baton inserted before Shihab or whoever he was, knew what hit him. And what hit him was the corporal's baton. Dazed, Sammy on his back could vaguely comprehended what was happening. They obviously were searching for a hidden suicide capsule, but from Kelly's point of view and to the viewers watching live, the cops, with direction of the police commissioner were assaulting another handcuffed FBI agent.

The world was again tuned in as the "Burk Show" as the "Joe Show" got bumped.

CHAPTER 34

WASHINGTON, DC

The White House: Oval Office and Rose Garden.

After just a few hours sleep, President Hilton, Secretary of State Kearney, and FBI Director Miller were all having coffee in the Oval Office and preparing for the 9 a.m. press conference in just about one hour.

Things had definitely gone south earlier this morning after the vice president left. The FBI director had called to say they had a problem in the Bronx. It seemed that Riley and Burk had interrupted the FBI search of Burk's apartment, secured the scene, dismissed the State Police, assaulted two federal agents, and impounded all the evidence and FBI property. He neglected to mention that Riley arrested the entire FBI team because Riley had in fact released most of them at NYC - FBI headquarters as soon as they got back to the city. But he did tell the president that two agents were detained. Instead of the president going nuts over this news she seemed to take it as just another nail in Bloomfield's, Riley and Burk's coffin. The tricky part was that Special Agent Hoar and another FBI forensic tech, Sammy Khan, were under house arrest, and Special Agent Hoar, should he talk, could lead the planting of evidence right back to him and then to the president. Without access to the police commissioner's office and many unreturned phone calls, FBI Director Miller had no idea what was going on inside police headquarters and what, if anything, Hoar had told the police. FBI Director Miller also had no idea why they had apprehended the forensic tech, Sammy Kahn, except that maybe they suspected him of planting the evidence, which of course, was not true. Kahn just did what he was supposed to do- discovered the evidence.

"Where's the vice president?" asked Secretary of State Kearney.

"Maybe he decided not to join us this morning," responded the president.

A knock on the door answered the question. "Madam President, Secretary Kearney, Director Miller," said the vice president as he entered to room.

"Where is the sword?" asked the president.

"They would not let me bring it in here. It's outside with one of the Secret Service agents."

"Well good, I am afraid you are going to need it, Joe," said the president.

FBI Director Miller was looking at the secretary to see if he knew what was going on but could read nothing from his stern expression.

"Ok everyone, it's show time," said the president. "Let's give them a damn fine show, shall we?"

On that, they all got up and headed out the door toward the Rose Garden followed by the Secret Service, cabinet members, and other agency heads.

The president stopped for a second to make sure the vice president picked up his package, then led the way out.

The media received the following announcement via social media yesterday, and everyone who is anyone rushed to get their clearance request in before 9 a.m. Because of the location, only one reporter from each media outlet would be allowed. Kelly Sullivan from *CNN* was on the list, but she decided not to attend. The release read:

President Hilton will host a Rose Garden news conference tomorrow morning. She will make opening remarks at 9 a.m. EDT and take questions from the media afterwards.

The news conference is open press.

Pre-set: 8 a.m.

Final Gather: 8:45 a.m.

Gather at the North Doors of the Palm Room

To attend, reporters must be cleared onto White House grounds. To obtain clearance, please email your full name, date of birth, social security number, and country of citizenship to press@who.eop.gov. The deadline to submit clearance requests for the news conference is 9 a.m. EDT today, Wednesday, November 13th.

There was no doubt that this would be a huge event as everyone expected the president to give a statement about Kingdom Tower disaster or as the story has been headlined by the *NY Post*: "Blown to Kingdom Come Tower." And if that wasn't enough there was the ongoing Burk story which was being hailed as the gift that keeps giving. Burk, the hero of NYC Bombed Bombs, had a warrant issued for his arrest. He was being skewed as the mastermind of the American Muslim Brotherhood, responsible for all the recent bomb threats, fires, lootings, shootings, injuries, deaths, and the worst economic and international tsunami to ever hit our shores. Burk has gone from hero to traitor in just a few days. If convicted on these charges, he would be sentenced to death, and it was overheard, around the *CNN* water cooler, that *CNN* and Kelly Sullivan would bring his execution to you live. Another first.

The Rose Garden sits in front of the west wing of the White House, and although larger venues were available, the president wanted this press conference intimate and controlled. The fact that it would be bitter cold today did not escape the president, and that is exactly why she wanted it held outdoors. All the reporters would have to decide to bundle up and look like babushkas or freeze while attempting to look professional. The president didn't care what they decided because either way they would not want to prolong their embarrassment or discomfort. The president intended to wear her navy blue Chanel suit with a white silk scarf. She would look presidential and in charge with her little American flag lapel pin and two big American flags behind her. The fact that the stage and podium were heated did not escape the president.

About 50 approved reporters, some babushka, some professional, all seated in a grid of chairs, with a single pooled TV camera, and awaited the President of the United States.

Without fanfare and exactly on time the president approached the podium and the press stood. Directly behind the president, were Vice President Joe Denning," Secretary of State John Kearney and FBI Director Robert Miller.

Back and off to the side were the rest of the president's entourage. The press corps continued standing.

The president, looking radiant and warm began. "Good morning every-body, please have a seat." Desiring to set an immediate easy tone, she said, "I hear you have some questions for me." Some chuckles emanated from the press and entourage. "But ah, let me make an opening statement and a few remarks at the top, and then I will open it up.

"On November 10, our fellow citizens, our way of life, our very freedom, came under attack in a series of deliberate and deadly terrorist acts. The victims were in cities, in their homes, schools and offices – secretaries, businessmen and women, military and federal workers, moms and dads, friends and neighbors. Thousands of lives were ended by evil, despicable acts of terror. The pictures of good citizens fleeing cities, homes and buildings, fires burning throughout the land, have filled us with disbelief, terrible sadness, and a quiet, unyielding anger. These acts that led to thousands of injuries and deaths and billions of dollars in damages were intended to frighten our nation into chaos and retreat. But they have failed. Our country is strong. A great people has been moved to defend a great nation. Terrorist attacks can shake our foundation, but they cannot crack the foundation of America. These acts were intended make us afraid, but they cannot dent the steel of American resolve. America was targeted for attack because we're the brightest beacon for freedom and opportunity in the world. And no one will keep that light from shining. This week, our nation saw evil – the very worst of human nature – and we responded with the best of America. With the daring of our rescue workers, with the caring for strangers and neighbors who came to give blood and help in any way they could."

As the speech went on, murmurs were beginning to be heard from the senior reporters and fingers were flying across smart phone keyboards. Many of the press realized the same thing – they had all heard this speech before. They all seemed to realize at the same time that it was same speech that President Bush addressed the nation with, right after 9-11. President Hilton was plagiarizing President Bush's 9-11 speech!

"Immediately following the first attack's threat," President Hilton continued, "I advised all three city mayors to trust but verify all the information before enacting evacuation orders and not to evacuate unless they were 100% sure the bombs would explode. But, that the final decision on evacuation was theirs and theirs alone. Unfortunately, only New York City and Mayor Bloomfield took my advice, over the objection of Mr. Burk, their terrorist consultant, who advised me to order evacuation. Disregarding that suggestion, I further implemented our government's emergency response plans. Our military is powerful, and it's prepared. Our emergency teams are working in Chicago, L.A and Washington D.C. to help with local rescue efforts. Our first priority was to get help to those who have been injured, contain the fires and to take every precaution to protect our citizens at home and around the world from further attacks. The functions of our government continue without interruption. Federal agencies in Washington are open for business. Our financial institutions remain strong, and the American economy is open for business as well.

"The search is underway for those who were behind these evil acts. I have directed the full resources of our intelligence and law enforcement communities to find those responsible and to bring them to justice. We will make no distinction between the terrorists who committed these acts and those who harbor them. The good news is that we have arrested the mastermind and many of his accomplishes to which I will ask FBI Director Miller to address.

"I appreciate so very much the support and advice of my good friend during these troubled times, Secretary of State John Kearney, and members of Congress who have joined me in strongly condemning these attacks. And on behalf of the American people, I thank the many world leaders who have called to offer their condolences and assistance. America and our friends and allies join with all those who want peace and security in the world, and we stand together to win the war against terrorism.

"Tonight, I ask for your prayers for all those who grieve, for the children whose worlds have been shattered, for all whose sense of safety and security has been threatened. And I pray they will be comforted by a power greater than any of us.

"This is a day when all Americans from every walk of life unite in our resolve for justice and peace. America has stood down enemies before, and we will do so this time. None of us will ever forget this week, yet we go forward to defend freedom and all that is good and just in our world.

"Thank you. And God bless America."

Even her cabinet and others present were shaking their heads. CIA Director John Bader turned to the Secretary of Defense Chuck Newel and said "I can't believe she stole fucking Bush's 9-11 speech. Does she think people are stupid and won't remember?"

"Unfortunately John," replied Chuck, "she did, she does, and they won't."

The press, unimpressed with the president's stolen pep talk, all, and as loud as they could, started asking questions, but it sounded like one big tremendous, thunderous roar. The press corps, who were not stupid and did not forget, were now on their feet and anything but controlled.

The president ducked back to allow FBI Director Miller up to the podium. Miller waved the press corps quiet and said, "Before the president opens it up for questions, she asked me to give you an update on the terrorist attack investigation."

That seemed to calm the press corps down or at least get their attention and one by one they began to set back down.

The director began to read his prepared statement. "Early this morning, FBI agents, with assistance from the New York State Police, and of course the New York Police force, raided Mr. Thomas Burk's apartment in the Bronx. Mr. Burk is currently in the custody of the NYC Police Department. The FBI has charged Mr. Burk in conspiracy with a known Muslim terrorist in the murder of IRS Agent William Skinner and its cover up. It is believed Agent Skinner had stumbled on the terrorist plot, but before he could inform the FBI of his suspicions he was silenced. Mr. Burk has also been charged, based on his actions and evidence found in his apartment, early this morning, with masterminding the three city bomb plots and the torching of America. Mr. Burk, a longtime friend and associate of New York Police Commissioner Riley, was engaged by Commissioner Riley and Mayor Bloomfield to assist in establishing, then aborting, the threat which it now appears he, Burk, created. Our investigation is continuing, and we will leave no stone unturned, and may the evidence lead us to prosecute to the fullest extent of the law, Mr. Burk and whoever is a conspirator or protector of Mr. Burk."

CHAPTER 35

NYC Police headquarters

In the police commissioner's office, Riley and Burk watched in total amazement what was on the screen before them. "How can he make this bullshit up?" asked Burk rhetorically. "I did not tell the president to order an evacuation."

"Yes you did," said Riley.

"No I didn't," Burk said.

Riley interrupted. "You did. Tommy, because you can't keep your big fucking mouth shut. It doesn't matter that you went on to explain why it was a bad idea to evacuate, they are going to use your own words. You said, 'You're the president, order us to evacuate.' Don't you understand how they use words and play games? We can never beat them at the 'he said she said' game. The president and FBI director have more resources and more importantly, more air time than the mayor and police commissioner of New York City."

"Then we just have to play a different kind of game. One they don't know how to play and we start right now." Said Burk.

"What have you got in mind?" asked Riley.

"It's not in my mind yet, it's more in my gut."

A knock on the door brought them back to business. The results were in on the initial chemical and toxic test from Agent Hoar's person and his personal Suburban. Both proved positive to the ammonia nitrate and the Cesium 137. The results from Hoar's person could be argued, but the Suburban positive results could not. Hoar and therefore the FBI had just been busted. Hoar had use the Suburban to transport the evidence to the apartment. But for now it would be Riley's and Burk's second best keep little secret. Part of the new game they were inventing as they go along. They decided to call it the "Frame Game." The first best keep secret was that their other FBI detainee, Sammy Kahn, was in fact the other looker Burk saw in the window standing next to Amid, the man who Burk felt in his gut was no messenger and no nobody. The way he disappeared from the apartment and building without a trace. No! This nobody was a somebody. This was Mr. Big, head of the American Muslim Brotherhood, but his day job was with the FBI. You couldn't make this stuff up.

"Let get back in there with FBI Special Agent Hoar and the FBI forensic tech Kahn," Burk said, "but I want to start first with Kahn. Where's my gardening bag?"

They went down to the detention floor and the two interrogation rooms that were side by side with a sliver corridor between containing AV equipment and two way mirrors looking into each room. Uniforms were stationed at each door. Riley and Burk passed Hoar's room and stopped in front of Kahn's. They needed to get their game face on before entering.

Special Agent Hoar meanwhile, like his neighbor across the corridor, had one hand cuffed to the metal chair, which was itself bolted to the floor. He had not been allowed to talk to anyone since police took him and his team into custody. As far as he knew, the rest of his team were somewhere in the same building and going through the same humiliation. He couldn't believe that Riley had the balls to arrest the FBI. Where does he get off? He knew he would be released within the next few hours, at least he keep reassuring himself that Director Miller or the president would intervene. The bigger problem, as far as he was concerned, was not if somehow they found out he planted the evidence, that couldn't hurt him because he was following orders. The problem that bothered him to no end was, that he and his team got arrested by the NYC Police.

There is no love lost between the two agencies. He knew, however, that wherever he went from now on: fellow agents, cops, secretaries, newbies and janitors would all be snickering behind his back. He would be forever known as the FBI Special Agent-in-Charge who got himself and his entire team attested by the cops. The FBI, Federal Bureau of Idiots led by Special Agent Stupid. His career was over unless his bosses, Deputy Director Johns and Director Miller came up with some fantastic cover story. If not, he might as well cop a plea of planting the evidence. At least he would be an FBI legend instead of an FBI joke.

He looked at his reflection in the metal table and saw above the gauze, covering his broken nose, that his left eye was now swollen. They had a doctor attend to his broken nose soon after he got there but not before they put him through all kinds of trace portal machines. Puffers-sniffer machines. He hoped the protective gear he was wearing, would block any traces of the ammonia nitrate and Cesium 137 residue. If not, he would just say it rubbed off after the suits came off. His impounded Suburban was an entirely different problem. But why did they go after his forensic guy, Kahn? He was just a tech nerd. Because Kahn's equipment detected the evidence? He was just doing his job. The evidence was real, and it was in the apartment. Riley and Burk are going down. He smiled at the thought of him being assigned, by Director Miller, to arrest Police Commissioner Riley and his buddy Burk. That would square things.

Riley had his office contact the FBI personnel department in Washington, to ask them to pull Sammy Khan's records, but they still had not arrived. Riley had no doubt, after what he did to Special Agent Hoar and his team, he and the NYPD were persona non grata with the FBI. The American Muslim Brotherhood leader's name and address they got from Amid proved good, but they found absolutely nothing incriminating in Samir Khan's apartment, not even a picture. His apartment looked like it was cleaned by ServePro. "Like it never even happened". In fact, it was too clean. And if you believed what you saw – or more importantly what you didn't see – in his apartment, this guy Samir Kahn could in fact be one and the same. Samir Kahn, leader of the American Muslim Brotherhood, was also Sammy Kahn, FBI forensic tech.

Burk and Riley had put it all together back in Burk's parking lot shortly after they tossed the tech guy Sammy Kahn. Sammy also known as Samir, and also known as Shihab, the nobody, the messenger. He was the second guy in the looker's room who had miraculously escaped.

The cop at the door opened it and Riley and Burk entered. The door closed behind them. As they sat down across from FBI forensic tech Sammy Kahn, they expected a lot of resistance. Would they be able to get to Sammy to admit to being Shihab then Shihab to admit to being Samir? Riley would again be the good guy, and Burk would be himself. Burk put his gardening tool on the table, noticed that he hadn't clean Amid's blood off, and they got ready for the long haul and some good old fashion blood and guts.

"Mr. Kahn, I am NY Police Commissioner Riley, and this is Mr. Burk, who is also associated with the NYPD. We have released most of your associates, but your boss, Special Agent Hoar, is rooming right next door to you. Shall I call you Sammy or Samir?"

Kahn was staring directly into Burk's eyes the entire time Riley was speaking. Neither Kahn nor Burk blinked or moved a hair. Kahn broke the ice with "I have seen you before, Mr. Burk."

"And I you, Mr. Kahn, through the looking glass, so to speak," said Burk.

"Yes," said Kahn, "through the looking glass. But I have also seen you on TV, Mr. Burk. You are the one who figured out the bombs would not go off, and for that and for discouraging the city evacuation, you became a hero. Then, as quickly as you were placed on the pedestal, someone kicked it over, and you came crashing down. I trust my tenure, as the precipitant of hero worship, will last a tad longer. I have also watched, with complete fascination, I might add, how you were, shall we say, credited for my smoke and mirror production. I have no real inside information about your involvement in the IRS agent's murder, but I sure as hell am not going to stand by and have you take credit for my masterpiece. Don't you agree, Mr. Burk? And if you haven't realized by now how absolutely cooperative I intend to be, you can show your appreciation by putting your garden pruner away. Thank you."

Burk looked at Riley then took the pruner off the table and placed it back into his jacket pocket. Burk looked back at Sammy. "Don't stop now, Mr. Kahn; you are, as they say, on a roll."

Kelly Sullivan was initially fired up for this press conference and had every intention of again asking the first questions. After her Burk show, she headed to Washington but when she landed she had changed her mind. Now she sat aboard the Washington/NYC shuttle in complete confusion and was about to land back at LaGuardia. She was deep in thought, putting it all together. She now understood that this whole thing had been a set up. She was the one used to set it up, and Burk was just a patsy. Hoar, Miller and even the president had lied to her. She knew what she had to do. She made up her mind to set it right. Kelly pulled out her phone and sent a text to Commissioner Riley.

Just then Police Commissioner Riley's cell phone beeped. He slid his hand in his jacket pocket, pulled out the phone and saw that he had a message from the *CNN* reporter Kelly Sullivan. He didn't remember giving her his unlisted number, but there she was.

Burk glanced over at Riley as if to say, *you're texting? What could be more important then what we are hearing now from Mr. Sammy?*

Riley looked up and saw the puzzlement in Burk's eyed and said, "You're not going to believe who wants to have a stop and chat."

CHAPTER 36

WASHINGTON, DC

The White House, Oval Room and Rose Garden.

The president now came back to the podium. With her hands, she gestured for the press corps to quiet down and when they finally did, she said she would open the floor up for questions.

Every reporter stood at that moment yelling and waving and hoping to be noticed. The president tired quickly of the press conference and had no intentions of answering any questions from this rabble. She would leave that to her subordinates. The president searched the crowd, looking for the press corps plant who would ask about the Kingdom Tower incident. The president would then take her leave and turn it over to Vice President Denning, who would, no doubt, appease the assembled in one way or another. The president had no intention of being present when either happened.

"For the first question I will ask…" The entire press corps had decided independently not to get "out yelled" by the reporter next to them, stood in unison and did their best to be noticed and picked. Unfortunately, the deck was stacked and the president found the plant in the third row left and pointed at him and said, "Jason." Everyone else quieted and sat down, wondering why Jason Stuart from *FOX* got picked. *FOX* never supported the president yet she honored *FOX* with the first question.

"Thank you Madam President, Jason Stuart *FOX TV.* Can you tell American people and the world categorically, that you and the American government had absolutely no involvement with the crashing of an American plane into the Kingdom Tower in Saudi Arabia?"

The president feigned disappointment and irritation by the question but seemed to take the high road and responded in kind. "Thank you Jason. As you and everyone here and around the country, and around the world can appreciate, FBI Director Miller, Secretary of State Kearney and I have been completely immersed in dealing with the New York, Chicago, and Los Angeles bomb threats, evacuations, and of course the forest fires that have devastated America. I am still following up with my promise to the American people to do what I call 'the four F's.'"

The secretary and director looked at each other in horror, anticipating the president would tell the world, her and Burk's high school sexual fantasy.

Accenting all four words with an F, she said "Find all those responsible. When we do —and it will be soon – make them Feel the full weight of American justice system. When they are found guilty – and there will be no mistaking about that – they will Fry. Eventually our great country will move on. We may not remember their names, but we will never Forget what they have done to us.

"Now to your specific question, Jason. Vice President Denning has graciously stepped in and offered his leadership and international experience to look into this unfortunate plane crash in Saudi Arabia. Working with his peers in our investigative agencies, he has developed new information that I am quite sure he would like to share with you." The president turned to the vice president and said loud enough for everyone to hear, "Joe, do you want to take a stab at this?"

The vice president seemed momentarily taken back by the president's deliberate dig but continued toward the podium. As the president stepped to the side, she whispered to the vice president, "Give them a good show, Joe." The president then walked off the stage followed by her Secret Service detail and senior cabinets and agency heads, leaving all second tier bureaucrats behind to sink or swim with the vice president.

The president's entourage rounded the corner and disappeared into the White House. The press corps had just been given the old bait and switch, but before they could check and see if they still had their wallets. The vice president, holding some sort of package at his side, stepped up to the podium and looked fully in charge. The vice president began. "First of all I would like to offer my and our entire country's sympathy to King Abdulla and all the great Saudi Arabian people for this horrific incident. Our prayers and hearts are with you, and America is here for you. God bless you, King Abdulla, and God bless the great Saudi Arabian people."

An audible grasp came from the entourage behind the vice president and from the press corps in front. Everyone seemed to be shaking their heads in amazement over the vice president's complete religious indifference. The vice president just kind of stopped looked around and said "What?" Oblivious of his ignorance, he quickly regained his composure and continued. "I want to make this perfectly clear. The president and America had absolutely nothing to do with this incident. My findings and those of Saudi and other international investigative agencies clearly conclude that this was an internal incident, carried out by traitors within the Royal Saudi Air Force. Yes, these traitors have claimed sympathy with America because of our recent troubles. Yes, the C-130 was purchased from the United States in 2011. And yes the Kingdom Tower was designed by an American firm. But that's as deep as a U.S-connection goes."

Jason was fast on his feet with a follow up question "Mr. Vice President, with all due respect, that's old news. What is the new information the president said you developed?"

"Had you not interrupted, Jason, I would have gotten to it. The new information is that – and this is very good news – the Kingdom Tower is going to be rebuilt. I spoke with King Abdulla this morning and pledged him $1 million for the rebuilding, and he graciously accepted. So only $29 billion and 999 million to go. With the way we piss away oil here feeding our cars, they should be able to make that up in a year or so."

Amazingly, and to the credit of the entire press corps, no one laughed but just looked stunned. Less enthusiastic about getting anything of substance from the vice president, the amount of hands up and yelling for attention seem to subside. The vice president decided to call on a local reporter.

"Mr. Vice President, Thomas Belk, *Washington Post.* A question and a follow up please. Why is the president not up here answering questions? My follow up is that my sources within the White House and in the intelligent community are telling me that the U.S. was involved up to their eyeballs in this Kingdom Tower plane crash. And that it was in retaliation for—not sympathy for—the city bomb threats and forest fires perpetrated by the American Muslim Brotherhood."

The vice president turned white and seemed to move in slow motion but suddenly speeded up and said, "Mr. Belk, the president is running the country and hunting down those who are responsible for attacking us. And as for your follow up, and let me make this perfectly clear, your sources in the White House, if in fact they exist, should be filed in your Rolodex as unreliable. Your sources in the intelligent community are just p-l-a-n-e stupid."

Hands went up and calls to be picked filled the garden. The vice president looked for someone easy and noticed a quiet dark-skinned man with a beard and wearing some sort of turban and robe. The vice president pointed to him, but reporters on either side of him seemed to think the vice president was pointing to them so they all jumped up and started to ask away. The vice president would not be bullied and said, "No. The gentleman with the turban, please. The others sat down and the gentleman with the turban slowly stood and said very softly, "Fayez Al-Omari, *Al Jazeera America.* Thank you, Mr. Vice President."

The vice president could barely hear him and said, "Mr. Fayez, can you please speak up here."

Fayez confused by what he heard, or exactly what the vice president meant, jumped up and briskly walked down the aisle and toward the podium and the vice president. Although older, he moved very fast and closed in on the vice president before anyone could react – except for the vice president security detail. Mr. Fayez Al-Omari of *Al Jazeera America,* who looked like a very short version of Osama bin Laden, was tackled to the floor by two Secret Service agents, in front of the press corps and the entire world. At the same instant the vice president's head security agent grabbed the vice president and pulled him down behind the podium in fear that Fayez Al-Omari had a bomb strapped to his body. This all happened in seconds and then there was complete silence. No bomb went off. No nothing. Mr. Fayez Al-Omari of *Al Jazeera America* offered absolutely no resistance. The press corps was too stunned to move. The vice president, sensing an opportunity to build on his tough guy reputation, wrestled away from his agent's grip and jumped up from behind the podium brandishing a U.S. Marine Corps officer's ceremonial Mameluke sword, a Scimitar-like weapon with a white ivory grip. The vice president pointed the sword at Mr. Al-Omari and ordered the security detail to release him. The Secret Service hesitated, but the vice president insisted. The two Secret Service agents climbed off Mr. Al-Omari. Mr. Al-Omari slowly got to his feet, quite shaken and bruised, brushed himself off and with a curved Persian looking sword pointed at him, said "My apologies, Mr. Vice President, I thought I understood you to say "Could I please come up here." The vice president quickly realized the misunderstanding and the embarrassment it was surely going to cause, especially with him pointing an Arab-looking sword at an Arab-looking man. The vice president realized very quickly that what he did in the next few seconds would change his fate and possibly that of the entire world. Known for thinking on his feet, Vice President Joe Denning had what is known as an "aha" moment. He raised the sword horizontally over his head and grabbed the blade with his left hand, He looked to the heavens and in his most solemn voice exclaimed, "Allahu Akbar."

A loud audible gasp arose from the press corps. The vice president instantly realized that he had not succeeded but in fact again made things worst. The vice president knew the world was watching and those who weren't would soon be seeing news alerts, Tweets and YouTube posts that would follow him for the rest of his life. Joe Denning, Vice President of the United States was a good man, an honorable man, a Marine and would not let these last few minutes define his entire life. In front of the press corps, his second tier team, his security detail and Mr. Fayez Al-Omari of *Al Jazeera America*, he took the US Marine Corps Mameluke sword and with both hands on the blade edge, pressed the sword tip tight to his stomach, put the swords pommel against the heated platform stage floor, and fell on his sword. This happened so quickly and was so unexpected, that the blade was in and out of the back of the vice president before anyone could react. And there, on the sword pommel, just proud of the vice presidents blood soaked hands and that no one had yet noticed, was a tiny decal of the American flag. Joe was a believer that the devil was in the details.

CHAPTER 37

WASHINGTON, DC

The White House, Oval Room.

The president, Secretary of State Kearney and FBI Director Miller had all watched *FOX News* in total amazement during the final moments of Vice President Denning's press conference. The president sensed something weird in the vice president's eyes as he narrowed his search for the next reporter to call on. Had he only picked one of the others with their hands up, everything would have ended so differently. But as the vice president searched, the president could see where he was heading and said aloud, "Don't go there Joe" But the vice president couldn't hear. Had this Mr. Fayez Al-Omari of *Al Jazeera America* been wearing his hearing aid and just asked his question, things would have certainly turned out differently. Even if the vice president had remained hidden behind the podium, it all could have been explained away.

A misunderstanding for sure, but an Arab man in a turban and robe, or anyone for that matter, approaching the vice president's podium uninvited would be restrained. It might have looked bad but it could have been pushed off to the overzealous Secret Service agents overly protecting their vice president. What happened next could not be explained away, except to say that the vice president had somehow just snapped – the Vice President of the United States coming from out behind the podium with a sword and pointing it at an *Al Jazeera America* reporter. Then lifting the sword and praising Allah. It just couldn't get any stranger. That was the *New York Post* cover. That was the Pulitzer Prize-winning story. But then, like leaving the football game in the middle of the third quarter, with your home team down 20 points and thinking it's over. But just as you walk out of the stadium you hear the home town crowd go wild and you instantly realize that you just made the biggest mistake of your life. So here is the vice president instantly realizing he has just made the biggest mistake of his life and there was nowhere to turn, no one else to blame and nowhere to go. Everyone was completely mesmerized by what was happening. Pin drop quiet. What was the vice president going to do next? Was this some sort of "Saturday Night Live" John Belushi parody? Where they being punked? They were watching the Vice President of the United States, standing above a short Osama Bin Laden looking character, sword raised, and praising Allah. Where could it possibly go from there? Then for better or worse, depending on your point of view, the vice president with tears in his eyes and looking so pathetic, all of a sudden mans up and brings the sword down and places it methodically between his stomach and the deck and proceeds to, in front of the world and without so much as a whimper, fall on his sword and commit a form of Hara-Kiri live in front of the entire world.

The secretary of state and the FBI director wisely felt it prudent, to allow the president to comment first, as they did not know how the president would react. The president looked at them and said almost admiringly, "Joe, I didn't realize you were that good. No one —and I mean no one – will be talking about anything for the next six months but our beloved vice president falling on his sword. I told him he had to keep it away from me or fall on his sword. Joe certainly exceeded my expectations."

CHAPTER 38

BANH MI SAIGON RESTAURANT

Grand Street, Little Italy.

After Burk read the text on Riley's smart phone, they continued to interrogate Sammy for another two hours. Burk and Police Commissioner Riley then left the interrogation room and headed out the building. At the building entrance lobby they picked up Riley's aid/body guard, Captain Bounty. Riley had his car waiting out front and told his driver, Officer Tanner, to head to Little Italy and Banh Mi Saigon restaurant. Tanner knew where to go as his boss often would eat lunch there. Burk asked Riley if he knew where this was heading and that Riley replied, "Sergeant Burk, I think it's all about to become crystal clear, so keep your mouth shut and don't fuck this up." On the way to the restaurant, they watched, in amazed silence, highlights of the president's press conference including Millers damming inditement and the vice president's suicide.

The black Chevy Tahoe double parked directly in front of the restaurant on Grand Street, between Mott and Mulberry. Riley, Bounty and Burk exited the Tahoe and headed toward the restaurant. The driver, Officer Tanner, stayed in the SUV and kept the motor running and the heat on. He knew from past experience that the commissioner could come running out at any second responding to an emergency, and he had to be ready to roll. He also knew that in a matter of minutes a rocky cop would pull up next him while he was double parked and tell him to move. It always happened because the black SUV's was pretty typical in the city and the commissioner didn't use NYPD plates.

The Banh Mi Saigon restaurant was not really a restaurant, but more of a Vietnamese sandwich take-out shop with limited seating. The owners always keep one table available in case the commissioner came in. Tanner, the good driver he was, usually called ahead to let them know they were rolling toward them for lunch. They had great sandwiches. The BBQ pork was perfectly seasoned and flavorful, and the baguette was perfectly toasty outside with a nice soft core.

Kelly Sullivan was already there and seated when they arrived. Riley asked her what she would like, and Kelly informed him that she already ordered. Riley and Burk grabbed a couple of stools at Kelly's table while Captain Bounty went to the counter and ordered four sandwiches and drinks. He then walked to the entrance and casually browsed a *NY Post* while the sandwiches were being prepared. All three knew each other, and after an awkward moment they all shook hands. A wall mounted LED was replaying all the press conference highlights and Riley, Burk and Sullivan watched in silence for a few minutes.

"Your dime," Riley finally said.

Kelly, wearing a black Armani suit with white pearls looked very fashionable—more suited for Madison Avenue than Grand Street—but Kelly could look good anywhere anytime. Burk was staring at Kelly and thinking, *"For a reporter, she really looks good. Had she not been trying to screw him every chance she got, he might have liked to screw her."*

Kelly said, "Yes Commissioner Riley, my dime. Thank you and Mr. Burk for seeing me. I–

Burk interrupted. "Ms. Sullivan, is this off the record, and can we assume it's not being recorded?"

Kelly responded curtly, "Yes and yes. May I continue, Mr. Burk?" Burk nodded. "I have recently come to realize that I have been taken for a ride, and I don't like where they took me. I have been used and I have unnecessarily and unfairly hurt some good people and my city. I also believe Commissioner Riley and Mr. Burk that, as I said in my text, I am being followed. And I believe soon I will have a new enemy. I am here with the both of you because when that happens we will have the same enemy."

Riley said, "Ms. Sullivan, we have already intercepted your tail, and although we ID'd them as FBI, we did not stop them. So yes, they know we are meeting but don't know what we are discussing."

"And neither do I," added Burk. "Just what are we discussing?"

Captain Bounty came over with the sandwiches and drinks, including Kelly's papaya salad with fresh mint and shrimp. Bounty took his and Tanners' sandwiches out to the Tahoe. For the next few minutes, they all proceeded to eat their lunch until it became a bit uncomfortable. Sensing that the time was right, Kelly spent the next 20 minutes explaining how she was contacted, why, and by whom.

When she was done, it became clear to Riley and Burk, that what they suspected, was in fact what had occurred. FBI Special Agent-in-Charge Hoar fed her information that she would let slip. Special Agent Hoar reports to FBI Deputy Director Johns. How much higher up it would go would soon be uncovered. Riley and Burk would figure it out when they returned to headquarters. But for the moment, Kelly was their new best friend. Burk, ever one to try and encapsulate a truce, took his diet peach iced tea and raised it to a toast and said, "Enemy Mine" to which he received blank looks from both Riley and Kelly.

Kelly said, "I think that's an appropriate toast, but I am not sure."

"May I continue, Ms. Sullivan?"

She nodded.

"It's a shortened version, ironically, of an old Arabic proverb which you may be more familiar."

"And that is?" asked Riley.

Burk still holding his bottle of iced tea, singular in the air said, "The enemy of my enemy is my friend." And to that end the other two drinks were joined in the air and the three clinked. Riley ended the toast with "To our newest, bestest friend, Kelly."

Not to be out done, Kelly added, "And to our newest bestest enemy, the U.S. Government."

Would you like to join us at headquarters, Ms. Sullivan?" asked Commissioner Riley. "We are going to have a chat with Special Agent Hoar, whom I believe would be furious if he knew we were seeing each other."

"I would, and thank you for lunch, Commissioner Riley."

CHAPTER 39

WASHINGTON, DC

The White House, Oval Room.

The president, Secretary of State Kearney, and FBI Director Miller were still discussing the improbability of what just occurred outside with the vice president, when Chief of Staff O'Donnell knocked and entered. Everyone seemed to immediately realize, with the appearance of O'Donnell that reality had just entered the room.

"Madam President, we need to talk," said O'Donnell.

"I know, Denis, we have been watching, but yes go ahead."

"Madam President," said O'Donnell, "Marine Two is landing now to take the vice president to Bethesda hospital and—"

"Excuse me Denis, what's the vice president's condition?"

"He died exactly eight minutes ago, Madam President, a severed artery," said O'Donnell.

The president, in a rare moment of remorse, suggested they all bow their heads and say a prayer for the vice president. A few seconds later, the president raised her head signifying the moment was over, and asked O'Donnell to continue.

"Madam President," continued O'Donnell, "I have the entire world press beating down the Rose Garden French doors wanting you or at least some sort of press release on the vice president's actions and death and about, what they are now calling, the "Mess Conference." I have your entire cabinet assembled in the Cabinet Room, assuming you want to confer with them. And you have to pick a successor to Vice President Denning."

"Exactly how does that process work, Denis?" asked the president.

"I just spoke to the Attorney General outside," said O'Donnell, and according to the 25th Amendment: Whenever there is a vacancy in the office of the vice president, the president shall nominate a vice president who shall take office upon confirmation by a majority vote of both Houses of Congress."

"Thank you, Denis," said the president, "Go tell the press they will be hearing something shortly and that I have ordered all flags to be lowered. Schedule a live 6 p.m. televised presidential address to the nation for tonight. Tell the cabinet I will be with them shortly and have Press Secretary Kerry and the head speech writer on standby outside."

After O'Donnell left and the door closed, the president buzzed her private secretary and filled her in what was going on and asked her to hold all calls.

The president led her two confidantes to the seating area and gestured for them to have a seat on the couch. "Gentlemen, we are at a pivotal point in this administration and this crisis, and we need to make some fast and rather important decisions. Before I call in my speechwriters and we leave for the Cabinet Room to meet with the cabinet, I want to make sure the three of us are on the same page.

"First, in the Cabinet Room, I will propose you John, as vice president, and you Bob as secretary of state. Now how does that sound?"

Both Kearney and Miller were effusive with their nods of agreement.

"Then that's it," said the president. "Bob, I'll need your recommendation for your successor. Now, to Burk and Riley. Why, after hearing their names, do I conjure up a vision two infamous characters?"

FBI Director Miller knew the answer, of course, but was reluctant to give it, sensing the president was baiting him or asking rhetorically. The president waited until Miller was forced to reply.

"Madam President," said Miller, "you may be thinking of Burk and Hare. Two early 19th century entrepreneurs who foresaw the shortage of cadavers for medical research, as a business opportunity and endeavored to address that shortage."

"Bob, you just reaffirmed my decision to nominate you for secretary of state. Now what exactly did you just say?"

Miller continued, "When they ran out of bodies to steal from graves, they streamlined the process by just selecting living indigent prospects and bopping them about the head."

"You mean they were murderers, Bob?" asked the president.

"Exactly," replied Miller.

"Just like our real life Burk and Riley?"

Neither Miller nor Kearney took the bait.

"Getting back on track, said the president, we have an old issue to deal with and a couple of new ones. Let's talk about our exposure to the old one first, shall we? She then turned the office voice recorder off.

Bob, your Agent Hoar managed not only to get himself arrested, but also his entire FBI team. Yes, Bob, I have my sources. That's got to set some sort of precedence, right? Hoar's locked up at One Police Plaza in New York, and if he talks it will implicate you. If that happens, Mr. Secretary of State-elect, the only state you will preside over will be state prison.

"Ha-ha," laughed the president at her own joke.

When the president regained her composure, FBI Director Miller replied, "He won't talk and they can't make him."

"What if they offer him some kind of deal?" asked the president. "Why don't you get with the attorney general and figure a way to spring him? I would feel much better with him out and about."

"I spoke with Attorney General Holler this morning before the press conference, and he is working on it. He feels Hoar will be released sometime today."

"What about the other agent they are holding, this Sammy Kahn character?"

"Not to worry," said Miller, "he is just a tech that knows absolutely nothing about anything."

"Not to worry huh, Director Miller?" Said the president. "That's right up there with 'No problem' or 'Trust me.' I would worry, Director Miller, if I were you. Now that brings us to our two new problems. First, the press conference."

Secretary of State Kearney thought to himself, "*Oh, you mean the fact that you plagiarized President Bush's 9-11 speech.*"

As if she could read Kearney's thoughts, she looked directly at him and said, "How can we turn the vice president's words and actions today, ultimately ending with him committing suicide, into a positive opportunity? Now guys, we've got to get creative here, ok!"

Director Miller had been on the carpet for the last five minutes, so he deferred to Kearney.

"Madam President," began Kearney, "I have been given this some initial thought and think I have found just the ticket. The vice president for the last week, ever since the bomb threats, had been acting very strange. I think we can all agree on that. What I suggest is that the vice president was a closet Arabophile."

"Jesus, John, is there such a thing?" asked the president.

"Of course," replied Secretary Kearney, "it's just not as out in the open as say an Anglophile or Francophile. His actions in the last week, and particularly this morning, support this. And we can postulate from that, that the vice president may have been a Muslim sympathizer. I mean why else would he have brought a scimitar to the press conference? Why in fact would he own one?"

"John, you know damn well I told him to bring the sword with him, and it was a U.S. Marine Corps sword not a scimitar."

"Well, how do you explain his calling on, of all people, an *Al Jazeera America* reporter, and raising the Marine scimitar over the head and reciting the most profound of all terrorist battle cry's, 'Allahu Akbar!' – which latterly translates to 'Allah is Greater?'"

"For Christ sakes, John, Vice President Denning was a former Marine, a real patriot," said the president.

"Well, be that as it may," countered the secretary, "he didn't raise the sword over his head in front of the entire fucking world and sing the Marine Corp hymn did he?"

The president, quite irritated, asked, "Where is all this going?"

"Back to Burk and Riley, that's where it's going," said Secretary Kearney. "They are both also, like the vice president, former Marines, and you know what they say about Marines, Madam President?

"What?" asked the president sarcastically, "the head doesn't fall too far from the scimitar?"

"That's very good Madam President, but no, I meant the secret saying that one Marine will only say to another Marine in Latin – 'Simper Fi!' which translates to 'Always Faithful;' Faithful to one another, that is."

"John, Bob," asked the president, "do either of you have any proof of them meeting?"

"None, but Marines are very sneaky."

On that thought, the president, secretary of state, and the FBI director all took a deep breath and leaned back into their seats. The president seemed to be thinking about Kearney's scenario that the vice president was some kind of Marine Arabophile terrorist. She then came back and said, "Ok, moving on. That brings us to our final new problem. What do we make of this meeting between that *CNN* reporter Kelly Sullivan with Burk and Riley? You want to take this one, Bob?"

Director Miller leaned forward and said, "Madam President, all three met at a Vietnamese restaurant in little Italy, for about an hour. Then Sullivan, Burk and Riley went back to police headquarters at One Police Plaza. That much we know for sure. Our agents tailing her were spotted. So now we know, that they know, that we know."

The president held up her hand for the FBI director to hold on for a second.

Miller sensing he was about to get taken down a notch for his agent's poor trade craft, slid back deeper into the couch and waited. Then the president leaned closer into the couch directly toward FBI Director Miller and said. "Bob, can you tell me what the fuck is a Vietnamese restaurant doing in little Italy?"

CHAPTER 40

NYC POLICE HEADQUARTERS

Riley, Burk and Sullivan headed back to One Police Plaza and directly to the interrogation rooms. Kelly was directed into the corridor room so she could see and hear what went on in either room but not be seen. Riley and Burk went straight in to visit with Special Agent Hoar. On the way back from Little Italy, Riley got a call from his deputy, informing him that Attorney General Holler's office is demanding Hoar's release today. They said if he is not released today by 5 p.m., Attorney General Holler and the FBI Director Miller, the FBI and if necessary, the National Guard would come down to One Police Plaza and literally come in and drag him out. Riley asked his deputy to "Kindly inform Attorney General Holler's office that he would very much enjoy hosting the FBI again, as it may not be possible to release Agent Hoar today. Special Agent Hoar will most likely be charged today with multiple crimes including: obstructing justice, aiding and abetting, evidence planting or tampering, extortion, falsely reporting a crime and offering or preparing false evidence, and last but least, multiple RICO charges, which may involve Attorney General Holler, FBI Director Miller and possibly the President of the United States."

Riley and Burk had the goods on Hoar but wanted to see what else they could get, and besides, they needed to charge him or discharge him. They opened the door and went in and sat down across from agent Hoar. Burk started to pull out his gardening tool but Riley stopped him with a quick kick to the shins. Burk recovered quickly and said, "What happened to your face, FBI Special Agent-in-Charge Hoar?" Hoar tried to look tough and did not take the bait. Burk continued, "You know what they are calling you and your team back at the bureau, Hoar?" Special Agent Barney Hoar in Charge, of the Mayberry Field Office."

With that, Hoar screamed, "You're a lying son of a bitch, Burk!" and was out of his the chair and across the table before either Burk or Riley could react. Even with his right hand right cuffed to the bolted down chair, Hoar managed to get most of his body splayed across the table and his left hand on Burk's jacket.

Riley's reaction was instinctive as he pushed back on their chair and reached for his gun. Riley's gun was checked outside, and Burk didn't have one. Burk didn't get as far back as Riley because Hoar had hold of his jacket. Everything kind of went into slow motion as Burk's hand came out of his pocket with the garden pruner. Seeing the pruner, Hoar decided retreat was the better part of valor and released his grip. Almost simultaneously, Burk grabbed Hoar's hand to prevent complete retreat. Now as fast motion returned, Burk in one fast swoop had the snipers in place and pruned Hoar's left index finger to the first knuckle.

Hoar screamed and shot back into his chair like he was tethered to it with a bungee cord.

"Christ, Burk, what the fuck is a matter with you!" shouted Riley. "What the fuck are you thinking?" Are you having flashbacks?"

Burk was up and across the table in a flash. He pinned Hoar's bleeding hand to the table with his knee and secured his neck to the back of the chair. Then with his free hand grabbed Hoar's crotch. With the pruner visible within inches of Hoar's face, Burk said, "The truth or your cock, Hoar."

Hoar had no doubt Burk would follow through but looked to Riley to intervene. When Riley didn't move, Hoar knew he had to tell Burk whatever he wanted or he would become a eunuch. Hoar did not think J Edgar Hoover would approve of eunuchs in the FBI. Hoar nodded and Burk ripped part of the gauze from his face and wrapped it around the bleeding stump. Hoar was cringing and near to tears.

"Just answer three questions Hoar," said Burk. "Did you plant the evidence in my apartment? Did Director Miller authorize it and why? Answer now, you piece of shit!"

Hoar sobbing, tried to gain his composure. "Are we off the record here?"

Burk answered, "Yeah, we're off the record"

Hoar then opened up. "Yes, I planted the evidence. And yes, Director Miller authorized it. Why? Why do you think, Burk? Because you embarrassed the president, the director and the country. Chicago and Los Angeles listened to the president's advice and evacuated. You saw what a mess that turned out to be. Because of you two, New York didn't listen and didn't evacuate. The president, her secretary of state, and the investigative agencies all missed this whole thing and were blamed for the evacuations and the international and economic debacle that it caused. They were taking all the heat while you two and New York City were heroes. The president wanted to create a distraction. Your shenanigans with the IRS agent and his murder opened up a whole rainbow of possibilities to us. It gave us an opportunity get the heat off us and on to you. You and Riley became the perfect patsy's."

"And what about that *CNN* Reporter, Kelly Sullivan – how did she fit into your blame game?" asked Riley.

Hoar laughed. "'Blame game,' that's good, Riley. She was a convenience. She served a greater purpose, and looked good doing it. Hell, we took a plain Jane reporter and turned her into GI Jane. We made her a *CNN* superstar."

"Did you sleep with her?" asked Burk, hoping to get him to say something embarrassing.

Before Riley could stop him, Hoar answered, "No, but I think the president did."

Now Burk felt like a real shit, but it was too late. The genie was out of the bottle.

Riley tried to minimize Burk's lack of discretion and said. "Thanks Hoar, you have been very helpful, as has your forensic tech," Samir Kahn next door."

"You said Samir; you mean 'Sammy,'" said Hoar.

"No I meant Samir," said Riley. "And on that score, you, Special Agent-in-Charge Hoar are in for a big surprise. But first we are going to charge you with obstructing justice, aiding and abetting, evidence planting, tampering, extortion, falsely reporting a crime and offering or preparing false evidence. And that's just to hold you here over night. Then we are going to get serious about what to charge you with, put all this together and go public. We have a reporter who is going to help us, I think you know her."

"You said this was off the record, Riley!" Hoar shouted, now visibly shaken.

"No I didn't," said Riley, "Burk did. And why would I believe that lying son of a bitch?"

Riley and Burk got up and left leaving Hoar sobbing and clenching his wounded left hand with his cuffed right hand. With his swollen, partially gauzed face and bloody gauzed hand pulled into his chest, he looked like a pathetic mummy.

Riley and Burk entered the corridor room and Riley told Captain Bounty to get a doctor in for Hoar and start preparing charges before the attorney general's people get here. "And don't let them see him," said Riley. They both kind of avoided direct eye contact with Kelly Sullivan.

She, to her credit, didn't even acknowledge their awkwardness. She did break the ice by saying. "Commissioner Riley, do you think I can get a copy of that tape for a prime time spot tonight?" There were smiles all around as they realized Kelly Sullivan was a real trooper.

CHAPTER 41

WASHINGTON, DC

The White House, the Cabinet Room.

From routine meetings to serious deliberations, the Cabinet Room's oval table and leather chairs have provided a stately yet comfortable environment for presidents to communicate their priorities and to listen to their cabinet's opinions and advice.

The oval mahogany conference table seats 20. When the cabinet meets around the table, each cabinet member is assigned a chair positioned at the table according to the date the department was established. The president occupies the taller chair at the center of the east side of the table and has a call button available to summon a White House steward.

The vice president sits opposite the president. The secretary of state, ranking first among the department heads, sits on the president's right. The secretary of the treasury, ranking second, sits to the vice-president's right. The secretary of defense (third) sits to the president's left, and the attorney general (fourth) sits to the vice president's left. The chairs bear brass plates indicating their cabinet position or positions and dates of service. When cabinet members conclude their terms of service, their cabinet chair is traditionally purchased by the rest of the staff and presented as a gift.

Overlooking the Rose Garden, the Cabinet Room contains likenesses of former presidents and statesmen, busts of Washington and Franklin and portraits of Theodore Roosevelt, Jefferson, Eisenhower, and Washington as well as a painting of the signing of the Declaration of Independence.

If the walls of the Cabinet Room could speak, they would tell of discussions and lively debate over national budgets, the state of the military, domestic and social issues and matters of national security. George W Bush convened a meeting on September 12, 2001, with his national security team in the cabinet room, where he declared that freedom and democracy were under attack. Nearly 40 years earlier, John Kennedy held intense discussions in the Cabinet Room during the days of the Cuban Missile Crisis.

The Cabinet Room is a little over 23 feet wide and 39 feet long, with 18-foot ceilings. There are no second floor rooms above the cabinet room or Oval Office.

Today, events on the level of the Cuban Missile Crisis and September 11 would be discussed.

Outside the Cabinet Room, the president pulled Attorney General Holler and FBI Director Miller aside and asked them if Agent Hoar had been released. FBI Director Miller and Attorney General Holler both looked a bit sheepish, but Holler, who must have earlier drawn the short straw, answered, "Madam President, the news is not good. They have charged Agent Hoar with numerous crimes including: evidence planting and tampering, falsely reporting a crime, and the list goes on. They won't let us near him or speak to him. This does not look good."

The president looked at both and in a low guttural tone, through gritted teeth said, "The both of you are letting a city police department trump the FBI, the Justice Department and the weight of the entire federal government? You, Bob, whom I was about to nominate as my secretary of state, let your agents get arrested and thrown into jail while you, Mr. Attorney General Holler, the nation's top cop, can't get them out. What am I missing here?" as Miller was about to answer, the president held up her hand. "Am I dealing with Frick and Frack here? Dumb and Dumber?" She could see they were steaming over the rebukes but didn't care and continued, "Both of you sit this cabinet meeting out until you can get Hoar out or find out if he talked. If he did talk, then have him killed or I will have both of your heads. Am I clear, gentlemen?" She didn't wait for an answer, she just turned and walked into the Cabinet Room and the door closed.

President Hilton entered the room, and everyone stood. She eased into her center chair and motioned everyone else to follow. The room was full, including the chairs along the walls, which held agency heads and staffers.

"Thank you all for coming," started the president. "We have a lot to cover and so little time. I have arranged for a live presidential address to the American people tonight at 6 p.m., and I intend to assure them that their president and their government is doing everything possible to restore order and put things right. So let's get to it and put things right.

"First of all, I want us all to offer our hearts and prayers to one of our fallen heroes. Vice President Joe Denning was a great vice president and a faithful friend. What happened today, in a few short minutes, is no way indicative of his long and meaningful service. He was, as you all know, an American hero, patriot and a Marine.

"Let's all bow our heads in prayer."

When the president raised her head a few seconds later, the others all followed suit, except Secretary of State Kearney, whom seemed to milk it a bit longer.

"John are you all right?" asked the president.

As he intended, everyone would now be focused on him. Kearney, with his hands folded on the table and head bowed, slowly extended his fingers to the steeple position then slowly raised his head and brought his finger tips to rest against his lips. He slowly looked left and right so everyone could see the tear rolling down his left cheek. "Today, I have lost another brother in arms. Every day there are fewer and fewer of us left. We served together in Viet Nan. I with the Navy and Joe with the Marine Corps. I feel I am on solid ground here, people, when I say…" Kearney now stood, looked directly at the vice president's empty chair, and brought his right hand up into a crisp salute. "Semper Fi, Joe."

The president shook her head slowly in total disbelief as she looked around the table. Several members were choking up, and she thought to herself. *This guy's good. A few minutes ago, he was painting the vice president a terrorist. Now he has him a hero and most of my cabinet in tears. I've got to check and see if I have my purse before I leave.* With the secretary back down in his seat, the president said, "That was very well said Mr. Secretary, and I think an excellent segue into the next order of business. I hereby put forth the name of Secretary of State John Fitzhugh Kearney to become the Vice President of the United States."

Most, if not all the cabinet members and agency heads and staffers, applauded and seemed resigned to the announcement. Not that they liked or respected John Kearney; it was just that it was expected. It was not out of the ordinary for a secretary of state to move up a notch.

Kearney stood and thanked the president and his soon to be former peers and simply said, "I am honored, and thank you, Madam President."

The president said, "Of course this is on the condition of confirmation by a majority vote of both Houses of Congress, but I don't see that as a problem. I am not going to nominate a replacement for secretary of state at this time."

This caught the cabinet a bit off guard, as there were a several qualified candidates.

"Now on to the agenda; you all have a copy," said the president. "I want to hear from everyone now on each item and then you will follow up with a written report."

Everyone had previously reviewed the agenda and were told by the president's Chief of Staff, Denis O'Donnell, to be prepared to answer but they all reviewed the list again. The president looked at the list and said: "

- Bomb Threats.
- Forest Fires.
- Evacuations.
- Lootings, Death and Injuries.
- The American Muslim Brother Hood and the arrest.
- The NYPD, Particularly Commissioner Riley and his terrorist consultant Burk, involvement and cover up.

"Plus all of the ancillary problems caused by the bomb threats and fires." added the president.

"They include:

- The Economy.
- China, Russia and Japan buying and selling as much oil as possible using the Chinese Yuan instead of standard dollar reserves currency.
- North Korea demonstrating a huge military presence on the DMZ.
- China is moving warships into the strait of Taiwan.
- The Syrian Cyber Army hacking into our electric grid and water supply.
- Egypt, Lebanon and the other surrounding countries making noise about the final destruction of Israel.
- Iran's new president, Hassan Rouhani making noise about launching a new test nuclear warhead missile capable of striking the U.S.
- Russia invading the Crimea.
- Illegal immigrants fleeing back across the border into Mexico.

The president continued. "People, I have a 6 p.m. address to the nation so keep your answers short and sweet. My Chief of Staff Denis O'Donnell and his writers will take notes. Your answers will form the basis of my address, so let's try and put a positive spin on things, shall we?"

CHAPTER 42

NYC POLICE HEADQUARTERS

Ms. Sullivan remained in the corridor room, but now along with the commissioner's A/V team, turned to the adjacent two way mirror that looked into Kahn's room.

Riley and Burk entered the room. Mr. Kahn seemed more relaxed. Since he seemed to be cooperating, Commissioner Riley had directed the innkeepers to let him use the facilities and had donuts and coffee brought in. His left hand, however, was still cuffed to the chair but he had finished off some coffee and a couple of donuts.

"Enjoy your lunch, Gentlemen?" asked Kahn.

"No, we decided to wait and eat yours," replied Riley.

"I never really understood what that meant," said Burk. "'I am going to eat your lunch.'"

"Does it mean I would eat it before you eat it or after you eat it? Either way, it doesn't sound appetizing."

Neither Riley nor Kahn responded.

Burk continued, "You were telling us about your Masterpiece."

"Yes," responded Kahn. "Shall I continue where we left off?"

"I am sure we will get back to that but we are in a bit of a time bind. How about we ask you some questions and you answer them. Ok?" asked Riley.

Burk started, "May I call you Samir?"

"You may," replied Samir.

"Are there any more surprises coming, Samir? I mean any more bombs, fires or anything? In, let's say, your third act?"

"No, nothing more. Wasn't that enough?"

"You outdid yourself," replied Burk.

Riley took over. "Are you the boss in the United States, or who do you report to someone?"

"Yes, I am the boss. I started the American Muslim Brotherhood, and I and I alone came up with the whole 'Fear Campaign,' as I refer to it. The American Muslim Brotherhood is in sympathy with the Arab Muslim Brotherhood, but I do not, however, report to them. I did present them my plan, which they approved and financed, but it was all done through encrypted emails and wire transfers. I have never been out of the U.S., except for one trip to Paris, and they have not, to my knowledge, been here. At least not to see me. I will give you my account information, for emails and banking, which I am sure you can triangulate, and both of which, are different from what you found in my apartment."

Riley continued, "Why ServePro your apartment when you're giving up everything now?"

"I wasn't ready to come out then but I am now. Besides events have seemed to influence that decision, wouldn't you agree?"

Riley said, "Are we to assume that besides Amid's cell here in New York, you also controlled the Chicago, L.A. and country-wide burn cells?"

"That is correct," said Samir.

"Samir, how and why did you get into the FBI?"

"It was quite easy to get in. I had a masters in chemistry from MIT didn't I? They, of course, being the FBI, vetted me pretty good, as one might expect, but I had a good solid clean record. An All-American boy, you might say. When I first joined, my heart did not belong to Allah."

"Did you contact the Muslim Brotherhood first or did they contact you?" asked Riley.

"They contacted me first while I was with the bureau. I was in a Starbucks on 14th Street by the Willard. I was just having an espresso latte and browsing the Internet and I received a message to contact the attached email. I thought it might be an FBI test of some sort. There was nothing else on it, and I looked around and no one was paying any attention to me. I figured it was someone with Bluetooth who didn't want to be known."

"An admirer perhaps," suggested Burk. "Yes, actually it was. The admirer turned out to be Allah, and I was, as they say, smitten."

"You know Samir, everything you have said has been recorded," said Riley.

"I hope so," replied Samir.

"One final question for now," Samir," asked Burk. "Did Special Agent Hoar or anyone else in the FBI know or suspect you were not who you said you were?"

"After I returned to Washington, shortly after the production, I was summoned to Deputy Director Johns' office and introduced to and put under the supervision of Agent Hoar. I was nervous at first then shocked that I, of all people, would be assigned by the FBI to investigate myself. This has to be a coincidence, I thought. Only later did I learn that they wanted me to sniff you out, so to speak. I would never have let you take the fall, Mr. Burk. This was my show. I hoped you would recognize me in the parking lot, and you did. You know the FBI, having the founder of the American Brotherhood in their ranks, is an added benefit to my production and something the bureau will soon not forget. But having FBI employee Sammy Kahn turn out to be the mastermind of the worst attack in America's history is what legends are made of. No Mr. Burk, the FBI didn't have a clue about me, and as far as I know still doesn't. I am sure they would love to talk to me. Will you accommodate them, Mr. Riley?"

"Samir, said Riley, when they find out what we have, they will definitely want to reach out to you."

"Right," said Burk. "When the FBI, finds out what we have, they are definitely going to want to reach out and touch someone. But not just you, my friend Samir, they are going to want to touch Special Agent In Charge Hoar, Police Commissioner Riley, Kelly and yours truly."

"That's not going to happen," said Riley.

"Right," said Burk. "I will bet you a nickel they are planning our unfortunate demise as we speak. We have not let them near Hoar and Kahn, and they are not stupid. As soon as you asked for Sammy's FBI personnel jacket, their little brains started ticking. They know Hoar knows everything and by now they know we know everything. Their little house of cards is about to fall and as far as they are concerned, they can't allow that to happen. Captain, they have to make the five of us do the Houdini. Somehow, someway in the next hour, you are going to get a phone call. It is going to be from someone you trust, setting up a meeting between them and us.

"Tommy, you're making this sound like the *Godfather* movie, for Christ sake," said Riley.

Burk, as if on cue from his straight man Riley, proceeded to recite in each characters voice the scene from the *Godfather* where their trusted capo Tessio sets up for a meeting to offer a deal.

"The Turk, he wants to talk? Badda-beep, badda-boop, badda-boop, badda-beep, he wants us to send Michael to hear the deal. We ought to hear what they have to say. Shooting your father was business not personal, Sonny!

"They want to have a meeting with me, right? It will be me, McClusky and Sollozzo. Let's set the meeting. We get our informants to find out where it's going to be held. Now we insist that it be held in a public place, a bar or a restaurant where there'll be other people there so I'll feel safe. But if Clemenza can figure a way to have a weapon planted for me, then I'll kill them both.

"What are you gonna do? Nice college boy, didn't want to get mixed up in the family business. Now you want to gun down a police captain. Why?

"You're taking this very personal Sonny. Tom, this is business and this man is taking it very, very personal.

"Where does it say that you can't kill a cop?

"Tom, wait a minute. I'm talking about a cop that's mixed up in drugs. I'm talking about a-a-a dishonest cop – a crooked cop who got mixed up in the rackets and got what was coming to him. That's a terrific story. And we have newspaper people on the payroll, Don't we, Tom. And they might like a story like that.

"They might, they just might, Michael.

"It's not personal, Sonny. It's strictly business."

"You're fucking crazy, Tommy," said Riley. "You memorized every word of every characters from the movie and have just been waiting for a chance to use it."

"Well not the entire movie, just the parts I felt interesting, and besides I thought it sort of captured the moment. Just insert our names here and there and 'the Godfather' becomes 'the Commissioner.'"

Samir, who you would think too young to have even seen the movie, clapped his hands and said, "Bravo Don Burk, bravo."

"Tom-anuch!" said Riley. "You're both fucking crazy." Just then the commissioner's cell rang. It was Mayor Bloomfield.

Burk smiled and said. "Et tu, Bloomtist?"

CHAPTER 43

WASHINGTON, DC

The White House, the Cabinet Room.

"OK, said the president, something has come up which requires us to address the ancillary problems first then we will jump back up to the bomb and fire, and other issues:

- The Economy
- China, Russia and our good friend Japan buying and selling as much oil as possible using the Chinese Yuan instead of standard dollar reserves currency.
- North Korea demonstrating a huge military presence on the DMZ.
- China is moving warships into the strait of Taiwan,
- The Syrian Cyber Army hacking into our electric grid and water supply.
- Egypt, Lebanon and the other surrounding countries making noise about the final destruction of Israel
- Iran's new president, Hassan Rouhani making noise about launching a new test nuclear warhead missile capable of striking the U.S.
- Russia invading the Crimea.
- Illegal immigrants fleeing back across the border to Mexico

"Ok," said the president, "the economy; you're up Lew."

Lew Jacobs, the secretary of the treasury, remained seated. "Thank you Madam President, I have conferred, this morning, with the Fed Chair Nanke Benns, and the heads of all our major financial institutions. As of yesterday morning, Wall Street is up and running, and the market is in a rebound. All the major banks are positive and lending again. Additionally, Fed Chair Benns told Congress that short-term interest rates will remain close to zero. The unemployment rate fell to 6.5 percent, and the annual inflation outlook is below 2.5 percent. While rates for...."

The president put up her hand for the secretary to stop. "Let's leave it there, shall we, Lew? Now that's good news. Well presented, concise and positive. Good job, Lew."

"I expect that kind of report from the rest of you."

"All righty. China, Russia, Japan, North Korea, Syria, Israel and Iran. John, you're up."

Secretary of State, Vice President-Elect John Kearney seated directly to the right of the president began "Madam President, I met this morning with Secretary of Defense Newel, CIA Director Bader and General Dumpy of the Joint Chiefs. Additionally, I have personally spoke with President Vladimir Putin of Russia, President Xi Jinping of China, Prime Minister Netanyahu of Israel, President Rouhani of Iran, Prime Minister Abe of Japan, Leader Kim Jong Un of North Korea, and president Park Geon-Hye of South Korea."

The president said, "John, you actually spoke to Kim Jong Un?"

"Yes Madam President."

"Well, he won't take my calls."

"Madam President, I believe he likes tall men."

She waved him on.

"Thank you, Madam President. To keep it simple, the oil deal, between Russia, China and Japan is still going forward but with the dollar not the Yuan. North Korea claimed it was only war gaming in front of the DMZ and said they have completed and terminated the exercise. China has recalled its warships from the straights of Taiwan. Egypt, Lebanon and others have agreed to sit down for further peace discussions with Israel. Iran's Hassan Rouhani is on his way over here to discuss nuclear disbarment. And finally, Russia says it is not invading the Ukraine or the Crimea but only filming a war movie. The troops and tanks you see are just extras and props. The film will be an updated version of Alfred Lord Tennyson's 'Charge of the Light Brigade' in Balaclava's 'Valley of Death'. Half a league, half a league, half a league onward, all in the Valley of Death, rode the six hundred.'" Anyway, the Russians won that battle but lost the war. In this adaptation of the movie, they intend to win both and it is rumored that Putin will play himself.

The president said, "John that is amazing news. I can't believe you pulled it off. I don't believe I have ever witnessed such successful international diplomacy. Mr. Secretary, how on earth were you able to pull us from the brink of Armageddon?"

The secretary, who had a habit of steepling his fingers and touching them to his lips before he would pontificate, did so. "Madam President, I fine-tuned my craft studying diplomacy from my predecessor. She was a master at playing and winning the strategic board game called international diplomacy."

The president smiled but thought, *And watching TMZ. What a bag of wind this guy is. I wonder if he would fall on his sword for me or shove in in my back?*

Secretary of State Kearney continued, "In speaking to each, I told them that these attacks have only made us stronger as a country and kindled our resolve. I told each, that we would remember who remained loyal friends and who deserted us because they felt we were weak. To the former, I promised continue friendship and support. To the latter, I read them the riot act and promised to discontinue all aid. They got the message."

"What did it cost us, Mr. Secretary, to keep our old friends and to make new ones?" asked the president.

"An additional 40 billion ought to do it."

"Thank you, Mr. Secretary," said the president, "not a bad price to pay for peace. War in any scenario, would have cost considerably more in dollars and lives.

"One last ancillary problem. Immigrations, Sally."

Sally Jewel the secretary of the interior began, "Thank you madam president. As of yesterday morning, the tide has begun to reverse and come in or in this case back. Illegal immigrants/undocumented workers are flocking back across the border. I spoke today with Mexico President Nieto, and he assures me he is doing everything possible to contain the flow.

The president interjected, "Madam Secretary, what do you think he means by 'containing the flow?'"

"I think he means he will hold on to those he wants to keep and let the rest return. In other words, our Latino voting base will be getting a bit larger."

"Excellent," replied the president. "OK, let's take a break and reconvene in an hour or so."

CHAPTER 44

NYC POLICE HEADQUARTERS

After he hung up on Mayor Bloomfield, Riley motioned for Burk to follow him out of the room. Outside the interrogation room they were joined by Captain Bounty and Ms. Sullivan.

"What did Tessio say?" asked Burk

"Will you get off that *Godfather* shit?" snapped Riley.

"If he wants to meet us at Louis Italian restaurant in the Bronx, count me out," said Burk. Ms. Sullivan and Lieutenant Bounty, who had been listening on the interrogation room speakers sheepishly smiled.

"The mayor is above all that political bullshit, Burk. He made me police commissioner for Christ sake. He wants us to take the two prisoners to LaGuardia. He will join our convoy at Gracie Mansion, then over the Triborough to the airport. The president blames all our bad press on bad reporting by an eager beaver reporter. I suspect she means you, Kelly.

Kelly made an "I'm sorry" face then looked down at her feet.

The president now believes us heroes and is sending Air Force 2 to LaGuardia to bring us down to Washington. The president would be honored to have us join her and stand beside her, as a show of unity and resolve, tonight, as she addresses the nation. I know what you're thinking, Burk. That Air Force 2 is the vice president's plane and he don't need it anymore and..."

"No," interrupted Burk. "actually that's not what I was thinking. "What I was thinking is we won't even make it to the LaGuardia. The feds will take us out on the way and put the blame on the Arab Muslim Brotherhood. Right after it happens, Al Jazeera will announce that the Arab Muslim Brotherhood took credit for taking out Samir so Satan could not prevent him from achieving his ultimate martyrdom. Well, El Capitan, I guess I'm Satan, so that makes you, Hoar and the mayor collateral damage."

CHAPTER 45

WASHINGTON, DC

The White House, the Oval Office.

FBI Director Miller was already in the Oval Office when the president and Secretary of State Kearney entered.

"Time's running out gentlemen," said the president. "Give me something good Bob."

Director Miller indicated to the president to silence the voice recorder.

"I didn't think you wanted the Attorney General to hear any of this, so I told him I would take the flack and he could rejoin the cabinet meeting when it reconvenes," said Miller. "He did not hesitate for a moment."

"OK give it to me," said the president.

"My source inside One Police Plaza says the police commissioner, Burk, and that *CNN* reporter Sullivan are all sequestered on the lower floor interrogation rooms. The whole floor is cordoned off. My source is close to one of the medical assistants in the infirmary, and according to this assistant, Agent Hoar was in bad shape. A lot of bloody gauze and bandages. Riley and Burk put a real hurting on Hoar. He also heard that both Hoar and the forensic tech Kahn had later gotten restroom breaks and were fed lunch. Obviously Hoar got medical attention."

"So what are implying?" asked Kearney.

"You don't give hall passes and milk and cookies to prisoners unless they are cooperating. I think Hoar spilled his guts. He knew we couldn't or wouldn't get him out, so he cut the best deal he could get and that was to sell us out. As far as Kahn goes, we put every resource we have to look into Kahn past to see if we missed anything."

"And?" said the president.

"And he was clean. Too clean and that meant he was covering something. We went deeper and found he was a deep sleeper. We don't have everything yet but enough to know we fucked up big time. This FBI forensic tech Sammy Kahn is Samir Kahn, leader of the American Muslim Brotherhood."

"Jesus Bob, who's on first?" said the president.

Both the president and secretary were shaking their heads in total disbelief.

"Excuse me Madam President," Miller said. "We can address this indiscretion later, but for now I have taken the liberty, a proactive option if you will, of setting in motion a plan to have these enemies of state and any potential problems they might have caused us, neutralized."

"Yes, we will address that little indiscretion, and I can't wait to hear that story, but tell me of the proactive option," said the president.

"Attorney General Holler and I called Mayor Bloomfield and explained the situation to him about our being denied access to Hoar and Kahn and that both of these federal agents are operatives and part of a bigger investigation critical to our national security. We told the mayor that Police Commissioner Riley and Burk were sandbagged by this eager beaver reporter Sullivan, who would do anything and drag anyone down to get a story. We told the mayor we need to have him, Burk and Riley here in Washington to be part of and honored at your 6 p.m. address to the nation. And we need Hoar and Kahn here for reasons of national security. We told the mayor we would have Air Force 2 waiting at LaGuardia to bring them all here to Washington. The mayor got Riley on the phone, read him the riot act and gave him his marching orders. We asked the mayor to give us the details of how it would go down. He did."

"And the mayor believed all this?" asked the president.

"Yes. He has higher political aspirations, and I hinted that you had something important for him.

"And why, Bob, do I want them on the stage with me tonight to be honored?"

"Madam President, they are going to have an unfortunate accident before they arrive."

"Very good, Bob. I think I will announce you as the new secretary of state."

"What exactly were those marching orders the mayor gave Riley, Bob?" asked Kearney.

"We know Riley won't fly in a helicopter so he—"

"Why is that?" asked the president.

"Because three different helicopters he was aboard in Viet Nam were shot down and he has never set foot aboard one since. They will instead, be taking a NYPD convoy up the FDR to Gracie Mansion, where the mayor's convoy will join them. Then straight over the Triborough to LaGuardia.

With a wink and nod to the president to turn on the recorder, FBI Director Miller continued, "According to recent chatter, we have intercepted, the Arab Muslim Brotherhood is planning to ambush the convoy. They must have a source within the NYPD. They want Kahn dead to keep him quiet and to allow him to be martyred. Riley and Burk will die because they think Kahn has spilled his guts to them. We have been trying to contact the commissioner, but he is not taking our calls.

I expressed concerns to the mayor that Riley is not taking my calls and asked him to try and open communications between us but so far nothing."

Kearney and the president looked at each other, then the president said, as if she only heard the first part. "Yes, Director, let's get them here. The country needs to know the terrorist responsible for all our troubles has been captured and is in FBI custody. And for the country and the world to see, standing beside me tonight, at my address to the nation, New York City's heroes. God bless them and grant them a safe trip here. Offer the FBI's help to the NYPD. That is, if they ever return your call."

CHAPTER 46

NYC Police Headquarters

While Police Commissioner Riley, Deputy Commissioner Turner, and Captain Bounty were setting up the convoy route and security, Burk and Sullivan had some time alone in the corridor room.

"I want to go with you; I want to follow this through to the end," said Kelly.

"That's not my call, but if it were I would say no," said Burk.

"Why, because I am a woman or because I am not a cop?" asked Kelly.

"Neither. It's because you weren't invited."

"Well, get me invited Burk – I am as much a part of this as you and Riley."

Captain Bounty returned and asked Burk and Sullivan to accompany him to the commissioner's office on the top floor. They went into the commissioner's conference room which was adjacent to his office. Burk keep going through into the commissioner's office. The conference room was a smaller version of the Office of Emergency Management Headquarters in Brooklyn. Around an oval table and up around the walls were mounted LED screens. Uniformed officers talking in groups were looking at images on the monitors.

As Captain Bounty closed the door behind them, Commissioner Riley and Burk came in through his connecting office door. Everyone came to attention, and Riley waved them down and told them to take a seat.

When everyone was seated, Riley said, "Ms. Sullivan, Mr. Burk, Officers, I called this Skull Session so everyone is on the same page and we all know what we need to. This is a tight group, and from here on down it's on a need-to-know basis only. You all know what's going on and what your jobs are. But I don't want any accidents or any of us hurt or killed, so let's recap.

We are going to release NYPD Convoy 1 at exactly 1 p.m. This convoy will leave from our One Police Plaza underground parking. Convoy 1 will be a placebo. It is our belief that Convoy 1 will be hit on route to Gracie Mansion or from there to LaGuardia. The FBI, who we have embarrassed, and whose agents we have arrested and who is complicit in the recent terrorist acts and its cover-up, have orders to make sure we don't make it to LaGuardia.

In Convoy 2, besides security, will be Ms. Sullivan, Mr. Burk, restrained prisoners Hoar and Kahn, Captain Bounty and myself." Convoy 2 will depart from City Hall underground parking, head north on Broadway toward Fifth Avenue. Convoy 2 will take a completely unexpected St. Patrick Day Parade route. That's up Fifth Avenue to Gracie Mansion or another possible location and hook up with the mayor."

Sullivan looked at Burked and nodded a thank you.

The commissioner continued, "We have SWAT and sniper teams along both routes. Traffic is being cleared as we speak and side streets, access ramps will be closed. The skies over the routes will be proprietary as well as our communications. All other aircraft will be grounded and all other communications will be jammed. The FBI are not amateurs and I guarantee they will have their best teams assigned. They know, from what the mayor and I decided to tell them, that the convoy will be going up the FDR at 1 p.m. They don't know about Convoy 2. But like I said, they are not amateurs and they will cover all the bases. If we get to LaGuardia that means they fail. If that happens, the FBI, as we know it, will cease to exist. They will be lucky if the whole bureau isn't reassigned as a minor department of the CIA.

"One more thing. Although we will have jammed all nonproprietary communications and grounded all nonproprietary aircraft over the city, we should not believe, for one New York minute, that the FBI and the NSA won't trump us with access to more sophisticated A/V technology. We have therefor developed a simple code, which you all have been read in on. It is simple but effective. By the time they break it, we will be in Washington. Regardless, let's keep the chatter to a minimum.

"Any questions?"

Of course, the only hand to go up was Burk's. "Commissioner, why don't we just take a chopper to LaGuardia?"

"You know damn well why, Burk, or have you forgotten our last chopper ride? Besides, a chopper would be an easy target for a surface to air missile. This is my town, and if they want us, they will have to work for it. I am not going to pull an evacuation off the rooftop like Saigon in '75."

"We are going in Convoy 2, and we are supposed to make it, right?" Burk said. "But who is going in Convoy 1 that is supposed to take the hit? Who volunteered for that?"

Commissioner Riley hesitated but decided to tell him. "The first and third Suburban's in Convoy 1 are all bullet and bomb proof. The tires are solid rubber. The Middle Suburban is not. The teams manning the first and third vehicles are all volunteers from the DESU, Department Emergency Service Unit. Lieutenant Savage, a former Delta Force member, is the convoy leader. We are Golf-1 and he is designated Golf 1-6. The DESU are the best, and they are expecting the fight of their lives."

"And?"

The Commissioner continued, "And the five doubles who represent us, have been volunteered."

"'Been volunteered' is not the same as volunteered. So what's that about, commissioner?"

Riley nervously looked around the room, but when his Deputy Commissioner Turner and Captain Bounty both nodded, he said, "The five doubles are part of Special Agent Hoar's FBI team that was not released. Each, as close as possible, matches one of us. You, me, Ms. Sullivan, Hoar and Kahn. Besides physical matching characteristics, our doubles will wear our clothes and have our IDs."

The room went silent. The bizarre admission just made by the commissioner was not lost on any one in the room. If the FBI succeeded today with their ambush of Convoy 1, they would be murdering their own.

"Who volunteered or who *was* volunteered to drive?" asked Burk.

"Neither," continued Riley. It's R/C, remote control. This Suburban operator is sitting in headquarters next to the drone operator. Cameras, GPS, and doubles. All smoke and mirrors, Burk. Any more questions?"

Burk's hand was up again.

"Yes Burk?"

"Will we have time to stop at Saks?"

"You got to be kidding right, right?"

"No, actually I'm not."

"What the hell for?" asked Riley.

"Did you forget commissioner that I had all my clothes and everything from my apartment confiscated by our friends the FBI, and now they are in boxes somewhere in your headquarters' basement? I want to look nice this evening standing beside the president.

"I am sorry, Mr. Burk," said Riley, "we won't have time this afternoon for shopping and lunch at Saks, but you should be able to find something in the airport shops."

"Yes Commissioner, I realize our time restraints, but all we have to do is pull up out front and do a stop and grab. Everything has been ordered and is ready. Saks has the best men's shop and personal shoppers. I should know - in my last life I designed the men's floor and Kevin has selected everything from suit to nuts for me."

The Commissioner just shook his head in defeat as Burk pulled out his iPhone and pressed speed dial.

"Hi Kevin it's me, can you be outside in front with my kit at, hold on a sec."

Burk looked at Captain Bounty who looked to the officer to his right and turned back to Burk and said, "1:13"

"Kevin, at exactly 1:13. Yes, Kevin, I understand they might be closing Fifth Avenue to traffic. But you have trust me on this. I will be able to stop in front and pop the trunk."

CHAPTER 47

WASHINGTON, DC

FBI Headquarters.

"Director Miller," said Deputy Director Johns, "we have the NY field office up."

Miller, Johns and the rest of the FBI intercept team all turned to one of six huge wall-mounted LED screens. The other screens show live feeds of One Police Plaza," sequential PiP, Picture in Picture, of the FDR Highway, Gracie Mansion, LaGuardia Airport, and PiP of their intercept teams. On the screen appeared FBI New York City, Field Office, Assistant Director George Veniz and his team. The A/V was completely encrypted and scrambled using NSA state of the art technology that the NYPD didn't have. The FBI New York Field Office at 26 Federal Plaza, just west of Chinatown, had been designated as the prime agency responsible for, as it had been designated, Operation Intercept.

Director Miller looking at Assistant Director Veniz and his team, said "Good morning Assistant Director Veniz and team. Please give us an update on your operational readiness and success assessment."

"Thank you, Director Miller," said Veniz. "We have five intercept teams. Five to six men in each team. Three along the FDR, one at the Triborough Bridge toll booths and one reserve team."

"Assistant Director Veniz," interrupted Miller, tell me about the teams? Who are the team members and where they from are?"

"The teams are sterile. Our overall group leader is Interceptor 6. The teams are T1-T5. The team leaders are T6's and are the only team member who know Interceptor 6, and Interceptor 6 only knows and reports to one of our undercover source attached to the Islamic Cultural Arts and Crafts Center, here in the city. We had these personnel, all ex-military, train together and be ready for an event such as this. They will be uniformed in the fashion of mid-eastern covert operators."

"Ex-military? Who's military?"

"They are all ex-military special forces and in America with temporary visas. They come from: Saudi Arabia, Iran, Egypt and Iraq."

"So, if I am following you correctly, Assistant Director Veniz, you have recruited Islamic ex-military types, who have temporary visas into the United States, and have absolute no knowledge of/or connection to the FBI. They are probably Al-Qaeda. What is, as they say in the movies, their motivation?"

"They are going to intercept and kill Police Commissioner Riley, his contractor Burk, FBI turncoat Hoar, and American Muslim Brotherhood leader Kahn along with any collateral interference. They are doing this; for Allah and because they believe they are furthering the cause, helping Kahn achieve martyrdom, and because the Imam Mohammed has told them to.

The NYPD has put in place their current generation A/V jamming equipment and have restricted aircraft fly over zones. Our NSA Communication equipment and satellite/drone equipment trumps anything they have."

"What is your percentage of success rate, Assistant Director Veniz?"

"100%."

"Outfuckingstanding, Director Veniz, because failure is not an option. I will let you get on with it and we will monitor you live from here. Your country, the bureau, and I, thank you and your team. God Speed and Allahu Akbar," said Director Miller.

The screen went white then black.

CHAPTER 48

NYC POLICE HEADQUARTERS

Commissioner's conference room.

"Commissioner, I just got off the horn with Captain Benson, our A/V communication specialist," said Captain Bounty. "She says she's registering an inordinate amount of overhead drone activity, besides ours that is. She can't determine satellite activity because her usual federal sources have all clammed up."

"To be expected, captain," said the commissioner.

"She is also hearing a lot of chatter and communications between the NYC and Washington FBI offices, where none was supposed to have been possible. We jammed everything but they seem able to circumvent our interference. She suggests NSA is helping them with more advanced systems. What if they try and shut our communications down?"

"They won't," said the commissioner, "because if they do, that will give me an excuse to shut down the convoy and they don't want that."

"Any of our assets on the ground and virtual see or hear anything?"

"We haven't seen any suspicious groups or movement along the drive but we are picking up some gibberish chatter. I have Benson bringing in some translators from the United Nations to see if we can decipher it. Keep you posted."

"Ok, 30 minutes 'til show time. Is Convoy 1 ready?"

"Ready. Sedated stand-ins for you, Burk, Ms. Sullivan, Hoar and Kahn are seated, belted in and ready to roll."

The Police Commissioner told Bounty to inform the FBI, as soon as Convoy begins to roll, that we are bringing some of the unreleased FBI agents with us in convoy 1. Make sure the message gets recorded so they have no deniability.

"All right," said the commissioner, "is everyone in place for Convoy 2?"

"Yes, said Captain Bounty, "our guest were driven individually to the secure parking level under City Hall. Just waiting for you and me."

"Let's not keep our guest waiting then, shall we?"

CHAPTER 49

NYC FDR Drive

Sutton Place and 57th Street.

Interceptor 6 had T-1 and T-2 at and around 57th. These were the strongest and largest teams.

The FDR Drive between 54th Street and 60th Street is covered—like driving through a tunnel, except one side of the tunnel is open to the East River and Roosevelt Island. Traffic going north is in the outbound lanes, closest to the river, while the southbound lanes hug the tunnel side wall but at a higher elevation. The tunnel ceiling, only 14-feet high, with one open side feels claustrophobic. Interceptor 6 put T-3 on Roosevelt Island in the Main Street parking lot next to the Goldwater Hospital, which was directly across the river from the FDR and 57th Street. T-3 is parked in a NY Presbyterian Emergency Services ambulance and for all intents and purposes the two men in the front seat looked like they were having lunch, which in fact, they were. The service portion of the ambulance was slightly modified with an interior stair and firing platform and a removable roof panel. A gunner and loader with two RPG-7, rocket-propelled grenade 7-V launchers, and four HE, high explosive rounds, sat patiently waiting.

On 53rd Street and 60th Street just off the drive, two eight-yard concrete trucks sat and waited. The trap was ready and would be sprung when the fly got to 56th Street.

Although this was the route given him by Imam Mohammed, the Imam also told him that the devil infidels were cunning and to take precautions in case of a diversions. This Interceptor 6 already knew…but where?

He had T-5 at the Triborough bridge toll booth area, as an ambush of last result. T-4 however, would be the positioned along FDR just 10 blocks south of the actual ambush site. They would be obvious and suspicious and in a similarly covered area of the FDR, right under the United Nations. But they would look and feel like the hit team and draw a lot of attention from the NYPD anti ambush teams and spotters. NYPD resources would be pulled from other areas to address this foreseen threat. But they and the threat would prove to be just construction workers and innocent bystanders and a big false alarm.

If the NYPD were to see similar suspicious activity a little later, let's say 10 blocks to the north, they might not cry wolf so quickly.

From the communication equipment Interceptor 6 and his team had, they were getting current live A/V links. Interceptor 6 would know in real time when the devil convoy has started to roll.

CHAPTER 50

NYC POLICE HEADQUARTERS AND CITY HALL

At exactly 12:45 p.m., all traffic on or near the FDR drive, Gracie Mansion, Fifth Avenue and north toward the Triborough and LaGuardia was halted and/ or rerouted. Police cruisers and motorcycle patrols stopped everything. NYPD spotters, surveillance cameras and low flying drones throughout the city were looking for anything out of the ordinary. Specifically they were focused on FDR Drive, Triborough Bridge and the route to LaGuardia airport.

New Yorkers, having just gone through a couple of horrific fearful days, were now thinking it was about to happen again. Most hurried back to their offices or apartments, locked the doors and turned on their TVs.

At 12:47 p.m., a threat alert came in simultaneously to operational control, and cameras, drones and spotters A/V were patched right to the commissioner: "Very suspicious activities and persons of interest have been spotted at and around the United Nations at 42ⁿᵈ and First Avenue. Heavy construction equipment, trucks and workers are where they don't seem to belong. Pedestrians have been spotted heading toward the FDR underpass carrying some sort of pipes and wearing backpacks." It was realized by all, very quickly, that it was a perfect ambush location and the significance of the location was not lost on anyone. Resources, as the report was surfacing, were being sent to verify the threat.

At exactly 1 p.m., despite the threat alert, Convoy 1, comprising of three black Suburbans with blacked out windows and take down light bars flashing, began to roll up from the One Police Plaza below ground parking ramp, turned left onto Frankfort Street then east to the FRD entrance ramp below the Brooklyn Bridge. This movement was immediately picked up by a NSA surveillance satellite and UAV Predator drones, who were zeroed in to One Police Plaza and transmitted the event, real time, to FBI Headquarters in Washington and New York but more importantly to Interceptor 6. Neither the drones nor the satellites could be seen or heard, but neither would miss a trick and were so good they could read a newsprint from miles up in space. Once Convoy 1 reached the FDR, at exactly 1:05 p.m., Commissioner Riley got in the shotgun seat of the middle vehicle of Convoy 2. Three black Suburbans comprised Convoy 2. Police Commissioner Riley gave the order to Captain Bounty in the forward Suburban to roll. Officer Tanner was behind the wheel with Commissioner Riley, Burk and Sullivan were in the furthest rear seats and Hoar and Kahn both restrained, were in the middle seats. Convoy 2 proceeded up Broadway to Canal then right to Fifth Avenue, the ruse being as simple as hoping no one would consider the second convoy to go north on Fifth when it was a one-way street going south. As good as the NSA satellite and drones were, it all comes down to the human factor. The mistake the NSA personnel, sitting in an office complex outside Arlington Virginia made, is that they were watching for a second convoy, if there was to be one, to come out of the same egress as Convoy1. Fortunately for Commissioner Riley, they were not focused on traffic just a couple of blocks west and completely missed Convoy 2 coming out from under City Hall.

NYPD would using Motorola #ASTRO SABER SSE-5000 encrypted phones and jamming on all other communications for the 1-hour convoy. NSA had a more advanced system, and they were in fact, not jammed at all. Everything NYPD said, NSA and the FBI heard.

Which was gibberish.

"Golf 1-6 to Golf 6 over."

"This is Golf 6 actual, go ahead Golf 1-6."

"This is Golf 1-6 actual. Yankees at mid-field. Halloween cancelled. Erector set torn down. GI Joe is watching a big year. Over."

"Roger that Golf 1-6, Golf 6 out"

What the police commissioner heard, after a little explaining from driver/ code breaker Tanner was: "SWAT team at 42nd Street. Threat not valid. Construction equipment has left the area. Pipes and packs are birdwatchers with telescopes."

The Feds would soon decipher all this, but not soon enough.

CHAPTER 51

FDR Drive and Fifth Avenue

Interceptors T-4, at the United Nations bogus ambush site, just south of the real ambush site, performed perfectly, drawing out valuable NYPD resources. T-4 regrouped and hurried up to Sutton Place to be used as reserves.

FDR Drive between 56th and 57th streets was the money shot, and Interceptor 6 had no intention of not taking it. The Triborough was a fall back and to be used only if they missed taking the money shot. Prudent, but not going to happen.

With Convoy 1 getting the all clear for the United Nations threat, they could keep rolling north until they reached Gracie Mansion or another threat was identified.

By 1:07 p.m., Convoy 1 was approaching FDR Drive and 42nd Street and the United Nations underpass. Convoy 2 was on Broadway just passing Union Square about to turn onto Fifth.

Convoy 1 made it through the United Nations underpass and was less than a minute away from the Sutton Place underpass and Interceptor 6's ambush.

Interceptor 6's T-1 and T-2, now supported by T-4, were in place, finished eating their lunches, folded their newspapers, got into position and pretended to go back to work. Engines for both concrete trucks were started. Across the river, T-3 loosened the roof panel and attached rockets to launchers. The NYPD low-level drone proceeding the convoy reported seeing a concrete truck coming to life and construction workers, and reported the possible threat to Golf 6. It was eerily similar to the previous threat, only the concrete truck seemed less a threat because it was on 54th Street facing west, and 54th. Street did not access the FDR drive because there was a 20-foot embankment drop that prevented vehicle access.

Lieutenant Savage, Golf 1-6, decided that Convoy 1 would accelerate and muscle on through.

Interceptor 6 had been following every movement of the convoy on his handheld. From his vantage point on the deck of the Sutton Place Apartments, he saw and heard the convoy approach. The lead Suburban was about to enter the 54th Street underpass when the 66-ton concrete truck at 59th Street, a half block from the embankment, put it in reverse, and floored it. The acceleration was tremendous, immediate and unstoppable. It sped down the slope and hurled itself over the embankment, over the southbound lane, over the meridian divider and into the northbound lane. Crashing with the force of an explosion into the overpass support columns. The rotating mixing drum, smashing into the under-pass ceiling, regurgitating its 30-ton load of wet concrete all over the FDR drive. At exactly the same time the second 66-ton concrete truck at 54th Street did the same but clipped the rear of the third Suburban as it entered the underpass. The concrete truck imploded, creating what looked like an enormous crater in the middle of the FDR north lane.

In an instant, Convoy 1 was trapped. It couldn't go forward or back. It couldn't cross over the concrete wall to the elevated southbound lane, and it couldn't go right over the low wall into the river. The convoy could not be seen from above. The only people who could see the convoy were those in it, those at that the receiving end of their transmissions and the rocket team across the river. Convoy 1 knew it was in big trouble, and it knew things were about to get worse.

Listening and watching live, Commissioner Riley, Burk, Sullivan, Hoar and Kahn, in Convoy 2, were fixated at what they saw. Although Officer Tanner continued his route north on Fifth, it seemed that they were now traveling in slow motion. Riley and Burk, having been in numerous ambushes in Viet Nam – both on the giving and receiving ends – knew what was coming next.

Lieutenant Savage's lead Suburban almost smashed into the mass of metal and concrete now blocking its front. If not for his driver's skill and ABS, Active Breaking System technology, they would now be indistinguishable from that mass of twisted metal and concrete. The third and last Suburban in Convoy 1, had its rear roof smashed in, by the plunging concrete truck, while entering the underpass and was stopped dead with its front end sea sawed up and wedged in the tunnel roof. The radio-controlled middle Suburban, the target vehicle with the doubles secured inside, braked to a screeching halt at 57th Street.

Burning rubber, smoke and steam were the fog of this ambush. A second of quiet before the storm, then all hell broke loose.

Across the East River just 340 yards as the rocket flies, the roof of the NY Presbyterian emergency services ambulance flew off, as one operative stood on the firing platform, his chest clear of the roof and from below the first RPG-7 was passed up. In one fluid motion the launcher was on his shoulder, aimed and fired. The rocket took less than three seconds to span the river and strike the middle Suburban. The detonation and explosion were thunderous. The RPG gunner discarded the spent launcher while another with the rocket attached was handed up and already in his shoulder.

Out from the apartment building basement where they were pretending to work, Teams T-1 and T-2 ran across the lawn carrying assault rifles and repelling gear. As they reached the underpass end, they hooked up to the safety rail and repelled over the parapet just seconds before the second RPG exploded into the third or last Suburban. The driver of the NY Presbyterian emergency services ambulance confirmed both hits to Interceptor 6. NSA and the FBI also received the transmission.

Lieutenant Savage and his three-man team were out of the lead Suburban just seconds after the first rocket struck, thus probably saving their lives.

An NYPD sniper on the Manhattan side of the Queensbury Bridge, sighting in his M82 Special Application Scoped Rifle with a 10-round, .50 caliber, BMG magazine, with an effective range of 1,969 yards, took the 429-yard shot across the river that blew the RPG gunner's head off. He then fired the rest of the ten rounds into the cab and body of the ambulance. The ambulance quaked, shuddered and was rammed almost ten feet further back into the parking lot from the impact it received from the .50 caliber rounds. An NYPD drone was airing all this live to headquarters, Convoy 2 and to Lieutenant Savage. The transmission then showed terrorists coming across the lawn and over the parapet. NYPD snipers on the Roosevelt Island side of the bridge opened up with extreme accuracy at their 429-yard targets. Of the 12, only 5 terrorists made it over the parapet and repelled down and swung in through the openings between the overpass support columns. A loud and terrible gun fight immediately erupted between the good and bad guys, even before the terrorists hit the deck. First to make it down was T-1, leader Musad, firing a HK 416, 5.56 with a 30-round magazine with under-mounted grenade launcher. His head-mounted A/V camera captured and broadcast in real time what no one, until then, could have seen from above: Two Suburban's completely destroyed and only four NYPD, DESU, Department Emergency Service Unit operatives returning fire. Within seconds, two of Savage's men were down, and only two terrorists remained.

Musad's mission ended when he could get close and personal with his targets. He needed to verify they were in the vehicle and if they were dead. With Musad surviving soldier providing cover, he rushed to the destroyed center vehicle with his cam recording every moment. As the fog of war cleared away for just a second, there through the blown away doors, through the fire and smoke, were the burning corpses of five bodies in civilian clothes—two of which were shackled to the seats. Musad saw out the corner of his eye his remaining soldier go down and two NYPD SWAT operatives closing in. His mission complete, he sprayed the bodies in the vehicle until his receiver flew open, then turned the barrel of the grenade launcher into his body and pulled the trigger.

The wall 20 yards behind Musad exploded. Musad, still standing, turned toward Savage who was now less than 10 feet away. What NSA, the FBI and Interceptor 6 were now seeing through Musads camera, was a NYPD, DESU operator pointing an M-4 carbine assault rifle directly at Musad but holding up his hand in a sign of peace. What Lieutenant Savage and his remaining team member saw was the last terrorist standing there like Wile E. Coyote with a large smoking donut hole through his stomach. The perceived peace sign was

Savage telling his man not to fire. As if in slow motion, Musad gurgled out "Allahu Akbar" then fell flat onto his back. Those watching Musads camera, which then focused on the underpass ceiling, were beside themselves with the success. In the last few minutes, not only did they verify that NYPD Police Commissioner Riley, Burk, Hoar and Kahn were dead, but Musad, in his last words, let the world know who was responsible. Just as they were slapping each other on the backs, they heard voices and rustling. Then a face, now distinguishable without his helmet, appeared in focus. The face was that of a grizzled hard looking DESU operative and his hand again seemed to be showing peace. But that changed quickly as he folded all but the middle finger and said, "Fuck you asshole. He's alive."

NYPD quickly closed down Sutton Place and Roosevelt Island. Remnants of T-4 remained trapped and in a serious above ground firefight, which they would lose. Interceptor 6 had moved out after the first RPG hit. He was now on his way to the Triborough to pick up Team 5. He watched the events on his hand held and praised Allah for his success. His Teams 1, 2, 3 and 4 were now completely wiped out.

CHAPTER 52

FIFTH AVENUE, UPPER EAST SIDE

Directly across town at 49th. and Fifth, while the ambush on Convoy 1 was taking place, Convoy 2 and Burk were picking up his kit from Kevin in front of Saks. Under the current circumstances, an act Burk was now sorry and embarrassed he had requested. By the time they reached 72nd and Fifth, the ambush was over. Reports from Lieutenant Savage were not good. The entire Department of Emergency Service Unit team in the third Suburban had been incinerated. Lodged in the upright position, the Suburban's doors and windows were crimped and wouldn't open. The gas tank exploded from the rocket impact.

The FBI stand-ins in the middle target vehicle and two the DESU operatives from Savages vehicle were all dead.

All fifteen attackers, including those in the ambulance, were dead and four more from T-4, above ground who refused to surrender were taken out. Wile E. Coyote, as Musad was being called, was alive. Paramedics checked him for hidden poison pills, his uniform was cut off, and was on his way under heavy security to Lenox Hill Hospital. The grenade passed through Musads soft body, like a big bullet, without detonating, until it impacted the wall behind him.

It was 1:30 p.m. when Convoy 2 turned off Fifth over to Third and headed north again. Over the Third Avenue Bridge into the Bronx, 895 to 95 North, and then about 23 miles to Westchester Airport, just north of Purchase NY. Mayor Bloomfield would be waiting for them with his private Gulfstream 650.

Riley looked at Burk and said, "Slight change of plans."

Ms. Sullivan asked the commissioner to please put *CNN* on so they could see what was being reported, and sure enough above the crawler the Breaking News banner appeared then video showing Convoy 1's ultimate destruction and final tomb.

With the volume turned up the *CNN* talking head said, "This just in. The heavy gunfire and explosions we have been reporting on from Sutton Place here on the Upper East Side of Manhattan, seemed to have taken an astonishing turn. Our sources inside Police Headquarters are now telling us that a NYPD convoy, carrying Police VIPs, was ambushed by Al-Qaeda terrorists under the Sutton Place Apartments on FDR Drive. We have a live feed from our local affiliate. We are going to watch this live together.

"It looks like smoke billowing from out of the underpass around 57th Street and the East River. There are cop cars all over the place, including on Roosevelt Island, and lights flashing everywhere. Ambulances and FDNY emergency vehicles are all over but it appears as though the firing and explosions are over and the police are, well, policing up.

"Hold on. I am just getting this from my producer. Unconfirmed reports are coming in that New York City Police Commissioner Riley was the intended target and that he and several yet to be named individuals have been killed in the ambush. I repeat, unconfirmed reports are coming in that New York City Police Commissioner Riley was the intended target of an ambush and that he and several yet to be named individuals with him in his vehicle are dead."

"Don't say it, Burk," said Riley.

After a moment of silence, Kelly asked, "Don't say what commissioner?"

"Don't encourage him, Ms. Sullivan," said the commissioner.

She looked at Burk but got nothing.

The screen came alive again.

"We have just received a report that Mayor Elliot Bloomfield will be addressing New Yorkers from Gracie Mansion any minute now. When he begins, we will patch into the host feed. To recap, hold on. Here is Mayor Bloomfield speaking from Gracie Mansion."

"Good afternoon my fellow New Yorkers and fellow Americans throughout the nation. It is with a very sad heart I have to report to you, this afternoon, the death of my very good friend, Police Commissioner Riley. He along with Tommy Burk, the hero who saved New York City, and the two terrorists charged with the recent NYC bomb threats, were being escorted to Washington at behest of the President of the United States. They were, along with myself, to fly aboard Air Force 2 this afternoon, to stand alongside and be honored by the president as she speaks to the nation tonight. The two prisoners were of extreme importance and were to be handed over in Washington to Homeland Security and the FBI. The commissioner's convoy to LaGuardia was ambushed along FDR Drive by a unit of, according to FBI sources, Al-Qaeda sympathetic to the American Muslim Brotherhood—the perpetrators of the bomb threats and wildfires in New York City, Chicago, Los Angeles and across the nation.

"On a personal note, I am relieved and heartened that this afternoon, before the convoy departed One Police Plaza, the president called and followed up with letter apologizing for the inaccurate, disparaging remarks and stories coming out of Washington and from a certain Atlanta news agency. These stories and news programs, said the president, painted Police Commissioner Riley and Mr. Burk as somehow being involved in the terrorist acts and were totally fabricated by unscrupulous low-level federal employees and news reporters. The reason was, undoubtedly, personal gain and TV ratings. The president has directed the FBI to put whatever resources necessary to track down the sources of their false and slanderous claims and prosecute them to the fullest extent of the law."

The mayor added that his office will distribute copies of the president's entire letter later today.

"Deputy Police Commissioner Turner has assumed overall control of the NYPD," the mayor continued. "All the terrorists involved it today's ambush have been killed or are in custody. The immediate threat is over, and I believe New York City is safe again. Tomorrow morning, Acting Police Commissioner Turner and I will hold a press conference at City Hall at 11 a.m. God Bless you, and God bless America."

Burk said in his best Hal Holbrook impression of Mark Twain, "The reports of my death are greatly exaggerated."

In a private conference room in the Westchester Airport, the semblance of his Gracie Mansion office were dismantled and the mayor boarded his jet to await the Commissioner.

Back in Convoy 2, getting closer to Westchester Airport, Police Commissioner Riley, after hearing the mayor's address, simply said to Burk and Ms. Sullivan, "In for a penny, in for a pound."

Burk looked at him and said, "You know, Captain, that's another of those silly sayings I don't understand. I mean if you said in for a penny, in for a dime, I would get it, *or* if you said, in for an ounce, in for a pound, I would get that too, but…"

"Sargent Burk…" Burk knew he was in for a lecture. "…here in America, in the 18th century, it was understood, that if one owed a penny one might as well owe a pound, as in pound sterling, UK currency. The penalties for nonpayment of either were virtually identical in severity."

Burk hated it when his Captain did that, but he had no one to blame but himself for asking a question he did not, but should have known the answer to. He would work on that problem and make sure he wouldn't get taught a lesson again.

CHAPTER 53

WASHINGTON, DC

The White House, the Oval Office.

The president, Kearney and Miller were back in the Oval Office. The president was seated on one couch, while the secretary and director were facing her on the other.

"OK, Bob," said the president. "The secretary and I have been watching *FOX News* and Shepard Smith, so we're pretty up on the unfortunate news coming out of New York. I will not watch CNN anymore after what they did to the mayor, commissioner and that poor Burk fellow.

"Can you believe what's going on there? Didn't you have information about an impending terrorist attack, Bob?"

"Yes, Madam President," said FBI Director Miller, "but as hard as we tried, the NYPD, and especially Police Commissioner Riley, would not respond. We just got stoned walled at every approach. Out agents were kept away from the convoy route. Very unprofessional of the NYPD and sadly unnecessary."

The charade they were playing was for the benefit of the hidden voice recorders that the president purposely let record their conversation. The president had a switch on her desk which could override the system but she wanted this conversation on the record.

"Bob," said the secretary of state, his voice now deeper and sounding vice presidential, "what can you add to what we have been getting from *FOX*?"

"When the NYPD lost control of the situation, we were invited in. I had teams standing by in case. The underpass looked like a battle zone. I have video that was taken by my agents just minutes after we were allowed in, which was not more than ten minutes after the last shots were fired. With your permission, Madam President." The president nodded, and the director flipped a switch and a large screen appeared. "This is raw film and quite graphic." Again the president nodded. The images that appeared were very clear and very graphic. Burning vehicles, black smoke, NYPD officers with guns drawn, DESU and SWAT teams holding assault rifles, NYFD emergency medics and firemen trying to put out the fires and bodies, body parts, and blood. It was absolutely frightening. Only someone who has been in combat can imagine how much more frightening it was when it was actually going down.

NYFD emergency responders were at the last Suburban attempting to cut access to the interior through heavy armored doors with the Jaws of Life, cutters and spreaders.

Some Homeland bureaucrat was ordering the NYFD first responders back because it was still too dangerous. A NYFD responder just looked at him and said "Danger is our job, asshole. Fuck off" then he continued cutting.

The center Suburban fire was out, the interior exposed, and bodies, or what was left of them, now cooled, were being removed.

This is where everyone sort of leaned forward to get a better look.

The first body pulled out from the shotgun seat was lying on the asphalt and looked to be the commissioner minus his right arm from the shoulder and the right side of his face.

Another body that was lying next to the Commissioner seemed to be that of a headless Burk. Inside the Suburban were three more bodies, and as the FBI agent got closer, they could see two charred bodies cuffed to the seats. They had to be Hoar and Kahn.

Surprisingly, another body was in the back—that of a woman.

The director mouthed "Kelly Sullivan," not wanting to be heard on the recording tapes. Both the president and secretary nodded and understood why acknowledgement that the *CNN* reporter was in the Suburban with Riley and Burk would lead to unwanted speculation.

Kearney, knowing what was now being said would soon become public, seized the opportunity to imbed potential sound bites for his future post vice president political aspirations said, "You know, Madam President," *his voice in an even deeper baritone now,* "I have seen this havoc up close while serving in Viet Nam. I have been wounded several times, and I can tell you it's like déjà vu for me watching these terrible terrorists assault innocents. Soldiers in Viet Nam have killed and have been killed, have raped, cut off ears, cut off heads, taped wires from portable telephones to human genitals and turned up the power, cut off limbs, blown up bodies, randomly shot at civilians, razed villages in fashion reminiscent of Genghis Khan, shot cattle and dogs for fun, poisoned food stocks, and generally ravaged the countryside of South Vietnam…"

The president reached across the coffee table and squeezed the secretary's shoulder, in what appeared to be an effort to console him but in actually to shut him up. *Jesus John, thought the president, you do run on, don't you? Where the fuck were you going with this?* "John, that was quite compelling and relevant. Thank you for serving." *She meant irrelevant but hoped that would just shut up and he would just drop it.* "Mr. Director, can you absolutely confirm at this time that these bodies are those of Police Commissioner Riley, Mr. Burk, FBI Special Agent Hoar, and FBI Tech Kahn?" *Where was the driver?*

"Madam President, the bodies were exploded, burned and shot up, but each matched the physical characteristics of Riley, Burk, Hoar and Kahn, and each carried identification identifying them as such. The driver's door was blown out and apparently he went with it. The NYPD has taken physical custody of the bodies but have allowed the FBI joint custody. We are working on gathering prints and dental comparisons, the results of which, we should have sometime this evening. Furthermore, the NYPD has accepted the bodies as their own, and the mayor with his earlier live address has confirmed the deaths of his commissioner, Burk, Hoar and Kahn. I can tell you, the FBI is 100% certain the final results will be conclusive."

"Bob," said the president, "I followed everything you said but your last sentence."

A bit irritated, Director Miller said, "What I meant, Madam President is that I am currently 99% convinced. But until the fat lady sings, I can't be 100% positive."

The president sat back into the couch, smiled at the director and thought to herself, *I am going to make you pay for that fat joke, Bob. I may still nominate you as secretary of state, because I need you and you know where the skeletons lie, but your first official visit will be to Antarctica where you will stay until you successfully negotiate a trade deal with the Eskimos to import fucking Sub Zero's.* "OK, let's get back to the Cabinet Room and finish up. I need some time after to get ready for my speech."

CHAPTER 54

WASHINGTON, DC

The White House, Cabinet Room.

"Thank you for all for hanging around and fitting this into your busy schedules," said the president. "We still have a few issues to settle and little time. I am still on for tonight at 6 p.m., so let's get to it.

"First of all, as I am sure you have all been watching on *FOX*. I want us all to offer our hearts and prayers to our fallen heroes: New York Police Commissioner Riley, Mr. Thomas Burk, FBI agents Hoar and Kahn, and their fallen comrades. What happened today—just a little over an hour ago—is another American tragedy. Let's all bow our heads in prayer."

This is becoming a habit she thought to herself.

As the president raised her head, she noticed Kearney still had his head lowered but this time she would not to take the bait and quickly continued.

"Ok," said the president, "let's continue." To the other cabinet members seated around the table she said, "I hereby put forth the name of FBI Director Robert Miller to become my Secretary of State.

All the cabinet members, with the exception of Kearney and most of agency heads and staffers appeared to be in shock.

"Bob has proven to me time and again his intelligence and ability to negotiate. Recently I have been working very closely with Bob and found him to be trustworthy, innovative and someone who can deliver what he promises."

Miller, not seated at the center table but against the wall, had no expectations of being warmly received by the cabinet. It was akin to having Himmler join the board of the American Retail Federation. Still, he stood and thanked the president and his soon to become peers and simply parroted Kearney's previous acceptance speech. "I am honored, and thank you, Madam President."

The president parroted her own previous response. "Of course this is conditional to confirmation by a majority vote of both Houses of Congress, but I don't see that as a problem."

"Now let's quickly get through the remainder of items that we didn't address this morning. Bomb threats and fires. FBI Director and Secretary of State-Elect Miller, would you like to start?"

"Madam President, cabinet and agency members and staff, we have been through an extremely rough week. Bomb threats, forest fires, the American Muslim Brotherhood and the false accusations issued against New York's finest and its hero, Tommy Burk. And of course today's terrorist attacks and the deaths of so many good souls. I will later address these in an investigative capacity and let the appropriate departments elaborate specifics, as they deem necessary.

"But I want to assure everyone that it's over! The bombs were duds as we, the president, the secretary of state, and I suspected and so advised the cities. The fires are mostly out. The arsons, all part of the American Muslim Brotherhood, are all in custody. The entire American Muslim Brotherhood has been neutralized, including the last team and the overall teams leader, found on the Triborough Bridge. The mastermind and founder, American-born and educated Samir Kahn, residing in Brooklyn, New York, was killed today in the ambush of the commissioner's convoy. He was the apparent target and was being escorted here to Washington by the NYPD. The terrorist group that attacked that convoy today, a splinter group of foreign Al-Qaeda operatives, were smuggled into the United Stated by the Islamic Cultural Arts & Crafts Center of New York and their leader Imam Mohammed Hikmah Al. The Islamic Cultural Arts

& Crafts Center of New York is now a crime scene and has been closed. The Imam has been arrested, and all but one of the terrorists are dead; and he is in critical condition in a New York Lenox Hill hospital, under tight security.

"The FBI along with the CIA, NYPD and Homeland Security will continue to investigate and incorporate procedures to make sure this kind of thing doesn't happen again.

"But as I said in the beginning of my statement, it's over!"

The director set down among murmurs from the cabinet members which sounded like, "Over my ass."

"Thank you, Director Miller, on behalf of myself and the cabinet, we welcome you," said the president. "Now what about the evacuations, lootings, death and injuries associated with New York, Chicago and Los Angeles? Madam Secretary, would you care to take this?"

Sally Jewel, the Secretary of the Interior, began, "Thank you, Madam President. Very early this morning, in a five way video conference, between myself, the director of Homeland Security Debra Wines, and the mayors of New York, Elliott Bloomfield, Chicago, Manny Rohm, and Tony Anthony of Los Angeles, I can, and with complete certainty, report the following. With the exception of New York City, which has its unique set of problems, we are still experiencing minor looting in Chicago and Los Angeles. In addition, in both cities, we are now having riots and several neighborhoods are on fire. Both Chicago's Mayor Rohm and Los Angeles' Mayor Anthony strongly agree their current problems started with terrorist threats but are actually a manifestation of inherent social and economic problems attributed to the availability of assault weapons to inner city children and racial profiling."

"So," said the president, "if I understand you correctly, New York, Chicago and Los Angeles have all three weathered the terrorist threats. The current problems in Chicago and Los Angeles are inherent to big cities. The problems could be eliminated or greatly reduced by passing stronger federal gun laws and eliminating stop and search. Does that about sum it up?"

"Yes," replied the secretary of the interior.

"Great," said the president, "we'll take care of those two problems. That's what we're good at—getting new laws on the books and ignoring old ones. Anyone have anything further to add? No? Good. Then that's it. Were finished here."

As the president was about to stand to leave, her chief of staff, Denis O'Donnell said, "Madam President, we have one more item we need to address before we can complete your speech for tonight."

"And that is?" asked the president.

"The Kingdom Tower incident, Madam President,"

"I don't want to touch that tonight, Denis, and besides I think the vice president's remarks and actions this morning were pointed and sliced right through the problem. Wouldn't you agree with that assessment, Chief of Staff O'Donnell?

"I think we're done here," responded Chief of Staff O'Donnell.

CHAPTER 55

WESTCHESTER COUNTY AIRPORT

White Plains, New York.

Convoy 2 arrived at Westchester County Airport at 2:30 pm. Captain Bounty and his security teams led the convoy around the back of the main airport to General Aviation parking, specifically to Hanger T, just to the left but far enough removed from U.S. Customs, to feel mildly obscure. No sense having a nosy custom agent peeking in the Suburban. Since the flight was domestic it did not require passports, and since it was the mayor's private jet, it only needed to file a flight plan to Washington DC's Reagan National Airport in Arlington Va. Captain Bounty with the jets pilot, filed the flight plan and a number of the mayor's guests with airport control.

The guest names were not necessary on this end as no one would check. The middle Suburban pulled into the hanger, right up next to the jet's fold down stairs. Police Commissioner Riley, Ms. Sullivan, Burk, and Captain Bounty went quickly up the steps and into the jet. With his security team guarding the hanger entrance, Officer Tanner gave the signal to have Hoar and Kahn uncuffed and quickly escorted out, up and into the jet. Once both were secured in the front two seats, the Golfstreams captain retracted the steps and closed the door. Tanner, the security team, and the three Suburbans pulled in front of Hanger T. They would stand guard there until the jet began to taxi to the runway, but wouldn't leave the airport until the mayor's Gulfstream 650 was in the air.

Mayor Bloomfield and Ms. Sullivan set aft on the two swivel chairs, and Police Commissioner Riley and Burk sat on the couch just opposite. On the bulkhead was a LED screen tuned to *FOX News*. Hoar and Kahn were forward, restrained, and had ear phones on, listening to music, not for entertainment but so they couldn't hear anything the mayor, Riley, Burk or Sullivan said. Captain Bounty, armed with his service pistol and black jack, set behind them. An attendant served coffee and cold drinks all around—even to Hoar and Kahn, who both had one hand free.

As soon as the attendant went forward to the enclosed galley, Burk, who felt left out since he was not read in about the whole Westchester Airport redirection, asked, "Is anybody going to tell me what's going on?"

"Look Tommy," said Riley, "the mayor and I have been developing the plan on the fly, so to speak. Here's what we got so far; I – we – are open for suggestions. Mayor, would you mind bringing us up to date?"

"Of course," said the mayor. "After my press conference this afternoon and after I received the president's letter exonerating Mr. Burk, and in a sense all of us, from complicity in the bomb threats, Commissioner Riley and I decided we should go to Washington for tonight's presidential address. After all, we were invited. I had my office contact the president's Chief of Staff, Denis O'Donnell, and let him know that I had decided it would be better for New York City to see me to be standing with the president tonight. O'Donnell was informed that I would be arriving Ronald Reagan Airport aboard my private jet at 5 p.m. I have three additional officials and associates aboard, not including the flight crew. Chief of Staff O'Donnell's office got back to us that they will have the Secret Service meet us at the airport and escort us back to Washington and to the White House. O'Donnell's office asked for a list of my entourage, and I had my office tell them that we would shoot it over to them before we take off. And that's where we are."

"So who are you going to tell them we are?" asked Burk.

Riley took over. "We don't know yet. That's as far as we got."

"So that's the plan?" asked Burk. "We are going to ride into Dodge and tell the sheriff that his posse got the wrong guys and we were just fooling around and can't we all just be friends? Are we going to do this before her address to the nation, during or after?"

"Look," said the mayor, "that's why we are sitting here now. We have a couple of hours to formulate a plan so we better get to it. Let's discuss what we think the president and her cronies know and as importantly what we want to achieve. Ok?"

Affirmative nods all around.

The mayor continued. "We embarrassed the president and the FBI by making the right call on the bomb threats. You, Burk, with your attitude and sharp tongue only took five seconds to get on the president's bad side. For whatever stupid reason the president and her inner circle, which I believe include Secretary of State John Kearney and FBI Director Bob Miller, decided to blame everything – bombs, fires, everything – on you Burk, and by association the commissioner and myself. Probably to take the heat off them, as Agent Hoar said." The mayor made a point to look directly at Ms. Sullivan to emphasize that point. Then looking back at Burk, he said. "Mr. Burk, an IRS agent, whom you were having, to put it mildly, suspicious dealings with, was murdered outside you apartment, a transgression that certainly left your character vulnerable for manipulation. But be that as it may, the president has officially exonerated us. Why? Because she knew all of us, including Hoar and Kahn, who they knew spilled the entire intrigue to us, would be dead before tonight's address. But they missed me and think I have rolled over because I am scared or want something from them."

"Look," said Burk, "here is what I think we should do. Let's send some false names to this chief of staff guy, and commissioner, you get us some false IDs to go with the names. If we sent our true identities, the Secret Service might take us to an outhouse instead of the White House.

"Your Honor, get us a meeting at the White House, say 30 minutes before the president's address. When we and the Secret Service have our meet-and-greet at Reagan, we need to appear to be whom our false id's say we are. It's cold, so we can have hats, scarves on. We can have glasses on or whatever. Just enough misdirection. When we get through the White House gate and out of the Secret Service cars, you, Mr. Mayor, call the president and drop the bomb. No pun intended.

Tell her we're all outside. Dead men walking. With all the staff and reporters around, she will have no choice but to hear us out. Tell her we have a win-win solution for everyone. To say she will be shocked will be an understatement but she'll see us, she'll have to."

"What's the win-win?" asked the mayor.

"I don't know yet," said Burk, "but I am on a roll so I am sure it will come to me before we get out of the Secret Service car. Just send the names and get us some ID's. What do you think?"

The mayor and commissioner nodded. Kelly remained neutral as she didn't feel she had a vote. Besides, nobody asked her.

"Can you get some ID's, Commissioner?" asked Burk.

"We have tons of confiscated ID's in evidence boxes from burglaries and pickpockets.

But I have a better idea," Riley said.

Riley got on the horn and called headquarters to get three ID's, some hats and scarves; he instructed them to fly them up by chopper but call with the names first. When the mayor got the names ten minutes later from the commissioner, he called his office and had his deputy call Chief of Staff O'Donnell with the names of his party and to get them a 5:30 meeting with the president.

"Tell him it is urgent we talk before the address," Riley said. "And if he presses you on what it's about and why it's so urgent, tell him there were more survivors of the ambush then originally reported."

CHAPTER 56

WASHINGTON, DC

The White House, the Oval Office.

Chief of Staff O'Donnell knocked and entered the Oval Office. The president, Kearney, and Miller were seated in the couch area.

"Denis, have a seat," said the president.

The president's chief of staff sat next to the president and across the coffee table from Kearney and Miller.

"Do you have tonight's speech, Denis?" asked the president.

"Yes Madam President, we are just finishing it up," said the chief of staff.

"Well Denis, is it going to be a great speech or just a good one?" asked the president.

"Great," answered Denis.

"Great as in Reagan's 'Tear down that wall' speech or Kennedy's 'Ask not what you can do for your country' speech or Martin Luther King's 'I have a dream' speech, or FDR's 'The only thing we have to fear is fear itself' speech?" asked the president. Without waiting for an answer, the president seemed to have another of her 'aha' moments. She stood and said, "Wait a minute, that's it. FDR's 'only thing we have to fear is fear itself' speech. That's what we should use. Updated of course. Change a word or phrase here or there; it's exactly what the country is going through now and needs to hear. I mean isn't this what it's all about? Fear. Denis, it is right there in front of you; all you have to do is borrow it. We still have time. Do a draft and bring it to me as soon as soon as it's ready. Anything else?"

"Yes, Madam President," said O'Donnell. "I told you Bloomfield is coming to the speech and bringing some guests with him, but his office just called and said it is urgent they meet and talk with you before the address. They suggest 5:30 p.m."

"Denis," said the president, "we don't have time for this nonsense. What does he want me to do? Have a meet and greet with some of his cronies before the most important speech of my presidency? Kiss some babies?"

"I don't think, so Madam President," said O'Donnell. "When I pressed them on what this is all about, they said, and I quote. 'There were more survivors of the ambush than originally reported.'"

The president waved O'Donnell out of the room with a warning to get her a speech that would become her legacy. "Wait, do you have that list of names?"

O'Donnell handed the president a piece of paper.

After the Chief of Staff left and the door closed, the president looked at Kearney and said "My chief of staff and his writers are not in league with Sorensen or Noonan, and I don't want my address to America to be remembered as a Bill Clinton's' 'I have sinned' speech."

The president, Kearney and FBI director all looked at each other with looks of confusion and uncertainty.

Then the president said, "What the hell is that supposed to mean 'more survivors of the ambush then originally reported?' What do you think he is up to, Bob?"

The FBI director responded. "We know that one terrorist went to the hospital, and we have been in to see him. The acting police commissioner is being very accommodating, unlike his predecessor. The surviving terrorist is in bad shape and not able to talk and if he could..."

"Excuse me, Bob," said the president, "I know all that. What I want to know is what they mean by having more survivors then originally reported. What is going on?"

"Madam President, I don't know, but I will find out if they're playing some sort of game. Can I see the names on the list O'Donnell gave you?"

The president glanced at the names, didn't recognize any, and handed it across the table to Miller. He perused the list: the new acting police commissioner, the team leader of the convoy Lieutenant Savage, and the mayor's press secretary. The mayor's guest list seemed to check out.

"I think," said Miller, "I understand what the mayor means by more survivors. One of the mayor's guests is the NYPD team leader who was in charge of the commissioner's convoy and put down the terrorist today in the ambush. The mayor is probably bringing him up here for you to pin a medal on him."

This seemed to appease the president for a second; then she looked at Kearney, and he nodded in agreement.

"OK," said the president, "keep an eye on it, Bob, but we'll go ahead have the meeting. But, Bob, you better be right."

CHAPTER 57

IN THE AIR

It takes about 43 minutes to fly from Westchester County Airport to Ronald Reagan Airport in Arlington, Virginia. Mayor Bloomfield, Police Commissioner Riley, and Burk continued developing their plan while Kelly took notes.

Burk said, "OK. If we make it through the White House gate, and with the Secret Service escorting us that should not be a problem, right? But as I said, when we exit the car, you, Mr. Mayor, make the call to the president. Kelly..." Kelly perked up when she heard she was being involved. "You call your camera crew – hell call everyone you know – and get them as close to the where we will be. Where will we be? I have never been to the White House. What gate do we come in and where is it?"

Neither the mayor nor Commissioner Riley seemed to have an answer, but Kelly did. "We will probably come in through Hamilton Place access and onto the east visitor's entrance."

"Does that put us inside the White House grounds and through the gate?" asked Burk.

"Yes," said Kelly. "We just walk a few yards to the entrance to the East Wing. But we will have to be on the VIP visitor's list, and we will be asked for identification again and have to go through metal detectors and trace puffers."

"By the time that happens," said Burk, "the jig will be up. Does everyone have their real ID's?"

Everyone nodded.

"OK, after the mayor makes his call, the president will know who's really here with the mayor. She's really going to be pissed after it all sinks in. We're all supposed to be dead, including you, Kelly. It was on TV, after all. But what can the president do? There will be reporters everywhere filming the mayor of New York City, along with his police commissioner and the hero of New York, yours truly."

Now feeling part of the team, Kelly pointed to the front of the plane and said, "Have we forgotten about those two?"

"Right," said Commissioner Riley, "we have to get them to a safe house as insurance or until we settle things. Captain Bounty will handle it. When we land, they will stay on the plane until we depart with the Secret Service. The Captain has some friends in the DCPD meeting him at the plane. They will hold out in the safe house until they hear from us. Kelly, you give Captain Bounty a reliable high profile media source he can trust. If they don't hear from us or if we disappear or have an accident, your source with Captain Bounty can go public. But that's just me being prudent because it's not going to be necessary."

"Right," said Burk, "but what are we going to do with them? We've got an FBI agent who was just following orders, misguided as they were. And another FBI agent of sorts who masterminded an attack on America that Osama Bin Laden would be in awe of."

Police Commissioner Riley said, "Samir is a bad guy who is going away for a long time or worse. The FBI, if it comes out that he was in their employ, will be devastated, and that could be a good bargaining chip for us."

"So," said Burk, "we keep Samir as Samir, and the Bureau makes Sammy disappear form their books. The FBI gets a win. You know, he's a bad guy, but I kind of like him. He could have stonewalled us, but he didn't. And besides the bombs were fake."

"Burk," said Riley, "the fires weren't fake nor were the deaths. A bleeding heart, you're not. What are you thinking?"

"Don't have it completely down yet. But I was thinking of what the president said in her letter to the mayor: she directed the FBI to put whatever resources necessary to track down the sources of the false and slanderous claims made against us and prosecute them to the fullest extent of the law. Well, that's not going to happen, but if the president doesn't want to play nice with us we can take her at her word and let Agent Hoar get some payback."

Kelly had been on the phone setting up camera crews and putting the word out about the secret VIP's en route to the White House. Now her contemporaries knew, she was still alive. She also told them to hold the photos and vids till she gave them the OK. She put her phone away and looked up and said, "I have some unverified breaking news. The press secretary hasn't released it yet, but the president has named Secretary of State Kearney to replace Denning as vice president and FBI Director Miller to move up to secretary of state."

No one said anything for a minute until Burk said, "I have a healthy hatred for scoundrels."

"Can we get back to our 5:30 p.m. meeting with the president?" asked the mayor. "We are on the list, we get through the metal detectors and puffer, and are getting ready to have a face to face with the most powerful person in the world, who five minutes before thought you two were dead and that I was playing ball. What happens next?"

"What happens," said Burk, "is we walk in like we own the place. She probably won't be alone; she will probably have Secretary Kearney, FBI Director Miller, maybe her Chief of Staff O'Donnell, and definitely Secret Service all over the place. But not the ones who picked us up because they will have been made redundant by now. She knows we know, and she knows we have Hoar and Samir, either of whom going public could tumble her administration. She is less than 30 minutes until show time for the most important speech of her life and has no idea what we want or what we will do. When she goes live at 6 p.m., will we be standing behind her smiling while she tells the world all is good and right, or will she be shooting from the hip because she knows we are going to bring her and her entire administration down right after she says, 'Thank you and goodnight America.'

"I think she will take what's behind door No. 1, don't you?"

The pilot's voice came over the address system. "Please fasten your seat belts. We are 10 minutes out of Reagan and have been cleared for landing."

"Ok," said Riley, "once we get in the president's office, why don't we let the mayor start it off, and I will jump in when the time is right. Agreed?"

"Sounds good to me," said Burk.

CHAPTER 58

REAGAN AIRPORT AND WASHINGTON, DC

The mayor's Gulfstream 650 touched down at Reagan National Airport on Runway 1-19 at 4:30 p.m. and taxied over to the General Aviation Terminal. When at its designated slot, the pilot shut down the engines. Looking out the jet's starboard portholes, the mayor and his guests could see three black Chevy Suburbans parked along the taxiway and several Secret Service Agents looking very secretive. The two detainees, along with Captain Bounty, moved aft to the windowless storage compartment. Both were gagged and had their hands and feet cuffed to the bulkhead and deck. Riley, Burk and Sullivan donned hats, glasses, coats and scarves to conceal their appearance as much as possible. The attendant opened the door and pushed the switch and the steps lowered. The mayor was the first one out, followed by Commissioner Riley, Burk, and then Sullivan. The Secret Service Agent-in-Charge, Agent Shila Robertson, introduced herself to the mayor, eyeballed and verified his guest names but no further introductions were made.

Agent Robertson directed the mayor, and his three guests to the middle Suburban. When all were seated, she did a whirlybird sign with her finger, climbed into the shotgun seat and into her lapel mike ordered, "Let's roll."

The convoy experience seemed eerily familiar to Riley, Burk and Sullivan. The three Suburbans moved out of the Regan National Airport onto George Washington Memorial Parkway north, with take down bars flashing and sirens chirping. They rolled to 395 north and over the Potomac via the Arland Williams Jr. Bridge, then the Francis Case Memorial Bridge, and into DC for a short ride to the White House. *So far so good,* thought Burk.

Before they knew it, they were rolling up Hamilton Plaza through the east gate and in front of the east entrance to the White House. Kelly had done her job, as outside the gate and near the entrance were several film crews and many reporters. Apparently, someone had tipped them off that some special secret VIPs were due at the East Entrance for a secret pre-speech meeting with the president. When the convoy stopped, Agent Robertson got out, as did several other agents, and the doors were opened. The mayor and his guests got out, and the jig was up. Riley and Burk looked towards the cameras and removed their scarves and glasses—just enough for their faces to be captured on film. Although Secret Service Agent Robertson started to direct the mayor and his guest to the entrance, the mayor said he had an important call to make and pulled out his cell. Now that Riley and Burk had their pictures taken, they covered back up and waited for the mayor to finish the call.

The film crews and reporters seemed to be the only ones to notice that two dead men were standing in front of the White House. And they got it on film.

The mayor's cell phone rang through to the White House, and after three rings the White House operator answered. The mayor introduced himself and asked to speak with Chief of Staff Denis O'Donnell. A few seconds passed, and O'Donnell picked up. "Mr. Mayor," he said, "you're outside; just come on up – we're here waiting"

"Denis," said the mayor, "put me through to the president, please."

"Is there a problem Mr. Mayor?"

"You could say that, Denis. Now may I please speak to the president?"

A moment of silence then, the president on the line said, "Mayor Bloomfield, what's keeping you, come on in. I am a bit pressed for time."

"Madam President, I am here with my guests, and I think you need to send word down to get us through security and in to see you."

"Mr. Mayor, I can assure you it's all been arranged. Is there a Secret Service agent with you?

"Yes," said the mayor.

"Put the agent on," said the president.

Bloomfield handed the phone to the agent.

"Agent-in-Charge Shila Robertson speaking."

"Agent Roberson, this is the president. Do you recognize my voice? Do you believe you are speaking to the president?"

"That's affirmative, Madam President."

"That's good," said the president. "Now, you personally escort the mayor and his guests here to my office immediately. Do not have them go through screening; just get them to my office now. That is a direct order. Do you understand, Agent Robertson?"

"Affirmative, Madam President." The line went dead. Agent Robertson again twirled her finger, and the mayor, his guests and the other agents were on the move into the East Wing.

Into the entrance they went. Agent Robertson spoke for a second to the Secret Service entrance security agent in charge and although unprecedented, ingress was unmolested and Agent Robertson and her charges were on their way to the Oval Office.

Burk whispered to Riley one of Napoleon's favorite sayings. "Never interrupt your enemy when he is making a mistake."

CHAPTER 59

WASHINGTON, DC

The White House, the Oval Office.

Secretary of State Kearney, FBI Director Miller, Chief of Staff O'Donnell and Press Secretary Jay Kerry were all seated on the two couches in the sitting area.

The president was behind her desk, putting the phone down. "What's going on, Denis?"

"I don't know, Madam President, but I have a feeling were in for a few surprises."

"Jay, let's go with the FDR's 'Fear' speech. Add the changes and my comments and get it up on the prompters. If time permits, I would love to do a run through in 10 minutes. Make it happen."

As Kerry exited the office, he passed Agent Robertson's incoming party. The mayor, Riley, Burk and Sullivan were removing their hats, scarves and coats as they walked down the hall. Kerry acknowledged the mayor, but stopped dead when he saw the Police Commissioner Riley, Burk and Sullivan. Carr just stood to the side with his mouth open. There was no time to alert the president as Agent Porter, the Oval Office door security agent's hand was knocking on the Oval Room door.

The door opened, and Agent Porter announced Agent Robertson, the mayor, and his guests were outside. Chief of Staff O'Donnell said to Porter "Ask Agent Robertson to escort them in." Agent Porter noticed who the guest were but assumed it was part of the presidents strategy. Agent Robertson, who now also recognized the guest, gave a look of bewilderment to Agent Porter as she passed.

Agent Robertson who had a direct order from the president to bring the mayor and his guest directly to the Oval Office came through the door followed by Mayor Bloomfield, Police Commissioner Riley, Tommy Burk, and *CNN* Reporter Kelly Sullivan.

At the same time, Kearney, Miller, and O'Donnell all stood and turned to face the mayor and his guest. The president remained seated behind her desk.

When Kearney, Miller, and O'Donnell looked past the mayor and saw Riley, Burk and Sullivan, they all kind of did that dog thing where the dog tilts his head and says huh? The president looked up at the mayor then his guest but made no effort to acknowledge them other than giving Burk a hard stare.

Agent Robertson felt awkward with the silence and was about to leave when Chief of Staff O'Donnell put up his hand indicating for her to stay. With another hand gesture, Agent Robinson was instructed to have the rest of her detail come in. Agent Robertson put her right hand on her service pistol and spoke into her lapel mike. Agent Porter and two more agents immediately came into the Oval Office through the main and side doors.

The Oval Office quickly took on the demeanor of Tombstone Arizona and the Gunfight at the OK Corral. The Clanton gang vs. Marshal Earp. Who was who remained to be seen, but only one side brought guns to this corral.

The president, switched off the voice recorder system and in a calm voice, while still seated, broke the standoff and fired the first shot. "Mayor Bloomfield, you have 10 seconds to explain yourself before I have you all arrested."

With this Agent Porter moved next to the president, and Agent Robertson and the other two agents moved to encircle the mayor, Riley, Burk and Sullivan.

The mayor held up his hands, palms facing the president in a gesture of calm, which came off as if he were already under arrest. "Madam President, there is no need for concern nor threats. We are here at your bequest. You called me and told me to get myself, Police Commissioner Riley, and Mr. Burk up here to be honored by you tonight, in front of the entire nation."

FBI Director Miller, sensing the need to do something or at least seem in charge moved forward and said. "FBI. Everyone on the ground, hands behind your back."

The president quickly realized what a ridiculous situation she had allowed herself to get in. She held up her hand for everyone to stop dead.

Looking around the room, the president saw that the mayor had his hands in the air, Secret Service Agents had their guns in their hands, and her FBI director had his head up his ass. There were two dead men and a *CNN* reporter standing behind the mayor. The tension in the room could explode at any moment and things were about to be said that she did not want certain people to here.

"Everyone stand down," she said. "Agent Porter, you and the other agents leave the room now."

Miller did not like this one bit and made it clear with a hand motion for the agents to stay.

The president barked, "Agent Porter, you and your agents leave now! Director Miller, don't ever countermand my orders again. Sit down on the couch or this fat lady will sit down on you. O'Donnell, you are also excused, and Mayor Bloomfield please put your hands down."

The agents left. Miller and Kearney sat down on the couch, and the mayor lowered his hands.

"Mayor Bloomfield," said the president, "can you please explain why you led me and the American public to believe Police Commissioner Riley and Mr. Burk were killed this afternoon when obviously that is not the case?"

"That, Madam President, is an excellent question and one I would love to answer. After you called me and invited the three us, and the two prisoners to Washington aboard Airfare 2, I directed Police Commissioner Riley to get Mr. Burk and the two arrested FBI agents to LaGuardia ASAP. As we were preparing the transportation logistics, we received credible information from the FBI and our own rakers assigned to our Demographic Unit that Al-Qaeda was preparing to assassinate Samir Kahn, the mastermind of the three city bomb threats and fires. The same Samir Kahn who started the American Muslim Brotherhood at night but had a day job with the FBI as Sammy Kahn. The same Samir Khan that we were to bring to Washington."

The president looked toward FBI Director Miller and shook her head in disgust.

The mayor continued. "The police commissioner and I took your invitation seriously, as we did the information and chatter we were receiving about an imminent attract on Kahn. The commissioner and I organized two convoys to LaGuardia-one up the FDR drive and another up Fifth Avenue. After I spoke to you, we received some additional information that required us to switch the commissioner's convoy from FDR Drive to the convoy going up Fifth Avenue."

"Well," asked the president, "who was in the convoy that did go up the FDR Drive?"

"Besides two Suburbans of NYPD security, the middle Suburban, which was supposed to have the Commissioner, Burk and the two prisoners, had instead, the rest of Agent Hoar's arrested FBI team."

"What!" screamed Miller? "You put FBI agents in a situation that led to their deaths?"

"No, Director Miller," said the mayor, "we didn't know for sure if we would be ambushed at all. We were just taking precautions by setting out with two separate convoys. Either could have been the target or not. We intended to release and drop the agents off at Gracie mansion." By the way, your office was notified of this, Director Miller." Said Riley

"This is crazy, Madam President," said Director Miller. "What were they doing with my FBI agents in the first place and who were they? What were their names?"

Burk stepped out from behind the mayor and yelled, "Stop it! Just stop it!"

Commissioner Riley put his head down as it he didn't want to see what was going to happen next.

"With all due respect, Madam President, let's cut to the chase, shall we?" Burk said. "You and your little pretty boys over there had no intention of allowing us to reach LaGuardia, let alone Washington. You know it, we know it, and your little Hoar knows it. And Hoar told us everything"

With that Miller was off the couch and halfway to Burk when Riley stepped in between. Riley was like a rock, and Miller was stopped cold.

Burk didn't flinch. "How you got Al-Qaeda teams into the country will be a topic for future discussion, but just so you know, your Al-Qaeda survivor Musad is now talking. He has a donut hole where his stomach used to be, but other than having severe tummy pains, he is going to live.

While the president remained seated, she was thinking where all this was going and who she would throw under the bus.

Kearney was but a mere formality away from becoming vice president of the United States and very possibly president. He saw both possibilities balanced on the precipice of a cliff and needed to step up and take charge before someone knocked them over. It had to end now and he was the one to negotiate some sort of deal or truce.

Standing, then moving next to Miller, Kearney said, "Everybody please calm down. Bob, calm down. Haven't you done enough? The secretary looked at the president, and she picked up immediately where he was heading. She decided to sit back and let it play out.

"Gentlemen, Madam President, I think it will serve us all greatly by—as Mr. Burk so eloquently suggested—cutting to the chase," Kearney continued. "Director Miller, I believe it would be more productive if you left the room.

FBI Miller knew this was a kiss of death. He knew he was about to be thrown under the bus, and the president wasn't going to stop it. His good friend Secretary of State John Kearney was now driving that bus.

"Are you sure you want to go this direction, John?" asked Miller.

"Bob," said Kearney, "I think your agency's intercourse with the mayor, police commissioner, Mr. Burk and Ms. Sullivan of *CNN* has become a stumbling point that will interfere with a timely solution to our little problem. Don't you agree, Madam President?"

Not even attempting to smooth over any awkwardness experienced by the director, the president simply said, "Bob, wait outside."

Miller did an abrupt about face and headed toward the door but not without first giving icy stares at Kearney and Burk.

Now with the FBI director gone, Kearney moved over next to the president and said, "I apologize for Director Miller's outburst; he has been under tremendous strain recently and frankly not himself lately."

Everyone in the room now seemed to now know where Kearney was taking this.

"The president and I are seriously considering moving Bob out of the agency and replacing him with more of a team player," Kearney said. "Bob has been going off on his own agenda lately, and regrettably that agenda is not in sync with that of the White House. What's done is done and I propose we all adjourn to the Press Briefing Room and join the president in addressing the nation. The president intends to bring the nation together tonight after a week of terror and fear. The president desires to have the three of you join her on the podium where you will be honored. After which we will come back here to finish up. Agreed?"

As it was almost 6 p.m., little alternative presented itself. The mayor, Riley and Burk all seemed to realize, that once the president honored them in front of the world, it would be a bit awkward to then have them arrested.

Burk looking at the president said, "No funny business, Madam President?"

"None, Mr. Burk."

"Then," said Burk, "what are we waiting for?"

CHAPTER 60

WASHINGTON, DC

The White House, Press Briefing Room.

The president along with Secretary of State Kearney, Mayor Bloomfield, Police Commissioner Riley, Burk and Sullivan headed out of the Oval Office, down the hall to the Press Briefing Room, where the president's live address to the nation would originate.

On the way, they picked up Chief of Staff O'Donnell and Press Secretary Jay Kerry.

Both O'Connell and Kerry walked close to the president for last minute instructions but also to see if everything was alright. If things were bad, the president sure didn't show it. She was calm and in control and about to make everything right.

The Press Briefing Room had a small stage with a podium. Two American flags and a small oval drawing of the White House provided the backdrop. Although the press were invited, there was no indication that the president would be taking questions. Three teleprompters were ceiling mounted in front of and to the left and right of the president.

Before the president and her entourage entered, Jay Kerry entered and laid out the rules of engagement to the press. He cautioned them that this was an address to the American people and therefore no questions would be entertained. He asked for their complete silence and professionalism.

Outside, Chief of Staff O'Donnell suggested to the mayor, Riley and Burk where to stand— next to, but behind the president, with Kearney and the mayor on one side, and Riley and Burk on the other. The lighting in the Press Briefing Room would be dark. What light there was, would be focused on the president. Ms. Sullivan would stand on the side with Kerry and O'Donnell.

With a nod from O'Donnell, Kerry said, "Ladies and Gentlemen, the President of the United States."

The lights dimmed. There was no fanfare, but everyone did stand only to be seated immediately. The president in a blue suit with white pearls entered the room immediately followed by Kearney, Bloomfield, Riley and Burk, who were behind her and in darkness. The other members of the president's staff, cabinet and agency heads filled in against the side wall. Conspicuously absent was Miller.

"Good evening, my fellow Americans.

"I intend to address you with a candor and decisiveness, which the present situation of our people impel. This is preeminently the time to speak the truth, the whole truth—frankly and boldly. Nor need we shrink from honestly facing conditions in our country today. This great nation will endure as it has endured, will revive and will prosper so, first of all, let me assert my firm belief that '*the only thing we have to fear is fear itself*'—nameless, unreasoning, unjustified terror paralyzes needed efforts to convert retreat into advance. In every dark hour of our national life a leadership of frankness and vigor has met with that understanding and support of the people themselves which is essential to victory. I am convinced that you will again give that support to leadership in these critical days.

"In such a spirit on my part and on yours we face our common difficulties. They concern, thank God, mostly material things and unfortunately some loss of life.

"More important, a host of homeless citizens face the grim problem of existence, and an equally great number toil with little return. Only a foolish optimist can deny the dark realities of the moment.

"Yet our distress comes from no failure of substance. We are stricken by no plague of locusts. Compared with the perils which our forefathers conquered because they believed and were not afraid, we have still much to be thankful for. Nature still offers her bounty and human efforts have multiplied it. Plenty is at our doorstep.

"Restoration calls, however, not for changes in ethics alone. This nation asks for action, and action now.

"Our greatest primary task is to put people back in their homes and into our national parks. This is no unsolvable problem if we face it wisely and courageously. It can be accomplished in part by direct recruiting by the government itself, treating the task as we would treat the emergency of a war, but at the same time, through this employment, accomplishing greatly needed projects to stimulate and reorganize the use of our natural resources.

"Hand in hand with this we must frankly recognize the fear of population in our industrial centers and, by engaging on a national scale in a redistribution, endeavor to provide a better use of the land for those best fitted for the land. It can be helped by insistence that the federal, state, and local governments act forthwith on the demand that their cost be drastically reduced. It can be helped by the unifying of relief activities which today are often scattered, uneconomical, and unequal. It can be helped by national planning for and supervision of all forms of transportation and of communications and other utilities which have a definitely public character. There are many ways in which it can be helped, but it can never be helped merely by talking about it. We must act and act quickly.

"Finally, in our progress toward a resumption of work we require two safeguards against a return of the evils of the old order: we must never allow terrorism to control our lives.

"There are the lines of attack. I shall presently urge upon a new Congress in special session detailed measures for their fulfillment, and I shall seek the immediate assistance of several states.

"Through this program of action we address ourselves to putting our own national house in order. Our international trade relations, though vastly important, are in point of time and necessity secondary to the establishment of a sound national economy. I favor as a practical policy the putting of first things first. I shall spare no effort to restore world trade by international economic readjustment, but the emergency at home cannot wait on that accomplishment.

"The basic thought that guides these specific means of national recovery is not narrowly nationalistic. It is the insistence, as a first consideration, upon the interdependence of the various elements in all parts of the United States—a recognition of the old and permanently important manifestation of the American spirit of the pioneer. It is the way to recovery. It is the immediate way. It is the strongest assurance that the recovery will endure.

"In the field of world policy, I would dedicate this nation to the policy of the good neighbor—the neighbor who resolutely respects himself, and because he does so, respects the rights of others—the neighbor who respects his obligations and respects the sanctity of his agreements in and with a world of neighbors.

"If I read the temper of our people correctly, we now realize as we have never realized before our interdependence on each other; that we cannot merely take, but we must give as well; that if we are to go forward, we must move as a trained and loyal army willing to sacrifice for the good of a common discipline, because without such discipline no progress is made, no leadership becomes effective. We are, I know, ready and willing to submit our lives and property to such discipline, because it makes possible a leadership which aims at a larger good. This I propose to offer, pledging that the larger purposes will bind upon us all as a sacred obligation with a unity of duty hitherto evoked only in time of armed strife.

"With this pledge taken, I assume unhesitatingly the leadership of this great army of our people dedicated to a disciplined attack upon our common problem of domestic terrorism.

"Action in this image and to this end is feasible under the form of government which we have inherited from our ancestors. Our Constitution is so simple and practical that it is possible always to meet extraordinary needs by changes in emphasis and arrangement without loss of essential form. That is why our constitutional system has proved itself the most superbly enduring political mechanism the modern world has produced. It has met every stress of vast expansion of territory, of foreign wars, of bitter internal strife, of world relations.

"It is to be hoped that the normal balance of executive and legislative authority may be wholly adequate to meet the unprecedented task before us. But it may be that an unprecedented demand and need for undelayed action may call for temporary departure from that normal balance of public procedure.

"I am prepared under my constitutional duty to recommend the measures that a stricken nation in the midst of a stricken world may require. These measures, or such other measures as the Congress may build out of its experience and wisdom, I shall seek, within my constitutional authority, to bring to speedy adoption.

"But in the event that the Congress shall fail to take one of these two courses, and in the event that the national emergency is still critical, I shall not evade the clear course of duty that will then confront me. I shall ask the Congress for the one remaining instrument to meet the crisis—broad executive power to wage a war against the terrorist, as great as the power that would be given to me if we were in fact invaded by a foreign foe.

"For the trust reposed in me I will return the courage and the devotion that befit the time. I can do no less.

"We face the arduous days that lie before us in the warm courage of the national unity; with the clear consciousness of seeking old and precious moral values; with the clean satisfaction that comes from the stern performance of duty by old and young alike. We aim at the assurance of a rounded and permanent national life.

"We do not distrust the future of essential democracy. The people of the United States have not failed. In their need they have registered a mandate that they want direct, vigorous action. They have asked for discipline and direction under leadership. They have made me the present instrument of their wishes. In the spirit of the gift I take it.

"In this foray against our nation, we humbly ask the blessing of God. May He protect each and every one of us. May He guide me in the days to come as he did in the days past."

The president gave it a couple of beats before she led into the next segment. She was also watching the reaction of the press corps to see if they had picked up on her borrowed speech. A few had.

The entire press corps, with the exception of a few of the older reporters thought they had just heard an exceptional speech. A great speech. The few older reporters sat there in complete silence as the president again shamelessly plagiarize another important speech. This time, Franklin D. Roosevelt, Inaugural Address of March 4, 1933.

The president, not the least bothered by being speech busted by the older press corps, bowed her head and came up with a very solemn expression.

"I want us all to offer our hearts and prayers to one of our fallen heroes. Vice President Joe Denning was a great vice president and a faithful friend. What happened today, in a few short minutes, is no way indicative of his long and meaningful service. He was, as you all know, an American hero, patriot and a Marine.

"Let's all bow our heads in prayer."

Raising her head, only this time with her Christ-has-risen expression, she said, "The Nation must move on. I hereby put forth the name of Secretary of State John Kearney to become my vice president of the United States.

"I hereby put forth the name of FBI Director Bob Miller to become my secretary of state.

"Of course both these nominations are conditioned to confirmation by a majority vote of both Houses of Congress, but I don't see that as a problem.

"My fellow Americans, we have been through an extremely rough week. Bomb threats, and forest fires, the American Muslim Brotherhood and the false accusations issued against New York's Finest: The mayor, the police commissioner and the city's hero Mr. Thomas Burk. And of course today's terrorist attack in New York City.

"But I am here to tell you it's over! The bombs were duds, as the secretary of state and I suspected, and so advised the cities. The fires are mostly out. The arsonists, all part of the American Muslim Brotherhood are all in custody. The entire American Muslim Brotherhood has been neutralized. The terrorist group that attacked that convoy today, was a splinter group of foreign Al-Qaeda, operatives, smuggled into the United Stated by the Islamic Cultural Arts & Crafts Center of New York and their leader Imam Mohammed Hikmah Al. The Islamic Cultural Art & Crafts Center of New York is now a crime scene and has been closed. The Imam has been arrested and all but one of the terrorists are dead. And he is in critical condition in a NY hospital, under tight security.

"The FBI, along with the CIA, NYPD and Homeland Security will continue to investigate and incorporate procedures to make sure this kind of terrorism doesn't happen again.

"But as I said in the beginning of my statement, it's over!

"My fellow Americans, I have the extreme privilege of having three American heroes on this stage with me tonight."

The lights came on, and the world and the press corps saw the mayor of New York City and two men, until this second, thought murdered today in New York City.

The press corps now gave off an audible sound of shock and disbelief as they realized who was standing beside the president. How could it be? Even the mayor said they were murdered, yet there they stood. Several reporters had the urge to rush out of the room to go live outside but decided to stay in case there would be another second act.

The president, having gotten the effect she wanted, continued. "I am proud to be here on stage with these American heroes…" She turned right and left to acknowledge and introduced. "…the mayor of New York City, Elliot Bloomfield, NYPD Commissioner Ray Riley, and a true American hero, Mr. Thomas Dean Burk.

"The terrorist that attacked today's convoy in New York City had every intention of killing these men and their prisoners, the mastermind of the terrorist acts, and another American traitor. But for Mayor Bloomfield, Police Commissioner Riley, and Mr. Thomas Burk's stealth, cunning and professionalism, the terrorists failed. We had to continue the ruse, not to keep the American public or the press in the dark but to guarantee they would arrive here tonight safe and sound. When the FBI successfully escorted them to the White House and informed me that all the terrorists were accounted for, in custody or dead, I could finally allow these three heroes to come forward tonight and receive the honors they so rightly deserve. They saved New York City by calling the terrorists' bluff and gave hope and direction to Chicago and Los Angeles, which both cities chose to ignore. These heroes, with the assistance of federal authorities, arrested the mastermind, and killed or captured his accomplices. These heroes averted a major catastrophe in New York City by listening to my council. I told them: *"'the only thing we have to fear is fear itself.'"*

The president then broke with tradition and turned and started to applaud, whereupon all the staff, cabinet members, agency heads and the entire press corps stood and joined in.

Riley could sense Burk staring at him, trying to get his attention, but he kept looking straight ahead. From the moment they arrived on the stage, Riley had his hand firmly around Burk's wrist in case Burk decided to reach out and touch someone. Riley knew if he looked at Burk, Burk would be smirking because of the size of the president's lies or because of the size of her balls.

When the president felt enough accolades have been bestowed upon New York's heroes, she turned back to the camera. This was her cue for everyone else to also stop applauding. "Now about the evacuations, lootings, death and injuries associated with New York, Chicago and Los Angeles terrorist acts," she said. "Sally Jewel, the Secretary of the Interior, and I began very early this morning with a five-way video conference, between myself, Secretary Jewel, the director of Homeland Security Rand Wines, and the mayors of New York, Elliot Bloomfield, Chicago's, Manny Rohm and Tony Anthony of Los Angeles.

"I can, and with complete certainty, report the following. With the exception of New York City, which has its unique set problems, we are still experiencing looting in Chicago and Los Angeles. In addition, in both cities, we are now having riots and several neighborhoods are on fire. Both Chicago's Mayor Rohm and Los Angeles' Mayor Anthony strongly agree their current problems, started with terrorist threats, but are actually a manifestation of inherent social and economic problems attributed to the availability of assault weapons to inner city children and racial profiling.

"New York, Chicago and Los Angeles have all three weathered the terrorist threats. The current problems in Chicago and Los Angeles are inherent to big cities. These problems could be eliminated or greatly reduced by passing stronger federal gun laws and eliminating stop and search. I intend to ask Congress to pass stronger federal gun laws and repeal stop and search. And I expect bills on my desk by the end of the week.

"I want to take a few minutes to tell you how happy I am that our country, our economy, and our international standing has come through this week as strong as ever.

"As for our economy. Lew Jacobs, the Secretary of the Treasury and I have conferred, this morning, with the Fed Chair Nanke Benns, and the heads of all our major financial institutions. As of yesterday morning, Wall Street is up and running, and the market is in a rebound. All the major banks are positive and lending again. Additionally, Fed Chair Benns told Congress that short-term interest rates will remain close to zero. The unemployment rate fell to 6.5 percent and the annual inflation outlook is below 2.5 percent. Now that's good news.

"Now internationally. Last week China, Russia and our good friend Japan began buying and selling as much oil as possible using Chinese Yuan as reserves currency instead of the dollar. North Korea began demonstrating a huge military presence on the DMZ. China began moving warships into the strait of Taiwan. The Syrian Cyber Army threatened to hack into our electric grid and water supply. Egypt, Lebanon and the other surrounding countries making noise about the final destruction of Israel. And Iran was back to developing a nuclear bomb. The Russians invaded the Ukraine and Crimea.

"Let me tell you the short version results of what Secretary of State Kearney and I negotiated. On China, Russia, Japan, North Korea, Syria, Israel and Iran, we met this morning with Secretary of Defense Newel, CIA Director Bader and General Dumpy of the Joint Chiefs. In addition, I have personally spoken with President Vladimir Putin of Russia, President Xi Jinping of China, Prime Minister, Netanyahu of Israel, President Rouhani of Iran, Prime Minister Abe of Japan, Leader Kim Jong Un of North Korea, and President Park Geon-Hye of South Korea. The oil deal, between Russia, China and Japan is still going forward but with the dollar not the Yuan. North Korea claimed it was only war gamming in front of the DMZ and said they have completed and terminated the exercise. China has recalled its warships from the straits of Taiwan. Egypt, Lebanon and others have agreed to sit down for further peace discussions with Israel. Iran's Hassan Rouhani is on his way over here to discuss nuclear disarmament. The Russians you see in Crimea are there to film a war movie and the troops and tanks are nothing more than cast and crew.

"My fellow Americans, we were able to pull ourselves from the brink of Armageddon. We told each that we would remember our loyal friends and those who deserted us. They got the message loud and clear.

"As for illegal immigrants fleeing back across the border into Mexico, Sally Jewel, the Secretary of the Interior, and I have confirmed, as of yesterday morning the tide has begun to reverse and come in."

Sensing an opportunity to build on her voter base the president decided to go off script a bit.

"We, as a country of immigrants, must welcome them just as our red brothers welcomed us to their country over 300 years ago. We must welcome these great Latino people who have contributed so much to America.

"Famous Latino scientists and inventors have made many discoveries and inventions that have greatly contributed to everyday human society. You probably have one of the most famous inventions in your kitchen closet: the mop. The mop was designed by the Spanish inventor Manuel Corominas, an air force engineer who was inspired after a trip to the U.S. in the 1950s to design a device to help with housework. He had observed Americans washing the floor with a flat rag that was subsequently wrung through rollers in a bucket. Corominas engaged the help of Emilio Bellvis, a military mechanic, and they launched the company Rodex, which began producing mops.

"Additionally, in the latter part of the 19th Century, an epidemic was affecting the agricultural industry. That epidemic was caused by a 'germ' in the terrain. In 1894, Fernando López Tuero, who was the head agronomist of the Agronomical Station of Río Piedras, discovered that the cause of the epidemic was the white grub, the very same insect that can destroy your lawn.

"Because of these great Latino inventors and scientists and because of the great Spanish people, our homes and lawns are clean and green."

The president just kind of stopped for a second when she realized what she just said. She left it hanging there and hoped the press and her own party would give her a pass. She was, after all, the champion of the proletariat.

The press waiting for the second act, had just gotten it.

"Thank you my fellow Americans and goodnight and God bless," said the president.

Abruptly the president, followed by Secretary of State Kearney Mayor Bloomfield, Police Commissioner Riley and Burk left the stage and headed back to the Oval Office. She gestured to Press Secretary Jay Kerry to stay and soothe the mob.

The first question Kerry had to field was from a reporter who wanted to know "who then was killed in today's ambush if not Police Commissioner Riley and Thomas Burk?"

Kerry had no idea and no answer. He decided to do what any press secretary would do when you don't know. You made something up. "The ambush and the terrorist were real but what you thought you saw, American casualties *and this is a phrase he has been hearing lately* were just 'smoke and mirrors.'

Thank you and goodnight."

CHAPTER 61

WASHINGTON, DC

The White House, Oval Office.

President Hilton, Kearney, Bloomfield, Riley, Burk and Sullivan were seated on the couches and side chairs.

"Well," said the president, "that went well, John, or should I say Mr. Vice President. Any thoughts?"

"Madam President, I think your address to the nation was brilliant," said Kearney.

"Do you mean brilliant as in the U.K. brilliant or the U.S. brilliant?" asked the president.

"I am not sure I understand the difference, Madam President," said the vice president elect.

"Brilliant in the U.K. means just good but here in the United States, brilliant means brilliant."

"United States brilliant," responded the vice president-elect.

The president looked across at her New York City contingent for some encouragement, and when no one seemed forthcoming, Burk volunteered and in his best British accent said. "Oh! Right. Brilliant, absolutely brilliant. What?"

Kearney, always the diplomat, was getting a bit tired of Burk's bad manners and lack of respect. He found it now, as vice president-elect of the United States, his responsibility to defend the president. Standing up, he said, "Mr. Burk, if you can't show respect to the president, please try and respect the office. You, Mayor Bloomfield and Police Commissioner Riley, have been honored tonight by the president for your selfless deeds. The people honor you, and I honor you. What then seems to be the problem, Mr. Burk?"

The president put her hand up. "It's OK, John, let Mr. Burk have his fun. I thought his accent was quite good. Besides, I thought all you Viet Nam veterans stuck together. Semper Fi and all that."

"Madam President," said Kearney, "as Viet Nam veterans, I look at Mr. Burk as mon frère d'armes, but as I was in the Navy and Mr. Burk was a Marine, esprit de corps is something that's needs to be earned."

Riley tensed as he knew what was about to happen.

Burk turned to face Kearney and said, "Earned like your medals, mon frère."

The vice president elect face turned white. He had been through all this before and did not want to revisit the controversy over his awards. A Silver and Bronze Star and three Purple Hearts. Many say he didn't deserve any of them. The third Purple Heart, which some say was self-inflicted, got him out of the war after only four months in country.

Kearney decided not to take the bait, but instead took the high ground. "Mr. Burk, I was only implying that we did not know each other well enough to have a common spirit of comradeship."

Burk said, "I know what you were implying and you know what I was inferring. We'll just leave it at that for now."

Riley stood and said. "Madam President, if the truth be told, we – New York City, Mayor Bloomfield, Burk and I – have been persecuted, slandered, ambushed, murdered, and honored all in the last few days. Your FBI director has been implicated by one of his own. How further up the chain that goes is not clear, but we have our suspicions. Someone is going down for this. We will leave that to you to decide but act quickly before we change our minds."

Mayor Bloomfield added, "Madam President, New York City has gone through hell in the last week, and our federal government has punished us to no end, including murder. This is criminal and unprecedented, and if it gets out, it will bring your entire administration down."

"Mr. Mayor, Commissioner Riley," said the president, "Vice President-Elect Kearney and I do not disagree with your observation or conclusion about FBI Director Miller. He is now my secretary of state-elect. Our country has been through enough. What would you have me do?"

"I don't care what you do," said Burk, "but what I want – what we all want – are some conditions to this truce."

"And they are?" asked Kearney.

"They are," said Burk, "that the federal government pay $10 million to each of the NYPD members present, killed or wounded, and each FBI agent killed in the ambush on FDR Drive this morning. Full college scholarships for all their children. Pay all the expenses NYC laid out for security in order to participate in today's charade. Ms. Sullivan gets her White House status back, and she is now your go-to source to leak information and stories. A federal 'get out of jail card' for Mayor Bloomfield, Commissioner Riley and any of his staff, Ms. Sullivan, and myself for anything that occurred last week until now."

"Is that it?" asked Kearney.

"Almost," said Burk. "The last thing is, that if anything should happen to any of us or our families, we will hold you responsible and everything that we know will go viral."

Kearney knew he could not make this call and looked at the president.

President Hilton nodded her head slightly while closing her eyes.

Looking at the president, Burk answered. "Is that a yes that you agree to the conditions?"

"Yes!" said the president. "But we want Hoar and Kahn."

Riley agreed but said the location would be emailed to them when he, the mayor, Burk and Kelly arrived safely back in NYC.

The mayor stepped forward and said, "Then that's it. We're through. With your permission and by your leave, Madam President, Vice President-Elect Kearney, we will return to New York."

Burk turned to Kearney and quietly asked him for his direct phone number. Kearney was not sure if he should give it to Burk, and besides he didn't know it. "Why do you think you will need to call me, Mr. Burk?"

Burk went closer to Kearney and in a lower tone said, "There is something I need to tell you, but not here and not now."

Kearney said he would leave word at the switchboard for Burk to be put through.

The president had no problem with them leaving. After all she had a rough day and was very tired. She buzzed Agent Porter to come in and asked him to have Agent Robertson escort the mayor and his party back to Reagan.

After they left and the door was closed, the president leaned back into her chair and Kearney sat in one of the chairs in front of her desk.

"What's your take on all of this?" asked the president.

"Look, Madam President–"

"John, when we are alone like this, please call me Diane."

"Diane, I can't believe I am going to say this, but I think we have a win-win. This morning we had to deal with the repercussions of another terrorist attack in the New York City, yet tonight it's all but forgotten because the dead have risen. We have, or will have, Kahn and Hoar. Samir Kahn we can exploit with a big trial right here in DC and Sammy Kahn can cease to exist. Hoar can disappear or be put on ice depending on what we do with FBI Director/Secretary of State elect Miller. The American people have heard a brilliant speech and must feel, by now, safe and reassured. We move on. The mayor, the commissioner and Burk also move on, and that's it."

"Don't you think some reporters are going to keep fishing; and what about the FBI agents killed today? What about the Kingdom Tower incident and Vice President Denning's involvement and death?"

"I think we have just the man to field and resolve all those questions," said the vice president elect.

"So you think we should keep him on?" asked the president.

"Yes, but on a very short lease. Tonight you have made everything right, and we don't need any more shoes to drop."

Kearney leaned in toward the president and pointed to the recording button on her desk. "I turned it off when they first arrived."

"Then this never happened," said Kearney.

CHAPTER 62

NEW YORK CITY-WASHINGTON, DC

Since they arrived back to New York City, the phones hadn't stopped ringing. The mayor had been on every local news and talk program, then on *CNN, FOX, O'Reilly, Meet the Press,* and more. The police commissioner was on to a lesser extent only because he chose not to. And Burk and Sullivan had just plain disappeared. Although in tremendous demand, Burk wanted no further exposure at this time.

When they first got back to Westchester Airport, the police commissioner had a security team waiting, with several cars assigned to take the mayor directly to his Manhattan apartment and another car to drop Burk off at his, then Sullivan to her apartment. Riley had his own car take him directly to police headquarters.

In his car, the commissioner called Captain Bounty and told him, based on their previous discussion from the jet, to notify the White House and set up a drop off for Hoar and Kahn – then get himself back to New York ASAP.

Burk, from his car, dialed the White House and asked for the vice president elect. After giving his name, he only had to wait a minute to be connected. Kearney picked up and said, "Well, Mr. Burk, I see you have landed and are heading home." Burk realized that the vice president either was assuming or more probably had eyes on the ground, which was all the more reason for what he was about to tell him.

"Kearney, it's just you and me now, so we don't have to play nice. The entire conversation in the Oval Office was recorded. You know that, right?"

"I am not at liberty to discuss White House procedure with you, Mr. Burk. But if it was recorded, it is proprietary."

"I am not talking about the White House recording system, you asshole, I am talking about the recorder that was in my pocket and microphone that was on my jacket collar."

There was a pause, then the vice president said, "Mr. Burk, do you expect me to believe you were able to get a recorder through Secret Service security screening when you first entered the White House?"

"Exactly," said Burk.

"Not possible, Mr. Burk."

"It is, thanks to your boss. She directed Agent Robertson to have us pass Go and collect $200. Don't you remember, or were you in the little boy's room?"

Kearney thought back and realized what Burk was saying was correct. He now knew that son of a bitch really had him and the president by the balls. "What do you want, Burk?"

"Nothing. It's just our insurance policy to make sure you remain faithful to our conditions. Besides, you can have a copy of ours, if you like, in case you accidently disengaged your propriety recording system."

The line went dead.

Kearney stood looking at the silent phone. He was very worried about the president—not the current one—he couldn't care less about her. He was concerned with the next president—President John Fitzhugh Kearney.

CHAPTER 63

EAST HAMPTON, NY

With every news agency through the world wanting a piece of him for interviews, and brands and marketing firms wanting him for appearances and endorsements, Burk had to get away. His apartment had been tossed by the FBI, except for some toiletries and dirty clothes. Then the NYPD had seized everything. Burk was broke and homeless. He had become closer to Kelly Sullivan and she had money and an apartment, but she was as much in the limelight as Burk. They tried sneaking into Kelly's Upper East Side apartment but got caught. A sharp reporter apparently had paid off one of the doormen, and got the tip off. They thought about flying off to some island, but that would mean passports and Burk's was somewhere in police headquarters. Besides, reporters were watching the airports. Riley promised to have all his stuff back to his apartment in a day or two, but Burk couldn't wait another minute. He had to disappear. Riley didn't really want Burk to travel too far and was procrastinating on returning his things—especially his passport.

Kelly's parents had a summer house on Egypt Lane in East Hampton, and Burk decided hiding among the rich and famous might be just the trick. Burk's car had been impounded, and Kelly didn't have one, so instead of renting they decided to take the bus, the Hampton Jitney, directly to the Hamptons from New York City. You could pay in cash and no IDs were required. Without a lot of luggage, they walked to their house from the East Hampton stop. East Hamptons, like all of the Hamptons, was packed in the summer and all the way up 'til New Year's. Then it was dead. But now, right before Christmas, it was packed. Not many day trippers from New Jersey, but many New Yorkers with homes in the Hamptons, would definitely be spending Christmas there, especially if they were predicting snow. Those same New Yorkers would then fly off to Vail or some such place for New Year's. Kelly's parents were away in the other playground of the rich and famous, Palm Beach, so Kelly and Burk had the place to themselves. It was still a few days away from Christmas and quite cold. It was close to 6 p.m. when they emerged from the house and ran freezing to the hot tub, which was actually attached to the pool. Burk with a glass of Champagne and Kelly with a vodka martini, eased into the hot bubbling water. The house overlooked Hook Pond, which was partly frozen and quite peaceful and beautiful.

Now as they leaned back against the pool sides, they contemplated each other.

"To new beginnings," said Kelly, to which Burk added, "To my enemies' enemies!"

They didn't plan it, but they were about to develop a strategy which would lead them on an adventure together that would define them and their beliefs. Neither could let go what happened to them. They were going to make it right and they were about to decide how. After an hour of just enjoying the bubbling water and its relaxing effects, not to mention the alcohol, Kelly moved over to Burk and snuggled close to him. This is as close as they had been together, although both realized something had changed with their relationship. Not facing Burk gave Kelly the courage to say, "You know, Tommy, I never apologized to you for starting this whole thing and getting you in so much trouble."

"Yes, that's right, and you owe me big time."

"What do you think I owe you," asked Kelly.

"Let's see how it plays out and then I'll decide," said Burk.

Kelly decided to let it lie. Things were going good and why push it if it wasn't an issue with him? "Did you see on TV this morning that Vice President Kearney has announced his bid for president, but that Madam President has yet to endorse him?"

"Saw that coming back when we meet in the White House. Kearney is an intriguer and has wanted this since he was a boy. He won't be stopped."

"You seem to know a lot about him," said Kelly

"Not a lot, but enough," said Burk.

Kelly, becoming more aware of Burk's darker side, again let it go. "New Jersey's Governor Christie, Florida's Senator Marko Rubio, or even Rand Paul could give him a run."

Burk ducked his head under the water and came back up to feel the cold air in his face. He waited a second and said, "Christie has a big mouth, and it won't take him long to alienate the gays, the women's movement, blacks, Hispanics and the college voters. He a bully and soon he will pick on the wrong guy.

Rubio is almost the same as Christie, except he's not a bully, won't alienate the Hispanics, just the white racist."

"And Rand Paul?"

Burk said. "Never trust a man with two first names. Besides the apple doesn't fall too far from the tree. Look Kelly, you're smart, you know the score. Kearney is an incumbent, a Democrat, former secretary of state and a former senator, a decisive position to be in. The Democrats killed the Republicans the last two times at bat and they are going to trounce them again. In 2008, all the Republicans could field was a foul-mouth old man and a dingbat. In 2012, they got a guy right out of central casting who still couldn't win. They have weak, ineffective leadership in both houses. The party is divided between the left, right and Tea Party. They shut down the government back in 13 for a misguided reason. They lost the youth, black, Latino, union, gay, right to life, women, liberal Hollywood, and all the media's vote. In other words, they lost the people that actually vote. Conservatives Biff and Buffy in Greenwich don't give a shit and don't vote."

"Then it's a done deal? Vice President Kearney will become President Kearney?"

"All he needs is for the fat lady to sing and he is in," said Burk.

"So what are we going to do about it, Tommy?"

"We are going to go in the house and make love, and then we are going to town to meet some friends."

Once out of the hot tub, the cold air persuaded Kelly and Tommy to make a quick dash back to the main house. Inside they went to their separate rooms to towel off and freshen up. Kelly had set out a guest robe for Tommy.

Kelly similarly attired, went to the kitchen and removed the martini and champagne glasses from the freezer and pored new drinks. She then put Sinatra on and found Tommy in the living room building a fire.

The fireplace was centered on the exterior wall with a pair of French doors flanking each side, with a view of the pond. The half frozen pond, the snow and the now sparking and crackling fire had the desired effect they both seemed to need. Both robed and with refreshed drinks they snuggled on the rug in front of the now blazing and warm fire.

Kelly asked. "Tommy, you mentioned meeting friends tonight. What is that about?"

Tommy replied. "The mayor and Riley are going to be in town tonight and invited us to dinner at the Palm."

"Sounds wonderful, but a bit of a coincidence. I thought we were trying to get away from it all."

"No coincidence. I have an idea that I want to share with the three of you. Riley thought dinner tonight would be a good venue."

Kelly said. "Ok. But are you going to tell me your idea or do I have to wait"

"You have to wait but it will be worth it" said Tommy.

"Ok I'll wait for tonight to hear your idea but outside you also said we were going to make love and for that, I would prefer not to wait. What about you Tommy?"

Tommy put his hand gently under Kelly's chin and brought his lips to hers and they kissed. As though choreographed to Sinatra now singing "The way you look tonight", both drinks disappeared onto the fireplace fender and both robes were slipped off. Their bodies now together, they embraced, explored and began to make love. "...There is nothing for me but to love you and the way you look tonight..."

CHAPTER 64

THE PALM RESTAURANT

East Hampton, NY

Police Commissioner Riley and Mayor Bloomfield were due in East Hampton earlier that night for a charity event. The mayor and commissioner were both there for political and social reasons. The mayor, a registered Democrat, crossed the line whenever and wherever he wanted. He was a good mayor and a great businessman and always picked the winners regardless of which party. East Hampton was absolutely, positively filled with the rich and famous and stars in their cars. They had money, power, property and priority. But when the mayor of New York City and his police commissioner's convoy of five big black Suburbans rolled into the village with blue take down bars flashing and sirens chirping, the village stopped dead. They pulled up in front of the Palm restaurant at 9:00 p.m., and the rich and famous and the stars in their cars became star-struck fans. After the event concluded, Officer Tanner called ahead for a table for four and had absolutely no problem getting a 9:00 p.m. reservation in an otherwise completely booked restaurant. Unlike other patrons who had to wait until their entire party arrived before they were seated, the mayor and commissioner, after they had their coats checked, were immediately escorted to a round table for six in the porch room. Bruce Bozzi, the co-owner, happened to be there, and took over the duty of maître d'—at least for the mayor's table. The Palm was the best steak-house in East Hampton but not very she-she looking. But with wood floors, tin ceiling, and white table clothes, it had a kind of a pub-like atmosphere, but not pub food. It's what the other co-owners, the Ganzi family, referred to as a "White Tablecloth Restaurant."

The restaurant and bar were packed, and everyone regardless of how uncool it was, eyeballed the two super famous people. Here tonight, among the crème of Manhattan, were the real supermoney and the real superpower. And with that, they got superpriority. Both men knew they were on display and both had impec-cable table presence. The mayor and police commissioner had dined in just about every city in the world and in most of the finest restaurants, but unlike presidents and premiers, the mayor and the commissioner dined unscripted and in pub-lic. They knew they were constantly observed and because of that, they had to perform. Their napkins were already on their laps, no elbows on the table, and cell phones were turned off. That was protocol, but in reality, Captain Bounty in plain clothes, sitting at the bar, had his cell on and could whisper in the com-missioner's ear if necessary. If not, the city would be in good hands tonight, with both their deputies in charge.

The waiter came over and asked if they would like to order wine or a drink while waiting for their guest. The mayor ordered a bottle of Tormaresca, an Italian Chardonnay.

The mayor and commissioner were discussing tonight's agenda, specifically Mr. Burk's role when they heard a disturbance arising from the bar area. Into the dining area came Burk and Ms. Sullivan, proceeded by matri'd Bruce. The mayor and commissioner stood while the waiter attended to Ms. Sullivan's seat-ing. When all were seated, the wine came; and after the mayor approved the selection, the waiter removed the cork and handed it to the mayor. He then poured the mayor a small amount to taste. The mayor approved it and the four glasses were half filled. The room then took on the air of the old E F Hutton commercial, as everyone adjacent became quiet to see if they could hear the expected toast or anything else.

They were not disappointed.

The mayor held up his glass and quietly said. "L'Chayim."

The others raised their glasses and said in unison "To Life" except Burk who said "Cheers."

The matri'd returned this time with a bottle of Crystal Champagne and a waiter with four glasses and an ice bucket. Upon their arrival, Burk ordered the champagne because he knew the mayor was a red wine guy and Burk only drank champagne. Burk did not like to compromise. The maître d' skillfully removed the cork and proceeded to give Burk an approval taste. Burk put his hand over the glass and said, "That won't be necessary, just pour."

When everyone's glass was poured, Burk held up his glass and said with a slight Irish brogue "Go mbeire muid beo ar an am seo arís." Everyone raised their glass in anticipation of an explanation, but Burk just held it out there for a moment than said "May we be alive at this time next year."

Whereupon the others said, "L'Chayim."

Burk savored the taste of his favorite champagne. He then said in his best cockney Irish accent, loud enough to be heard by most of the room and to everyone astonishment, except Riley who knew what was coming, "That's good foooking champagne!"

Their table was as private as it could be in the Palm but they could easily converse without being overheard. None had an affected or projected voice. Even Burk had an inside voice when necessary.

When Burk and Riley had spoken earlier on the phone, Burk gave Riley a brief suggestion of what he was thinking and Riley recommended they meet here tonight to discuss it.

The Palm is known for great steaks, seafood and accoutrements.

Kelly ordered the Gigi salad and the Atlantic salmon. Burk ordered the 9-oz. Filet Mignon charred, medium rare, and the mayor and Riley both ordered 14-oz. New York Prime Rib, medium rare. The three guys ordered the Classic Caesar salad, then Riley ordered creamed spinach and hash browns for the table.

The dinner was turning out to be a fun evening with good friends.

As soon as the waiter left all four leaned in conspiratorially.

"Did you decide what direction to take your life, Mr. Burk?" asked the mayor.

"Yes I have. I'm broke, unemployed, and famous. If I don't take advantage of my 15 minutes, I will be broke, unemployed and stupid."

"So what do you want to do and just as importantly, how can we help?"

"I don't like it here," said Burk.

"This is a great restaurant," said Riley, "the food is fantastic"

"No El Capitan, I am not talking about here, here." He gestured about the room. "I mean *here*. This time, this place in our history, our country. This is not the country I want live in, and it is not the country I want to leave to my children. Captain, we fought a good fight in Viet Nam, but we fought a bad war.

"Johnson let Kennedy be assassinated and the floodgates to Viet Nam opened. We believed Walter when he told us to go, and we listened to him when he told us to leave. We did what our misguided, uninformed, selfish, egotistical, elected officials told us was right. Not just Johnson in '64 but Truman 14 years earlier in Korea. It seems when things are slow at home or politicians need to divert attention, they have some sort of esoteric need to involve us in other people's civil wars. We don't learn. Politicians read polls, they don't read history. They make the same mistakes over and over again. Bush the son, couldn't stop after he punished the Taliban. He, Cheney, Rumsfeld and that shit Wolfowitz said the war in Iraq could be done on the cheap and that it would largely pay for itself. It ended costing us $800 billion and 500,000 dead, of which 5,000 were American troops. You do the math. Cheney said the WMD were a 'slam dunk,' but the only slam dunk that came out of that fiasco was the obscene amount of money Cheney and Halliburton made.

"I don't even want to get into what our country and particularly the four of us have just gone through and our government's involvement and cover-up.

"As a country, we are morally and financially bankrupt, yet we export our beliefs along with foreign aid to countries that hate us. We meddle in everyone else's affairs to hide the fact that we can't get our own house in order. One week we had money to bomb Syria and the next week we had to close the World War II memorial for lack of funds.

"We have become a country of dysfunctional families, morally diffident financiers—all led by delusional, corrupt politicians.

"I don't like what I see, and I am going to change it. I am going to make the dysfunctional, function. Overturn the tables of the money changers and instill the fear of God into the politicians."

Burk had worked himself into a sort of a frenzy, and the mayor, Riley and Sullivan all just kind of sat there in silence and stared at him. It was clear he had finished his ramble, so Riley said, "Jesus Christ, Tommy, you sound like Jesus Christ. Are you going to part the seas and raise the dead, too?"

With that, the salads arrived and everyone had a chance to reflect on what was just said and where it might be headed. Small talk ensued until after the main course arrived and the wine and champagne were refreshed.

The commissioner broke the ice. "Tommy, you acknowledge your availability and window of opportunity. You laid out much of what ails our country, but what are you going to do about it?"

"I want to integrate my experience, integrity and common sense into my 15 minutes and parley that into politics."

To say everyone at the table was shocked was an understatement. Never would anyone think Tommy Burk would make a good politician or more to the point, want to be one.

The mayor, who had not known Tommy long but had grown to admire and like him, spoke first because, as one would assume, he was the only politician at the table. "Tommy, that's outstanding. I am very proud that you would even consider entering politics. We need more nonpoliticians in government. Have you given any thought where you would like to start? I know of a couple positions in my administration, and there are a couple of state congressional district openings coming up."

Burk remained passive and the mayor looked over to Riley, who was looking down at his steak, slightly shaking his head and closing his eyes. The mayor then looked at Kelly, who didn't seem to have a clue.

Riley knew Burk so well, he knew where Burk was going. Burk was not a team player, not now, not ever. But he wasn't going to spoil the fun. He had no intention of stealing Burk's punch line or thunder. Although Burk did confide in him yesterday, what he had just disclosed, his guess was Burk was thinking a bit higher.

Burk said, "Thank you, Mayor. Let me think that over, but please, let's eat before it gets cold." Burk looked at Riley. Riley had that 'cat that swallowed the canary' look on his face. Burk said. "I would like you to do something for me, Captain."

"And what would that be," sergeant?"

"Captain, please pass the salt."

Riley, enforcing his table manners, passed Burk both the salt and pepper, as neither should ever be separated.

After everyone had finished, the waiters cleared the table, cleaned the table cloth, took coffee and desert orders, and left.

Burk said, "That was delicious. Thank you, Mr. Mayor, for inviting us. I have given some thought as to your offer but feel it's necessary to begin my political career in Washington in order to correct, as the commissioner so eloquently stated, much of what ails this country."

The mayor turning toward Riley to see if he was being put on. "Washington, that's quite ambitious."

Riley just leaned back. "You have no idea, Mr. Mayor."

Burk continued. "Yesterday, Vice President Kearney announced his bid for president"

"That was expected," said the mayor.

"Yes," replied Burk, "but we can't allow that to happen."

The mayor looked at Burk and in almost a whisper said "What are you suggesting Mr. Burk, that you are going to Washington to kill the vice president?"

Burk face didn't flinch; he sat stone faced.

The mayor looked to Riley and Sullivan for some sort of help or understanding but just got shoulder shrugs. He looked back at Burk who finally said, "Your Honor, why do we have to put up with this? The same politicians every four years. The same lies. This country deserves better. This country was built on the backs of citizen soldiers and citizen politicians. Where does it say, we have to continue year after year perpetuating dynasties? Mr. Mayor, I am not going to Washington to kill the vice president, just to beat him senseless. I am going to Washington to become president."

This announcement didn't shock Riley, but for the mayor, hearing it said aloud, was like a bolt of lightning. Kelly was as shocked as the mayor. Finally the mayor feeling he was being the brunt of some sort of joke or worst said to Riley. "Commissioner, what's going on?"

"Mr. Mayor, I am hearing this for the first time." He looked at Burk who remained stone-faced. "I have known Tommy for a long time, Boss, and never, and I mean never, have I heard him say anything he didn't mean. And to that end he always does what he says."

Burk realized he had just taken their dinner party to another level and tried to take it down a notch. People in the adjacent tables were starting to glance over at a seemingly excited mayor. "Mr. Mayor, I am serious, and I need your help. We cannot allow this country to go through another four or eight years of business as usual."

"Mr. Burk," said the mayor, if you are serious why not support someone who can actually win. "Chris Christie of New Jersey, or Marco Rubio of Florida, or Rand Paul?"

Burk looked at Kelly then repeated the answer he gave her to the exact same question only a couple hours earlier. "The Republicans are no different or better than the Democrats. Christie has a big mouth and it won't be long before he falls off the bridge and alienates the gays, the women's movement, blacks, Hispanics and the college voters. Rubio is the same as Christie except he won't alienate the Hispanics, just the white racists. As far as Rand Paul, never trust a man with two first names. Besides the apple doesn't fall too far from the tree.

"Look, Kearney is an incumbent, a Democrat, former secretary of state and senator. A decisive position to be in. The Democrats killed the Republicans the last two times at bat and they are going to trounce them again. In 2008, all the Republicans could find was a foul-mouth old man and a dingbat up. In 2012, they got a guy right out of central casting who couldn't win. They have weak, ineffective leadership in both houses. The party is divided between the left, right and Tea Party. They shut down the government back in 13 for a misguided reason. They lost the youth, black, Latino, union, gay, right to life, women's, liberal Hollywood, and all the media's votes. In other words, they lost the people that actually vote. Conservatives Biff and Buffy in Greenwich don't give a shit and don't vote.

"I can win. But as an independent. Everyone in the country is waiting for a knight on a white charger to ride in and save this nation. That's going to be me, but I need your help."

The table got silent again. No one knew quite what to say.

The mayor knew Burk was right but how could he possibly become a nominee or even be considered.

Riley said, "Look, Tommy, you helped save New York and now you want to save the country. I for one am in." He placed his had in the center of the table followed quickly by Kelly's and then, a bit reluctantly, the mayor's.

Burk held back a second then placed his hand on the top saying "In for a penny, in for a pound."

The waiters brought three Lavazza Italian coffees, a Tetley tea for Burk, and a bag of warm donuts with cinnamon sauce – a special Palm desert.

It was a little after 11 p.m., and the joint was still jumping. They needed tables so the waiters were hovering around some non-celebrity tables to get them moving but the mayor's table could stay all night. After tasting a donut and his coffee, Riley excused himself and headed to the restroom. As he passed the bar, he stopped to converse with Captain Bounty. Bounty had finished a light supper at the bar and had gotten take outs for Tanner and the rest of the security team waiting by the Suburban's. He then walked into the men's room and to the urinal, unzipped and started to relieve himself. The door opened and without looking, Riley said "God bless all here and you, too, McSorley."

"Didn't know you had eyes in the back of your head, chief," said Bernard McSorley, executive producer of the popular long-running "Midas in the am" TV/radio show. McSorley eased over to the stall next to the commissioner, and as men do while relieving themselves, kept face forward as they spoke.

"I saw you when you came in with your friends," Riley said. "What are you our here for?"

"I might ask you the same thing, chief," said McSorley.

Both men seemed to finish at the same time and turned to the sink to wash their hands. Not until the hands were washed and dried did they face each other and give a warm hand shake and man hug. These two guys went way back and were good friends.

"Nice company you keep, chief," said McSorley.

"Oh! So you spotted me across the room and our meeting here in the little boy's room is no accident," asked Riley.

"Hardly chief. Everyone is trying to get a piece of Burk, and I just thought–"

"Just thought what, Bernie?" said Riley.

"I just thought, an introduction. I mean I would love to book him on our show, but what's the chance of that happening?"

"Bernie, you know what they say about timing." said Riley.

"That it's everything, chief."

"Right, but you also need what?"

"Luck. Timing and luck. Right chief."

"Bernie you're a lucky guy."

"Why's that chief?"

"Because your timing is impeccable. Follow me."

The commissioner led Bernie back to the table and made the introductions and asked Bernie to join them. Everyone knew of McSorley because, besides being the show's executive producer, he was also one of the show's on-air personalities.

"You know," said the commissioner, "meeting Mr. McSorley here tonight could be just what we are looking for."

McSorley tensed. He couldn't believe his good luck and timing. If this was going anywhere near where it appeared to be going, he would pull off the biggest coup in broadcasting.

Burk looked at McSorley and said, "May I call you Bernie?"

"Of course."

"Bernie, I watch your show every morning or at least every morning before all this stuff happened. I did, however, miss the show that got you guys canned."

"Yeah. Well that was unfortunate, Mr. Burk, but we moved on."

"You know, Tommy," said the commissioner, "this might be just the right venue for your opening shot. What do you think?"

"Don't know, Captain. What makes you think they would even want me?"

"Bernie?" said the commissioner.

"Oh yeah!" said Bernie. "We want."

"Bernie," said the commissioner, something big is in the works, and if it materializes, Mr. Burk may announce it on your program. It might be a good idea to touch base before the show. When do you think you would have him on?"

"The Midas is back Monday January 4. Is that too soon?" asked Bernie.

"Bernie," said Burk, "that's perfect and my manager, gesturing to Kelly, can, if it's ok with you, work out the details beforehand."

Kelly didn't realize she had just been made his manager but seemed to accept it. Burk was on a roll, after all, and she intended to roll with him. She had a quick flash that if Burk actually managed to pull this off, she could become his press secretary.

"Kelly, are you OK?" asked the mayor. She seemed to snap back from somewhere, and the mayor continued. "OK! Sounds like a plan. Let me get the check and we'll get going. We have a long hard road in front of us."

Bernie just couldn't believe his luck. He had just gotten an exclusive TV appearance for the hottest personality in New York. Possibly the country. On top of that, something big might be launched on the same show. Doesn't get any better.

After goodbyes, handshakes and cell phone numbers exchanged, the mayor, Riley, Kelly and Burk left the restaurant. Bernie sat back down at the mayor's table, pulled out his phone hit speed dial and said, "Boss, it's me. You're never going to guess who I just had coffee with and who I just booked for the show."

There was a brief pause as he listened to his boss correctly guess. After a few back and froths the line went dead. McSorley, feeling at the top of his game just leaned back into his chair, put a smile on his face and said, "O snap."

CHAPTER 65

White House, Oval Office

Vice President Kearney, Secretary of State Miller, and Chief of Staff O'Donnell sat in the Oval Office sofa and chairs, while President Hilton, at her desk with her phone to her ear, was, from what they could overhear, having girl talk with German Chancellor Angela Merkel. Why not, thought Kearney, the guys do it. Vice President Kearney and Secretary of State Miller were both approved for their current positions by Congress as required by law. It was a near run thing for both but the president stepped in and told both speakers to get it done. She said the country didn't need any more drama right now.

The president was laughing at something Merkel said then said goodbye and hung up. She got up and went over to the guys and asked, "Ok, where are we?"

Vice President Kearney said, "Madam President, my announcement and your endorsement have taken our numbers up some but not great. This Sunday, I do all the talk shows and then we wait to see who steps up, as challengers, from the dark side."

Chief of Staff O'Donnell said, "The usual suspects are lining up and commenting on John's bid announcement. Christie, Rubio, Paul, and now we have Senator Ted Cruz. *FOX* is fair and unbalanced as usual but I have noticed *CNN* and the senior's stations are not towing the line. Affordable Health Care is killing us in the polls."

The president bristled at the mention of her dream program. Her legacy was in trouble from day one. Couldn't get the college kids to sign on and the website was still an embarrassment. It had being going south since it launched. She wished she had never listened to the two idiots: Melosi and Tweed. They pushed the launch before it was ready and she was holding them responsible. But at the end of the day, it was her name on the bill, not theirs. The president said, "We need to get the Affordable Health Care Program back on track or it will bring us down. More specifically, bring you down, John. It's been two years and all the promises we made have turned to shit. We should have shitcanned Cibelius after the first week. Listen, all of you start spinning the hell out of this. Get everybody on it. The Affordable Health Care Program is working. Get the best PR firm to get it out there. Get doctors, nurses, patients, providers to do testimonial about how well it's working. If enough people hear it's working, then it's working. It's all about perception.

"If not, then I expect you, Bob, as my new secretary of state to find us a diversion—a nice small city or country to attack, or better yet invade, something like Mogadishu, Kosovo, Rwanda or Haiti. Hell, Bill was a master at it. He attacked all those shit holes and even bombed Iraq - and all with excellent results. The public and news channels eat this stuff up. Everyone loves to see the Marines landing on some beach somewhere and kicking ass. Bill left office with the highest end-of-office approval rating of any presidents since World War II—even with the blow job in the Oval Office. Hell, he even got impeached but refused to quit and still came out on top. That tells you something: even if you're caught with your pants down, don't admit it. Lie, divert, shed a tear, blame others. Praise the Lord and pass the ammunition."

CHAPTER 66

NEW YORK CITY

January 4th.
Fox Entertainment Network.

Andy Midas, as a radio/TV personality, has been going strong since the early Seventies. Today "Midas in the am" is broadcast throughout the United States by Columbus Media Networks and simulcast on television by the *Fox Entertainment Network* in New York City. The show is funny, unscripted and irreverent. It is one of *Fox's* highest-rated shows, which means it is one of the top shows anywhere, anytime. Midas has evolved over the years and is still funny, unscripted and irreverent, but is now pro-gay, pro-same sex marriage, and basically now pro most everything for the underdog. But it was not always that way.

As early "shock jock," Midas and his crew, mainly Bernard McSorley, repeatedly made controversial remarks through skits and character impersonations in what they considered a comical format that critics labeled as racist, misogynist, homophobic and anti-Semitic and xenophobic. He was also known for making offensive remarks.

In a 1984 interview, answering a question about Howard Stine, Andy Midas said, "Yes, Howard's a slut, too, Lloyd...plus a Jew bastard, and should be castrated... put in an oven." As reported by *The New York Times* columnist Bob Hurbert, Midas said that McSorley was hired to perform "nigger jokes." Midas has also repeatedly referred to Arabs as "ragheads."

The show's routines sometimes contained derogatory epithets for homosexuals, including "faggot" and various terms describing homosexuality. But Midas has also made fun of the Irish, Jews, Italians, other ethnicities, and all political positions. Midas referred to former Speaker of the House Newt Vonrich as "disgusting" and a "fat repulsive pig."

But all that ended on April 4, 2007, during a discussion about the NCAA Women's Volleyball Championship. Midas characterized the Princeton's University women's volleyball team players as "rough girls," commenting on their tattoos. His executive producer, Bernard McSorley, responded by referring to them as "hardcore hos." The discussion continued with Midas describing the girls as "nappy-headed hos," and McSorley remarking that the two teams looked like the "jigaboos versus the wannabes,"

On April 9, Midas appeared on Al Ripton's syndicated radio talk show, *it's real with Al Ripton*, to address the controversy. Sharpton called the comments "abominable," "racist" and "sexist" and repeated his earlier demand that Midas be fired. Midas said, "Our agenda is to be funny, and sometimes we go too far. And this time we went way too far. Here's what I've learned: that you can't make fun of everybody, because some people don't deserve it."

On April 11, 2007, Steve Papus of *NBC News*, announced that *MSNBC* would no longer simulcast Bernie McSorley effective immediately. While the decision came on the same day that a few advertisers left Midas, the network also said employee concerns played a role. The next day, *CBS Radio* canceled *Midas in the am* effective immediately.

But just eight months later, on December 3, 2007, Midas was reborn. He returned to the airwaves on *ABC Radio* and *RDF-TV.* When asked about Midas's return to radio, Ripton said in an interview, "We'll monitor him; I'm not saying I'm going to throw a banquet for him and say welcome home. He has the right to make a living, but because he has such a consistent pattern with this, we are going to monitor him to make sure he doesn't do it again." On April 4, 2008 Jesse Jameson appeared on "Midas in the am" to discuss the 40th anniversary of the assassination of Martin Luther King—a booking that would have seemed impossible nearly a year before, when Jameson joined 50 demonstrators in Chicago demanding that "Midas Must Go." Many media commentators declared Andy Midas's rehabilitation complete.

In 2008, Little Richard appeared as a guest artist on *The Midas Christmas Record* to help raise funds to benefit sick and dying children, as well as to debunk the notion that Midas was racist. In September of that year, Midas signed a multi-year deal with *Fox Entertainment Network* to simulcast his radio show *Midas in the am*. The program airs Monday through Friday from 6 to 9 a.m. and was first broadcast on October 5, 2009.

The Midas in the am show was now neither left, right nor in the middle. It could be, at any moment, and on any issue, in one, none or all three camps.

And this was the show that Tommy Burk, with the support of Mayor Bloomfield, Commissioner Riley, and his Campaign Manager, Kelly Sullivan, was about to appear on and announce his bid to run for the next president of the United States.

Just having Burk, the hero of New York, on his show was a big deal. Everyone but everyone would be watching, and Midas intended to make the most of it. There was no script, no pre-approved questions, no nothing. The only thing that was even remotely scheduled was which segment and for how long the guest would be on. And with Midas, even that could change. It all depended on what happened in Midas's personal life the night or hour before the show. If his wife, Dede, out of the blue, championed Mark Savin's knowledge over his or his Starbucks coffee was not just right or his shoulder hurt, he could spend a half hour off on a tangent. And when a guest finally did appear, Midas more as likely would either find he/she boring, and talk instead about himself. Or if he really didn't like his guest or his guest said something to offend Midas, he more than likely would throw you off the show. But that's why the show was watched everyday by so many. You just never knew what was going to happen.

But this morning, at 6 a.m., Andy Midas was in good form. His regulars were all here.

Tony Power, Ron Bart, Warner Fox, and Dagen McCain, Lou, Guns, Bo, Bigfoot, Diane and Carly were all around the set. Sitting to Midas's right was

Connell McFhane the news anchorman and a unique appearance, at least on the same set, was Bernie McSorley, the guy who set it all up.

This was going to be as good as it gets, and Midas just wanted Burk, McFhane, McSorley and himself on camera, at least for now. Any other TV show would hold Burk back to the middle or end of the program to keep viewers locked on, but Midas wasn't anybody. He beat to his own drum, and besides he knew everyone would stay tuned as he and the gang exalted or savaged the guest after the guest had left.

Midas was about to go live with the most sought after person in New York, if not world, as his guest—the mysterious Tommy Burk, who had saved New York, was killed, along with the police commissioner in an ambush, but then arose from the dead, who sliced off the terrorist's finger during interrogation, and possibly killed an IRS agent. And that was before Midas started probing. He had some general questions written down about the IRS agent and the New York City bombs, but he had no knowledge of the Washington DC bomb that Burk was about to drop.

At 6:05 a.m. a canned baritone voice announced, "Ladies and Gentleman, Midas in the am."

The show began with Midas complaining about some ill or another and his cold coffee.

He did everything but mention his guest. He had Connell do the news, Dagen report on business and NASCAR, then asked Warner, "Who won last night's game?"

And then he asked for and got a Bernie briefing.

Midas told the audience he had Fat Elvis and Little Richard in the house. He then put his hand up to his ear and with a studied fast jerking movement he signaled Bigfoot to go to break.

During the entire break Midas said nothing. That was not unusual, especially if something was bothering him.

During the break, Tommy Burk was led in and given the seat closest to and across from Midas. Bernie McSorley was setting to Burk's left. Midas barley acknowledged Burk, and Burk was feeling he may have made a big mistake.

When the break was over, Midas knew instinctively and looked at Burk although the camera was on him and said, "Ladies and Gentleman, a few months ago we almost lost this city but for the courageous acts by Mayor Bloomfield, Police Commissioner Riley, and a Mr. Tommy Burk. And there may have been some others who helped, but we don't care about them. Mr. Burk had some sort of instinct that told him the bombs were fake and what the terrorists were trying to do was scare us to death. Because of Mr. Burk, the terrorist spilled his guts, and that averted a bigger disaster in New York City and possibly Chicago and L.A. There's a dead IRS agent, an ambush, and some other stuff in there, too.

"Please welcome to the program, Tommy Burk."

The camera than focused directly on Burk who said to Midas, "Thank you, Midas and Semper Fi."

"Semper Fi to you, Mr. Burk."

"Burk or Tommy, please."

"So Tommy, tell me, you look about my age, possibly a little younger. Were you a Marine fighting the Cong in the jungles of Viet Nam the same time I was there?"

"No," said Tommy, in an obvious lie, "I was a bugler in Lejeune."

"You mean Pendleton," corrected Midas.

"Whatever," replied Burk.

People usually didn't turn things around on Midas, but he seemed to appreciate Burk's humor and let it go. "So before we begin, I always ask my guest what their five favorite songs are. So what are yours, if you don't mind my asking, and if you do, I don't care."

"Not in any order, and they change according to how I feel, but today I would say: 'Try a Little tenderness' by Otis Redding, 'Good Day Sunshine' by the Beatles, 'Slip Away' by Bowie, 'Waiting on a Friend' by The Stones, and 'Ave Maria' by the Vienna Boys Choir."

Midas pondered that for a second then asked, "Schubert or Bach."

Burk replied "Schubert."

"Well," said Midas, "those are some great songs. Don't get much better than 'Try a Little Tenderness,' but tell me about 'Good Day Sunshine.' How the hell did that make your list?"

"When I was finishing my tour in Viet Nam, November '67, it rained most every day. We were always out on operations and always soaked. It was during monsoon and on my last patrol somewhere between HUE and the Hi Van Pass. The rain was pouring down. I had a 60-pound pack and ammunition on my back, which when soaked, felt like 80. I started singing to myself 'Good Day Sunshine,' and the rain stopped and the sun came out, and for the briefest moment I felt alive. I always associate that song with me leaving Viet Nam alive."

Midas looked like he was going to say *"That was way too much information,"* but he gave Burk another pass and instead said, "We've all been there."

For the rest of the segment, Midas, Connell and Bernie had Burk tell the terrorist bombing story and about the convoy ambush, but it was clear that there was not enough time. Midas asked if Burk could stay on for an unprecedented second and third segments, and Burk agreed.

Burk wanted to get right to the announcement when they came back, but with Midas you never knew.

While Midas was eating some fruit in a cup, Burk leaned over to Bernie and said, "Bernie, I got something big to announce and I am hoping you give me a lead in. You won't regret it."

"You got it, Tommy," said Bernie.

"Please welcome back to the program, Mr. Tommy Burk," said Midas.

Bernie, true to his word asked, "Ok Tommy, you saved the city if not the country. Terrorized the terrorist. You were framed, accused of murder, murdered and unmurdered then honored. That about it?

"Just about," replied Burk

"Ok then," said Bernie. "What's next? What do you do with your 15 minutes?"

Burk was perfecting his monologue and repeated his Palm restaurant mantra. "I don't like it here."

"You don't like the studio? What?" said Bernie, wondering if he just got set up.

"No Bernie, I am not talking about here." He put gestured and looked about the studio. "I mean here. This time, this place in our history, our country. This is not the country I want live in, and it is not the country I want to leave to my children. We fought a good fight in Viet Nam, but we fought a bad war. Johnson let Kennedy be killed and the floodgates to Viet Nam opened. We believed Walter when he told us to go, and we listened to him when he told us to leave. We did what our misguided, uninformed, selfish, egotistical, elected officials told us was right. Not just Johnson in '64, but Truman 14 years earlier in Korea. It seems when things are slow at home or politicians need to avert attention, they have some sort of esoteric need to involve us in other people's civil wars. We don't learn. Politicians read polls; they don't read history. They make the same mistakes over and over again. Bush, the son, couldn't stop after he punished the Taliban. He, Cheney, Rumsfeld and that shit Wolfowitz said the war in Iraq could be done on the cheap and that it would largely pay for itself. It ended up costing us $800 billion and 500,000 dead, of which 5,000 were American troops. You do the math. Cheney said the WMDs were a 'slam dunk,' but the only slam dunk that came out of that fiasco was the obscene amount of money Cheney and Halliburton made.

"I don't even want to get into what the country and the four of us have just went through a few weeks ago.

"As a country, we are morally and financially bankrupt, yet we export our beliefs along with foreign aid to countries that hate us. We meddle in everyone else's affairs to hide the fact that we can't get our own in order. One week we had money to bomb Syria, and the next week we had to close the World War II memorial for lack of funds.

"We have become a country of dysfunctional families, morally diffident financiers, all led by delusional, corrupt politicians. I don't like what I see, and I am going to change it. I am going to make the dysfunctional function, overturn the tables of the money changers and instill the fear of God into the politicians."

Midas seemed to roll his eyes back in to his head and said in his best evangelist voice, "Amen. Jesusss Goddd. Praise the lord!"

Everyone kind of just sat there, but Burk looked at Midas and said, "Yeah, I've been be getting that a lot."

"Burk, just where exactly are you going with this?

"Where I am going, Andy Midas, is Washington. Today, right now, right here on the *Midas in the a.m.* show, I am announcing that Mayor Bloomfield,

NYPD Commissioner Riley, and Kelly Sullivan have formed an exploratory committee to put my name forward in nomination to become President of the United States."

"Jesusss Goddd!" said Midas again.

"It just doesn't get any better than this, does it, Boss?" said Bernie.

"You know," said Midas, "Vice President John Kearney is a friend of mine. I think he's a jerk and a pompous ass, but he did do a pretty good job as secretary of state. We still like him, don't we Bernie?"

"We did, but I think we have made a new best friend this morning, Boss."

"What I think," said Midas, "is that this is my show, and it's supposed to be about me. I don't know how our viewers and our radio listeners, who can't see us, will react to a show not about me! But in this instance, and this instance only, I am willing to let Mr. Burk continue. Didn't I tell you Kearney was a looser, Bernie?"

"Tommy," said Bernie, "what about Governor Christie, Rubio, Rand Paul and the top running Republicans?"

Burk looked at Bernie then continued his mantra. "Bernie. I am not running as a Republican or Democrat or as a Tea Partier. I am going to run in a party that represents all the people. We can't have four or eight more years of Democrats. We are $13 trillion in the hole; in eight more years we will have a $40 trillion deficit. The Affordable Health Care Act is in the toilet ready to be flushed, and that's the Democrats take. The Congress is completely ineffective, and our president clearly represents only half of America.

"The Republicans or the Tea Party will not win. Christie has a big mouth, and it won't take him long to alienate the gays, the women's movement, blacks, Hispanics and the college voters. He can fall off the bridge anytime. Rubio is the same as Christie except that he won't alienate the Hispanics, just the white racists. And Rand Paul. Never trust a man with two first names. Besides the apple doesn't fall too far from the tree.

"Look, Kearney is an incumbent, a Democrat, a former secretary of state and senator— a decisive position to be in. The Democrats killed the Republicans the last two times at bat, and they are going to trounce them again. In 2008, all the Republicans could find was a foul-mouth old man and a dingbat. In 2012, they got a guy right out of central casting who still couldn't win. They have weak, ineffective leadership in both houses. The party is divided between the left, right and Tea Party. They shut down the government back in '13 for a misguided reason. The lost the youth, black, Latino, union, gay, rite to life, women's, liberal Hollywood and all the media's vote. In other words they lost the people that actually vote. Conservatives Biff and Buffy in Greenwich don't give a shit and don't vote.

"I can win. But with an American Party. A party for all the people. Not of the liberals or conservatives. Not of the whites or blacks or browns or reds or yellows. Not of the rich or poor. But a party for all the country.

"I am going to shake this country up. Everyone in the country is waiting for someone else to do something. That someone is going to be me, but I need your help and I need all your viewers and listeners out there to help make it happen.

"I am going to make America great again. I am going to make America into a great American corporation. We are going to make money for the people, not take it from the people. We have a Gross National Product of $15 trillion, but our debt is $15.5 trillion. We should be making money not losing money.

"We are going to be a benevolent America, but not export our values. We are going to 'Walk softly but carry a big stick.'"

"Sounds to me like we're all going to be living the dream, boy." said Midas. "Don't know about that big dick stuff."

"Big stick," corrected Connell.

Midas said, "Oh sorry! Seems my hearing aide came out."

In the background Deegan, Guns, Carly and the entire Imus show were whooping and hollering.

Midas continued, "Burk has got it going on, McSorley. You done good with this guest, Bernie."

"Thanks, Chief," said Bernie. "I think that's the first time you ever gave me a compliment."

Midas said, "Burk, I want to see you make it, brother. I want you to be president of this country. I want to see this country great again before I leave it. I and this show will help you on your journey, brother."

The show went to break but when it came back it was either over or Midas had suddenly developed a British accent.

CHAPTER 67

NEW YORK CITY

January 4th.
FOX Entertainment Network
Midas Private Office.

In Midas office after the program, Andy Midas and Bernie McSorley sat down to discuss going forward with Mayor Bloomfield, Commissioner Riley, Kelly Sullivan and Burk.

After introductions, Kelly said, "To run as an independent, there are some steps we need to follow, and we have hired John Renson out of New York. John is an independent political consultant who will offer us perspectives and insights for independent and third-party political candidates. More importantly, he will walk us through the required steps.

"First we checked to ensure Tommy meets the qualifications for the office of president as established in Article II, Section 1 of the U.S. Constitution. Candidates must be natural-born citizens, 35 years of age and have lived in the United States for 14 years. He does.

"With John's help we have already formed an exploratory committee, and engaged in 'test the waters' activities that include polling, canvassing and making phone calls to gauge public support. So far so good, but after today's show we'll blow the roof off.

"We are forming a campaign committee. It's a rudimentary committee before filing any paperwork, but keep in mind that our committee cannot begin electioneering in excess of $5,000 raised or spent before you have declared Tommy's candidacy.

"Today we will file a Statement of Candidacy with the Federal Election Commission. This basic form requires the candidate's name, address, phone number and information about the campaign committee chair. We must also send this form to the declared opposing candidates.

"We will then organize the campaign committee and file a Statement of Organization with the FEC within 10 days of declaring candidacy. This form registers a treasurer and custodian of records for the campaign with the FEC.

"Here's where you can help. We need to get on the ballot in all 50 states. Independents must obtain a certain number of petition signatures in each state to appear on the ballot. The threshold for getting on the ballot varies by state. Tommy must appear on nearly every state's ballot to obtain the 270 out of 538 electoral votes needed to win the election. Launching ad campaigns in television markets nationwide can garner name recognition and may expedite the process of gaining signatures. Mr. Midas, your show reaches across the country, and that's what we're counting on.

"Once that's done, we begin campaigning, and file quarterly financial reports with the FEC to document contributions and expenditures to qualify for matching funds."

Midas said, "I will get the message out, but why not hit all the talk shows? *O'Reilly, Hannity, CNBC* – although why bother, no one watches them or *CNN.*"

"I'll answer that," said Burk. "Because we don't want to come across as too right or too left. Your show, Andy, is on *FOX,* but everyone knows you're down the middle, and that's where we want to be. We also want this to be grass roots and not another slick production. No big money, no big lobbyists. We are going to use 'Midas in the am' and social media, then let the American people take it and run with it. We need you and your show to be our middle of the road voice.

Midas looked at everyone. "What you are doing makes me feel alive again. *The Midas in the am* show will support you today, tomorrow and through to the White House. It don't get any better than this. Isn't that right, Bernie?"

"You got that right, Boss," said Bernie.

Midas said, "This is going to be the most exciting, best, erection on the face of the planet."

Kelly looked at Bernie to see if she heard Midas correctly, but Bernie kind of closed his eyes and gently shook his head as an indication for Kelly to let it go.

CHAPTER 68

WASHINGTON, DC

White House, Oval Office.

The president asked Kearney, Miller, O'Donnell and Kerry to join her to watch the *Midas in the am* show—something none of them, with the exception of Kearney, would ever consider doing. They all knew of Midas and his past problems. They knew about his off the wall show and crazy antics, but that morning they would watch because of who Midas had as his guest.

During the show, which ran about three hours, many comments and quite a lot of laughter and snickering occurred.

But toward the end of the program when Burk announced his intention to run for president, everyone became very quiet. The thought that Burk would even consider running for office never occurred to them. Why should it? If it were a local office, they wouldn't care, but this was different.

The laughing stopped, and the president asked the vice president, "I thought I heard Midas say you were friends. But now it sounds like Burk is Midas' new best friend. Before the show, you said Midas would tear Burk a new one. It looks now like you underestimated both your friend and your enemy."

"Madam President, I don't think we need to worry about Burk being my competition and certainly not becoming president. He is a murderer, after all, and the Republicans are touting Christie, Rubio and Paul.

"Did you forget that little something he has, John? If I were you I wouldn't underestimate him again."

O'Donnell said, "We have 11 months left until the election. Not a lot of time. John, you need to bring in David Arod to run your campaign."

"That's a good idea, Chris; why don't you and Jay go get it started," said the president.

After they left the room, the president turned the recorder off and said, "John, against Christie, Rubio and Paul or that Cruse fellow, you were a shoe-in, but with Burk it's a new ball game."

"He will use the tape recording, he made in this office, against me."

"Don't be ridiculous, John. Burk, the mayor and police commissioner stood in the Press Briefing Room, no so long ago, and in front of the entire nation accepted hero accolades bestowed on them by me and the United States of America. They can't use anything they have against us. We would bury them. But just to be on the safe side Bob, get all you can on that IRS murder and find out about Burk's relationship with that Kelly Sullivan reporter. Better yet, have the FBI dig deep into Burk's past and have it ready in case we need it. Burk will be a tough opponent, especially if he has Bloomfield's money and Midas's voice. He's going grass root, and that might be brilliant or he might just self-implode.

"And Bob, if we need him to self-implode, I want you plant the bomb."

"I would be more than happy to plant the bomb personally," said Miller.

CHAPTER 69

BURK FOR PRESIDENT HEADQUARTERS

1111 Lexington Avenue, NYC.

The Burk for President Headquarters took up an entire brownstone on Lexington between 76th and 77th. The ground level was a storefront that acted as the retail end for the campaign (staff, volunteers, walk-ins, literature, etc.) while the top three floors were used for offices. The Lexington Avenue subway entrance was right on the corner. The area was both residential and business, and the Lexington Hospital was around the corner. There were plenty of places to eat, drink and shop and that meant plenty of people.

The grass roots movement to get Burk on the presidential ticket had paid off. Burk was on the ballot for all 50 states and all according to the FEC rules. The Republicans were not standing still, but one week Christie was in the lead, the next week he fell off the bridge, and then it was Paul or Rubio. Ted Cruz and Tea Party Republicans we're gaining ground but confusing the traditional Republican platform. It would be back and forth between the four of them as one would move up, as the others said or did something stupid. Usually it was about same-sex marriage or immigrants. The Republicans had already started planting the seed, in case they lost, that Burk's independent run had split their party and taken away much needed votes. The Republican Party just couldn't get over themselves. The Democrats weren't much better, although they seemed to realize that it was better to attack the Republican Party leaders than the party's constituents. Regardless, both parties had long since proven that once elected to the office of President of the United States, the president quickly became the president of the people who brought em.

"That was not going to happen when I win," Burk told voters. He would be president of all the people. Those that voted for him and those that didn't. Burk was running on a very different platform than all the others. Term limits were one of the platform planks, and Burk intended to walk the walk. If elected, he would only run for one term. Let the other candidates top that. But Burk could afford to make that stand because he has a little secret in store for America. But that's for later. Now he was an independent candidate, and this was his Declaration of Independence.

Before there was a Constitution and almost a year after Concord, there was an idea that was put down on a piece of parchment. This idea, often overshadowed by the Constitution, was what escalated everything.

"When in the course of human events it becomes necessary for one people to dissolve the political bands which have connected them with another and to assume among the powers of the earth, the separate and equal station to which the Laws of Nature and of Nature's God entitle them, a decent respect to the opinions of mankind requires that they should declare the causes which impel them to the separation. We hold these truths to be self-evident, that all men are created equal, that they are endowed by their Creator with certain unalienable Rights, that among these are Life, Liberty and the pursuit of Happiness.—That to secure these rights, Governments are instituted among Men, deriving their just powers from the consent of the governed,—That whenever any Form of Government becomes destructive of these ends, it is the Right of the People to alter or to abolish it, and to institute new Government, laying its foundation on such principles and organizing its powers in such form, as to them shall seem most likely to affect their Safety and Happiness. Prudence, indeed, will dictate that Governments long established should not be changed for light and transient causes; and accordingly all experience hath shown, that mankind are more disposed to suffer, while evils are sufferable, than to right themselves by abolishing the forms to which they are accustomed. But when a long train of abuses and usurpations, pursuing invariably the same Object evinces a design to reduce them under absolute Despotism, it is their right, it is their duty, to throw off such Government, and to provide new Guards for their future security.—Such has been the patient sufferance of these Colonies; and such is now the necessity which constrains them to alter their former Systems of Government. The history of the present King of Great Britain is a history of repeated injuries and usurpations, all having in direct object the establishment of an absolute Tyranny over these States. To prove this, let Facts be submitted to a candid world."

The Declaration of Independence of 1776 paved the way for our Constitution. Our Constitution of 1791 has been amended 27 times, for good and not so good.

Burk's strategy so far had been to avoid participating in Republican or Democratic debates. They were as far as he, and obviously many of his supporters were concerned, a bunch of buffoons.

There was nothing wrong with the individual beliefs of either party, but when you put them together in a platform, they end up alienating half of the population.

Burk's strategy and philosophy was simple. Believing that all people should be allowed to live their lives in the way that they want to. Life, Liberty and the Pursuit of Happiness. A euphemism for that phrase would become Burk's "No Name Party's" slogan, "Live and Let Live." Burk's polls and numbers were off the wall and across the board.

Democrats, Republicans, Independents and Tea Partiers were all deserting their usual suspects and coming over to Burk's campaign. Burk's manager, Kelly Sullivan, was no David Arod, but she was a quick study, and besides they weren't running a traditional campaign. It was crazy. Women from both pro-life and pro-choice, gay and straight, gun control and NRA, Christian, Non-Christians, secularists, atheists, Muslims, right and left were all coming together and working together to elect Burk. It seems when people adopt the "Live and Let Live" policy, they can not only work together, they can also be friends again.

Burk's rise in the polls and increased media coverage were very reminiscent of President Hilton's own run eight years previously.

But Burk himself was just starting to get his momentum and he was about to announce his running mate – and that would really shake things up.

CHAPTER 70

WASHINGTON, DC

White House, Oval Office.

The president, Kearney, Miller, O'Donnell, Carr and Arod were meeting in the Oval Office and feeling very good about themselves. Just over a month ago, Kearney hired Arod, a political consultant based in Chicago. Arod was a top political advisor to President Bill Clinton as well as campaign advisor to President Hilton. Arod was now the architect for Kearney's presidential campaign. Kearney had gathered them, at the request of President Hilton, to pick his vice president.

Everyone was seated around the coffee table in the sofas and side chairs.

David Arod began by listing several possibilities. "I think we should strongly consider; Senator Kirsten Gillmartin of New York, Governor Brian Shuster of Montana, Senator Mark Weiner of Virginia, and Governor Martin O'Balley of Maryland. Let's take them down one by one. The three primary factors we should look for in your running mate are: image. And by that I mean how they look, and as importantly, how they look standing next to you. Votes. And by that I mean what states they can deliver. And finally, loyalty. And by that I mean will they be your puppy dog and get your newspaper or will they be a pit bull who wants their name in the paper.

"All four have been phase 1 vetted and after we narrow the list today, to one or two, we will start vet phase 2. Madam President, any thoughts?"

The president went to her desk. "I think you summed it up correctly, David, so why don't you and John decide, then I'll weigh in."

The vice president seemed to agree and started out. "Ok! And in no specific or relevant order. Governor Brian Shuster of Montana: he reminds me of Tim Russert, and I don't understand those silly little cowboy neck ties he wears"

David raised his hand. "The fact that he looks like Tim Russert could be a benefit. Tim was well liked and very smart. Those little ties he wears are called bolo string ties and he wears them to because he is a cowboy. That's what they have in Montana: cowboys. In fact that's what a lot of important men wear in Dallas, Las Vegas, Vail, and some of the middle states."

"Regardless," said the vice president, "He looks silly and probably only a million people live in the entire state of Montana and most of them are Indians who don't vote. Let's move on, shall we? Senator Mark Weiner of Virginia is goofy looking, and besides his state is too close to Washington."

David countered, "He is very smart and can bring in some southern votes."

"You did say a primary factor was image and how they looked, didn't you?" said the vice president. "Anyway let's move on. Now Governor Martin O'Balley of Maryland is someone I could work with. He looks like a vice president; hell he looks like a president; and now that I think about it, I don't like him. Is Maryland considered a southern state?"

Now the president jumped in. "John, don't worry about O'Balley looking more presidential than you. No one looks more presidential than you. And Maryland is considered a middle state and won't bring in many southern votes."

"Agreed," admitted the vice president. "Well that leaves Senator Kirsten Gillmartin of New York. I think she's hot, and together we would look fantastic—like a real couple on a real date. She is smart, beautiful and a senator, not governor or one of those representatives from the House. Do you know what President Johnson said was the difference between the Senate and the House? I'll tell you. One is chicken salad, and the other is chicken shit."

David replied, "I agree that she is smart, beautiful, and a senator and that she will look good on your arm, but she is married, and so are you for that matter.

Do we want the media spending time speculating about the two of you? Besides, she is from New York and won't bring in any votes that you don't already have in your pocket."

"Look, said the vice president, you cited: image, votes and loyalty. Hell, as Meatloaf said, two out of three ain't bad."

"John," said the president, "I do agree she complements you. I say she should be on your short list, and if the media wants to speculate then let them. And John, I think you're dating yourself."

"You mean, Madam President, my reference to Meatloaf?" asked the vice president.

"No John," said the president, "she is smart, beautiful and a senator. When you're together on your date, you'll look like you're dating yourself."

"I don't get it" said the vice president.

The president turned to take a phone call but said, "Can someone please help the vice president get it?"

After lunch, Kearney and David Arod adjourned to the vice president's office just down the hall. "Why don't we call Gillmartins's people and see if she is interested?" asked the vice president.

David took out his cell and talked to one of his people, listened for a couple of minutes and then clicked off. He turned to the vice president and said, "Were on it, but something alarming is happening with Burk's campaign. That was Dunn, one of my top people, and he said Burk is polling out of the ballpark, and we had better do something to get our numbers up.

"He said Burk is about to announce his VP, and that he is completely ignoring the Republican candidates. He won't even debate them. Word has it that he thinks it's between you and him and that everyone and everything else is irrelevant. His man inside Burk's campaign said they leaked it to the Times that Burk wants to debate you."

"That piece of shit couldn't debate a high school sophomore, let alone me," said the vice president. "I will kill him. Bring him on."

"Not so fast, John. He might be looking to elevate himself to your level. Get tons of respect and free media attention. Remember, the presidency is yours to lose, John. Burk may not be a debater, but he damn sure is a gunslinger. And if you give him a debate, he will ambush you."

"You have no idea," replied the vice president. "There are some things I can't tell you, David. Suffice to say, they are national security matters and on a need-to-know basis. If there comes a time for you to know, I'll read you in. Until then, you'll have to trust me."

"Let's break his balls a little," said David. "I'll let it slip you'll be happy to debate the top Republican and/or the top opposition candidate. Let them slug it out first. In the meantime, my team will pursue Sen. Gillmartin of New York and Governor O'Malley of Maryland for vice president.

"You need to get the president to get the Affordable Health Care Program working, and I mean working real good. You better get a couple million young people enrolled before the program implodes. If it does, you can kiss moving into the White House goodbye.

"If you debate Christie or Burk or whomever, you will kill them in foreign affairs and international relations. We also need to get all the financial and world leaders to endorse you.

"I disagree. I think we need go after Burk now and debate him now. It's really coming down to Burk and me. Why bother with the Republicans. And besides, I was an officer and Burk was of the 'other ranks' for Christ sakes. He was just a corporal and I was a commander. A commander!" Said Kearney.

"Burk was a sergeant not a corporal" replied Aron.

"Not much of a difference. Corporal, sergeant. Look what those two little corporals did to Europe. What did they achieve? Had they been 'Commanders' things would have certainly turned out differently." Said Kearney.

"John, comparing Burk to Napoleon and Hitler's shortcomings or yourself, for that matter, as someone who could have succeeded where they failed is, I believe, a disastrous strategy.

I suggest you keep your historical war lord fantasies filed away. Somewhere deep, dark and alongside Genghis Kahn." suggested Arod.

Vice President Kearney knew Arod was right but sometimes he just couldn't help himself. Sometimes he just couldn't keep his mouth shut. Especially about his past.

CHAPTER 71

BURK FOR PRESIDENT HEADQUARTERS

1111 Lexington Avenue, NYC.

A lot of activity was transpiring at Burk's Lexington Avenue headquarters. At the street level, volunteers were lining up down past St. John's Cathedral down to 74th and Lexington. Police were assembling wooden saw horses and controlling and directing people and traffic. It was a scene, but some locals considered it a mess.

Midas was pushing Burk, and Burk was finally pressured to appear to on *CNN*, *FOX* and Sunday morning's *Meet the Press*. The *Wall Street Journal* called him a social media Messiah. *The Washington Post* and *The New York Times* both endorsed him.

Burk's numbers were soaring into the stratosphere. His "Live and Let Live" platform was something liberals, moderates and conservatives, young and old, gay and straight, Christian and atheist, white, black, brown, yellow and red could and were embracing in huge numbers.

He had Ronald Reagan's conservative Republicans, who wanted tax cuts, a greatly increased U.S. military budget, deregulation and family values. He had the Conservative Christian morality voters, who typically opposed abortion, gun control, and gay marriage.

But he also had liberals, whose political philosophy or worldview was founded on ideas of liberty and equality. Liberals espouse a wide array of views depending on their understanding of these principles, but generally they support ideas such as free and fair elections, civil rights, freedom of the press, freedom of religion, free trade, and private property. Liberal voters typically supported abortion, gun control, and gay marriage.

The Republican top runners were still battling it out to see who would get the nomination, while Burk and Kearney were starting to go at each other. In fact, Kearney's people were now knocking on Burk's door for a debate. Kearney was losing points in the polls, and he was trying to distance himself from Hilton's still floundering Affordable Health Care Act.

Burk, Kelly Sullivan, and their team set around a plywood table on the third floor trying to decide between two vice presidential candidates. Both candidates had joined the party and volunteered their names and support before they were told they were being considered for vice president. Burk was listening to the back and forth between what either running mate would bring to the table. But Burk already knew who he wanted and when he announced who, it would set the incumbents and GOP so far back that there would be no hope for a rebound. But he would keep that name close to his vest until he was ready.

Burk liked the direction they were heading and was enjoying the malaise emanating from both mainstream parties.

Burk's team put out daily issues, beliefs and ideas in the form of bullet points. Kearney and the Republican hopefuls had to spend most of their time on the defensive. They could accept, refute or dodge the bullets. But before they could shoot back, another bullet was fired from Burks camp and heading their way. Most of – but not all of Burk's offensive – was through social media, such as Facebook, YouTube and Twitter. The youth of America had grabbed on to Burks mantra: "Live and Let Live" and were taking it viral.

Burk was very independent in his thinking, but many undecided still saw him as a wild card if not a wild man, what with his IRS speculation and terrorist interrogation antics. But most of America was willing to overlook, if not champion, those minor indiscretions because of what he was preaching.

"The Bill of Rights:

"'That all power is originally vested in, and consequently derived from the people. That government is instituted and ought to be exercised for the benefit of the people; which consists in the enjoyment of life and liberty and the right of acquiring property, and generally of pursing and obtaining happiness and safety. That the people have an indubitable, unalienable, and indefeasible right to reform or change their government whenever it be found adverse or inadequate to the purpose of its institution.

"'The civil rights of none shall be abridged on account of religious belief or worship...The people shall not be deprived or abridged of their right to speak, to write, or to publish their sentiments; and the freedom of the press, as one of the great bulwarks of liberty, shall be inviolable. The people shall not be restrained from peaceably assembling and consulting for their common good; nor for applying to the legislature by petitions or remonstrances for redress of their grievances...The right of the people to keep and bear arms shall not be infringed.'

"Today, however, the executive branch of the government is immensely powerful, much more powerful than the Founding Fathers had envisioned or wanted. Congressional legislative powers have been usurped. There is no greater example of that usurpation than in the form of the presidential Executive Order. The process totally bypasses Congressional legislative authority and places in the hands of the president almost unilateral power. The Executive Order governs everything from the Flag Code of the United States to the ability to single-handedly declare Martial Law.

"Since the enactment of Executive Order 13603, the only thing standing between our democracy and dictatorship is the good character of the president and the lack of a crisis severe enough that the public would stand still for it."

When President Burk said he would fix the biggest problem facing America—an ineffective, corrupt, self-serving congress—he would fix it by instituting Executive Order 13603.

You see, Burk had no desire to be the man who would be president. Burk wanted to be the man who would be king. But he would be a benevolent king. As

Burk said, "If our form of democracy is to survive, it must first die, be cleansed, and then reborn."

Burk would only have four years to accomplish this metamorphosis, or possibly a little more. You see, Burk secretly harbored Mel Brooks' philosophy, "It's good to be the king." And as Lord Acton said "Power corrupts, and absolute power corrupts absolutely."

CHAPTER 72

WASHINGTON, DC

White House, the Vice President's Office.

The vice president and David Arod were sitting at the vice president's desk. Polls hadn't improved for the vice president. His campaign was floundering. The only blessing was that he was running unopposed. Debates had been set against the Republican candidate Christie but nothing was confirmed yet with Burk. He had to debate Burk to get his numbers up. He was losing his voter base to Burk and had to stop the hemorrhaging while wooing some Independents and Republicans.

Kearney selected Gillmartin of New York as his running mate. And what was worse, is that Governor Christie chose Sen. Mark Rubio of Florida as his running mate. Now even the Republicans were going to steal his Latino votes.

Burk won in the Iowa caucuses, New Hampshire, Colorado, Minnesota, Missouri, Utah, Nevada, south Carolina, North Carolina, Arizona, Michigan, Colorado, Oregon, Oklahoma, Tennessee, Texas, Virginia, Mississippi, Ohio, Illinois, Louisiana, Maryland, Wisconsin, Connecticut, Massachusetts, Vermont, District of Columbia and Rhode Island.

Christie won in Delaware, New Jersey, Pennsylvania, Indiana, Nebraska, West Virginia, and Florida.

Kearney was running unopposed within his party and didn't have to participate in the caucuses.

Kearney and Arod were waiting for a return phone call from Kelly Sullivan, Burk's campaign manager, agreeing to three October debates. When the phone rang, the vice president picked it up. It was the White House operator seeing if he would be available for Ms. Kelly Sullivan. He said, "Yes, put her through" and handed the phone to Arod.

Arod said, "Kelly, good to hear back from you." As the vice president listened, Arod nodded, said "good," and gave a thumbs up to the vice president.

"Are you with the vice president? asked Kelly.

"Yes" replied Arod.

"Then you should tune in now to *CNN*" She then hung up.

When the call ended, Arod told vice president. "We got the debate for October 16th, but that's it. They will give us only one shot. Oh! And she said we should turn on the TV.

Arod took out his cell to notify his staff, while the vice president turned toward the two monitors in his office – one to *CNN* the other to *FOX*.

"Holy shit," said the vice president.

Arod turned to see to what the vice president referred to and then repeated those exact sentiments.

There on the screen was Burk, standing at the podium preparing to make an announcement. Mayor Bloomfield and the person who Burk would nominate as his vice president, stood behind him.

Kearney said, "Don't you do it, Burk."

Burk seemed to looking right at Vice President Kearney and said, "My fellow Americans, it gives me immense pleasure to introduce to you, the next Vice President of the United States – Cassy Hilton."

Both the vice president and Arod slumped down into their chairs as Kearney counted down "3, 2, 1." At that, there was a disturbance at his door and the president came storming in.

"When did you know about this, Kearney? And if you didn't, you should fire this sniveling boob sitting next to you. I am not going to have this embarrass me, Mr. Vice President. I am this close…" *She extended her middle finger.* "…to pulling my endorsement from you and giving it to Burk and my daughter." With that, she stormed out of his office.

The vice president looked at Burk's happy team, live on both *CNN* and *FOX*. They were still congratulating each other and shaking hands and pointing to friends in the audience. A new banner was unfolding in the background, proclaiming "Burk and Hilton. Live and Let Live."

Cassy Hilton loved her mother but hated John Kearney. She was young and an idealist and believed the country needed new leadership. The Country needed Burk and she was going to bring the left and female vote. A graduate of Harvard Medical School and practicing general physician, she was smart, gorgeous and independent.

It was turning out to be a contest between two sets of handsome candidates right out of central casting. Like a high school prom. Kearney-Gillmartin and Burk-Hilton. Who would become the homecoming King and Queen?

CHAPTER 73

October 16ᵀᴴ Debate, Hempstead, NY

VICE PRESIDENT JOHN F. KEARNEY AND TOMMY D. BURK
PARTICIPATE IN A CANDIDATES DEBATE, HOFSTRA UNIVERSITY,
HEMPSTEAD, NEW YORK
SPEAKERS: THOMAS D. BURK, I-NY
VICE PRESIDENT JOHN F. KEARNEY, D-MASS
MODERATOR: JIM LEER of the *PBS News Hour*

LEER: Good evening from Hofstra University, Hempstead, New York. I'm Jim Leer of the *PBS News Hour*, and I welcome you to the first and only presidential debate between Vice President John Kearney, the Democratic nominee, and New York Bombing Hero, Tommy Burk, the Independent nominee.

This debate is sponsored by the Commission on Presidential Debates. Tonight's 90 minutes will be about domestic issues and will follow a format designed by the commission. There will be six roughly 15-minute segments with two-minute answers for the first question, then open discussion for the remainder of each segment. Thousands of people offered suggestions on segment subjects or questions via the Internet and other means, but I made the final selections. And for the record, they were not submitted for approval to the commission or the candidates. The segments, as I announced in advance, will be three on the economy and one each on health care, the role of government and governing, with an emphasis throughout on differences, specifics and choices. Both candidates will also have two-minute closing statements.

The audience here in the hall has promised to remain silent – no cheers, applause, boos, hisses, among other noisy distracting things, so we may all concentrate on what the candidates have to say. There is a noise exception right now, though, as we welcome Vice President Kearney and Mr. Thomas Burk.

(APPLAUSE)

"Gentlemen, welcome to you both. Since you are both veterans let me begin by saying, thank you for serving. Let's start the economy, segment one, and let's begin with jobs. What are the major differences between the two of you about how you would go about creating new jobs? You have two minutes. Each of you have two minutes to start. A coin toss has determined, Mr. Vice President, you go first."

KEARNEY: Well, thank you very much, Jim, for this opportunity. I want to thank Mr. Burk for joining me and Hofstra University for its hospitality.

You know eight years ago we went through the worst financial crisis since the Great Depression. Millions of jobs were lost, the auto industry was on the brink of collapse. The financial system had frozen up.

And because of the resilience and the determination of the American people, we've begun to fight our way back. Over the last 30 months, we've seen 5 million jobs in the private sector created. The auto industry has come roaring back. And housing has begun to rise.

We are on the right track and it is working.

But we all know that we've still got a lot of work to do. And so the question here tonight is not where we've been but where we're going.

Mr. Burk has a perspective that says if we cut taxes, skewed toward the wealthy, and roll back regulations, we'll be better off. I've got a different view.

I think we've got to invest in education and training. I think it's important for us to develop new sources of energy here in America, that we change our tax code to make sure that we're helping small businesses and companies that are investing here in the United States, that we take some of the money that we're saving as we wind down two wars to rebuild America, and that we reduce our deficit in a balanced way that allows us to make these critical investments.

Now, it ultimately is going to be up to the voters – to you – which path we should take. Are we going with top-down economic policies that helped get us into this mess or do we embrace a new economic patriotism that says America does best when the middle class does best? And I'm looking forward to having that debate.

LEER: Mr. Burk, two minutes.

BURK: Thank you very much Jim, Mr. Vice President. Jim, I know you are a former Marine so I want to also thank you for serving.

So far so good, thought Riley, seated in the audience along with Mayor Bloomfield and Kelly Sullivan, but he held his breath for what he knew was about to come.

And while we're at it, I would also like to thank all the waiters and waitresses for serving.

Some chuckles were heard, but must people just didn't seem to get it. Burk hated that condescending "thank you for serving" comment almost as much as he hated politicians who wore American flag pins on their lapels. Riley more than anyone knew that Burk would not let this charade go on much longer and knew of his hidden agenda. Leer let Burk's response go.

I'm concerned that the path that we're on has just been unsuccessful. The vice president's policies have a view very similar to the view the president has had for eight years. That bigger government, spending more, taxing more, regulating more – if you will, trickle-down government – would work. It hasn't. It won't. The vice president hasn't a clue about my perspective.

It didn't take Burk long to begin to veer off course toward his own agenda, Riley thought.

The problem with America is its people have been lied to, bullied and coerced by our leaders. Not just in the last eight years but since World War II. The American people today are confused about the past, uncertain about the present, and scared to shit about the future. Our government is out of control with spending and taxes. We have a Congress that has been incapacitated, presided over by a president who is dysfunctional and a vice president who is incompetent.

This is not why I served, and not why our fathers and their fathers served. We deserve better than this. I demand better than this, and I will deliver better than this. We have a $15 trillion debt. The world thinks us a joke. We are unemployed, uninformed and unwitting. No Mr. Vice President, it's not working."

LEER: Mr. Vice President, please respond directly to what Mr. Burk just said about… well, about everything he just said.

KEARNEY: Well, yes, but it troubles me that Mr. Burk somehow feels it necessary to demean sincere sentiments made by our grateful citizens, who find it in their heart, desirous to thank our service men and women for wearing the uniform our country. This is not about Mr. Burk's cynicism. It is about our grateful citizens and one of the few ways they can show thanks and respect.

I served with honor in a dirty war many years ago and…

BURK: Are you sure you want to go there, John?

LEER: Mr. Burk, please let the vice president finish.

KEARNEY: As I was saying, I served with honor in a dirty war many years ago, and the nation honored and awarded me a Silver Star, Bronze Star and three Purple Hearts for my service. But many soldiers, sailors, airmen and marines were not so honored and a simple gesture of thanks can make a difference. Mr. Burk, have you been similarly honored?

LEER: It seems as though we are getting a bit off course, but let's see where it takes us. At least for a while. Mr. Burk, would you like to respond?

BURK: John, I saw a lot of action Viet Nam and carried many dead and wounded to the choppers for evacuation. But when the choppers left and the rotor noise died out, quiet resumed. I and the other survivors picked up the dead's and wounded's gear, added it to our kit and continued the mission. They didn't give out medals to survivors. I was not a hero but I walked among them.

I respect those who went to Viet Nam. Those were troubled times, and it was not until many Americans and Vietnamese died before we found out it was all a big Johnson lie. But at least we did something. Some of us drank Walter's Kool-Aid and went to Vietnam. Some of us went to Canada. Some of us protested. But we did something. Hell, even Fonda did something. At least we didn't sit on the sidelines and get bum knee deferments or marry to get out of the draft.

My problem with you, John, was not your going to Viet Nam or even your "Winter Soldier" protest against the war when you got home. My problem is what you did while you were there. During your time in the Viet Nam War, you were seen by colleagues as a self-serving, 'loose cannon' who came only to launch a political career. You arrived in the country with a self-serving determination to build a foundation for your political future. You only served about four months of a 12-month tour of duty in Vietnam, winning the Silver Star and Bronze Star. After receiving three Purple Hearts, you requested and received reassignment to the United States. Many took exception to the Purple Hearts awarded to you. Your wounds were suspect, so insignificant as to not be worthy of the award of such a medal. That you would seek the Purple Heart for such wounds is a mockery of the intent of the Purple Heart and an abridgement of the valor of those to whom the Purple Heart had been awarded with justification. A normal tour of duty in Vietnam was at least one year for all personnel. You requested to leave Vietnam after four months. You're also the only known Swiftee who received the Purple Heart for a self-inflicted wounds. None of your Purple Hearts were for serious injuries. They were concededly minor scratches at best, resulting in no lost duty time. Each Purple Heart decoration is very controversial, with considerable evidence – and in two of the cases, with incontrovertible and conclusive evidence – that the minor injuries were caused by your own hand and were not the result of hostile fire of any kind. They are a subject of ridicule within your unit. A witness to two of your war wounds and Bronze Star say you're a fraud. There were those in your Coastal Division who turned down Purple Hearts because, when the medals were offered, these honorable men felt they did not really deserve them.

To cheat by getting a Purple Heart from a self-inflicted wound would be regarded as befitting the lowest levels of military conduct. To use such a fake award to leave a combat sector early would be lower yet. Finally, to make or use faked awards as the basis for running for President of the United States, while faulting one's political opponents for not having similar military decorations, would represent unbelievable hypocrisy and the truly bottom rung of human conduct. Anyone engaging in such conduct would be unfit for even the lowest rank in the Navy, to say nothing of the commander in chief.

John, there was another JFK. The real one. The one you aspire to be. He also was from Massachusetts and skippered a little PT boat similar to yours, but in World War II and in the Blackett Straits. Kennedy was later awarded the Navy and Marine Corps Medal for his heroics in the rescue of the crew of PT 109, as well as the Purple Heart Medal. He was everything you and many of us wanted to be. John Fitzgerald Kennedy was a great man and a great president. You, John Fitzhugh Kearney, are not a great man and will not be a great president. Kennedy took us to the moon. Kearney will tax it.

Applauds and laughter emanated from the audience until Jim Leer held up his hand to quiet them.

KEARNEY: Mr. Burk, I knew John Kennedy, and yes he was my hero as much as you are not. You were not there with me, and you have no right or solid ground to regurgitate those false accusations. You have turned this debate into a referendum on my honorable service not to mention a self-serving attempt to further your own cause.

BURK: John, I told you not to go there.

LEER: Ok Gentleman, I believe that is enough of a detour. Let's try getting this back on tract.

They continued for the next hour back and forth but the damage was done and neither was relenting or giving an inch. Finally, it got so bad and out of control that Jim Leer had to shut it down.

LEER: Gentlemen, it's unfortunate that things turned out as they did, but I can see no further gains to be had by continuing. That brings us to closing statements. It was a coin toss. Mr. Burk, you won the toss and you elected to go last, so you have a closing two minutes, Mr. Vice President.

KEARNEY: Well, Jim, I want to thank you and Hofstra University, but I think the debate was hijacked. I will at least try and end with optimism.

You know, eight years ago, we were going through a major crisis. And yet my faith and confidence in the American future is undiminished. And the reason is because of its people, because of the woman I met in North Carolina who decided at 55 to go back to school because she wanted to inspire her daughter and now has a job from that new training that she's gotten; because a company in Minnesota who was willing to give up salaries and perks for their executives to make sure that they didn't lay off workers during a recession.

The auto workers that you meet in Toledo or Detroit take such pride in building the best cars in the world, not just because of a paycheck but because it gives them that sense of pride that they're helping to build America. And so the question now is how we build on those strengths. And everything that I've tried to do, and everything that I'm now proposing for the next four years in terms of improving our education system or developing American energy or making sure that we're closing loopholes for companies that are shipping jobs overseas and focusing on small businesses and companies that are creating jobs here in the United States, or closing our deficit in a responsible, balanced way that allows us to invest in our future, builds on those strengths.

All those things are designed to make sure that the American people, their genius, their grit, their determination, is – is channeled and – and they have an opportunity to succeed. And everybody's getting a fair shot. And everybody's getting a fair share – everybody's doing a fair share, and everybody's playing by the same rules.

You know, eight years ago, I said that I wasn't a perfect man and I wouldn't be a perfect secretary of state. And that's probably a promise that Mr. Burk thinks I've kept. But I also promised that I'd fight every single day on behalf of the American people, the middle class, and all those who were striving to get into the middle class. I've kept that promise, and if you'll vote for me, then I promise I'll fight just as hard as your president.

LEER: Mr. Burk, your two-minute closing.

BURK: Thank you, Jim, Mr. Vice President, and Hofstra University. And thank you America for putting up with this.

This is an important election, and I'm concerned about America. I'm concerned about the direction America has been taking over the last 60 years.

I know this is bigger than an election about the two of us as individuals. It's bigger than our respective parties. It's an election about the course of America. What kind of America do you want to have for yourself and for your children?

And there really are two very different paths that we began speaking about this evening.

But they lead in very different directions. And it's not just looking to our words that you have to take in evidence of where they go. You can look at the record.

There's no question in my mind that if the vice president were to be elected, you would continue to see a middle-class squeeze with incomes going down and prices going up.

I'll get incomes up again.

You'll see chronic unemployment. We've had 43 straight months with unemployment above 8 percent.

If I'm president, I will help create 12 million new jobs in this country with rising incomes.

If the vice president is elected, the Affordable Health Care Program should finally be fully up and running. In my view, that's going to mean a whole different way of life for people who counted on the insurance plan they had in the past. Many will lose it. You're going to see health premiums go up by some $2,500 per family.

If I'm elected, we will make the Affordable Health Care Program work and make everyone join it—including the president and congress. We'll put in place the kind of principles that allow each state to craft their own programs to get people insured and we'll focus on getting the cost of health care down, deductibles down and co-pay down.

If the vice president were to be elected, you're going to see a $716 billion cut to Medicare. You'll have 4 million people who will lose Medicare Advantage. You'll have hospital and providers that'll no longer accept Medicare patients. I'll restore that $716 billion to Medicare.

And finally, military. If the vice president is elected, you'll see dramatic cuts to our military. The secretary of defense has said these would be devastating.

I will not cut our commitment to our military. But we will not interfere with other countries politics and problems. I will keep America strong and get all Americans working again. Get Congress to once again function. Get the sick and the elderly cared for. The young educated, and the disenfranchised welcomed. I will abolish the IRS and institute a flat sale tax and make our out of control big government be once again responsible to the people. All the people.

I will pay down the $15 trillion deficit, created by the last four Republican and Democratic administrations. It has been their tactic to kick it down the road for our children to inherit, but not on my watch!

Thank you, Jim.

LEER: Thank you, Mr. Burk.

Thank you, Mr. Vice President.

Burk knew he won whatever there was to win and Vice President Kearney knew he lost. Riley was thankful that Burk behaved himself and had not walked across the aisle and punched the vice president in the face in front of the entire world.

CHAPTER 74

WHITE HOUSE, OVAL OFFICE

The next morning, the president had the vice president in her office at 7am. She had not renounced him, but after the previous night she could see he was a defeated man.

"Get yourself together, John," said the president. "You can beat this guy. You need to beat him senseless. I want my daughter out from under his Svengali grip. You just need to push the right buttons and he will come unglued. He will snap. You got to get one more debate with him and get him to lose it in front of the nation."

"I am afraid it will take more than that," said the vice president.

"Where do you mean John?"

"Madam President, we have too much at stake to allow Burk to be president. Enticing your daughter into his web is a slap in your face, and that's just the beginning. If he gets in, he will destroy everything we have built and then he will come after us. We should have taken care of him the first time but for Miler's ineptitude."

Now Kearney seemed to be coming into his own. It's like the debate shook him awake, and he was now going to sink or swim on his own. His honor has been challenged in front of the world and he is now going to throw down the gauntlet. *He should have challenged Burk to a duel right then during the debate. It could have been the Burr–Hamilton duel all over again. With himself in the roll of Vice President Burr mortally wounding Hamilton.*

"You know Madam President I have an idea. Why don't you put pressure on Burk's team, through the media, to get me another debate. I don't care how you do it, but do it. I don't care where, but make it someplace warm and outside. Weehawken New Jersey would be nice. I just need one more shot"

The president, seeing for the first time her prodigy coming into his own, did nothing to dash that illusion.

CHAPTER 75

BURK FOR PRESIDENT HEADQUARTERS

October 17th.

Burk, Cassy Hilton, Kelly Sullivan, Riley and team sat around a plywood table on the third floor of their Lexington Avenue campaign office. Riley had resigned as NYPD police commissioner to join Burk's team as security director. He will take over the FBI when Burk gets into office.

Kelly said she had been getting pressure from the media to schedule another debate between Burk and Kearney She said her state campaign leaders were also getting pressure, and the media was going to put it out that Burk was scared and hiding something. The entire team was against it. The race was now Burk's to lose, and the election was only three weeks away.

"Kelly, did anyone from Kearney's office contact you?" asked Burk.

"Yes," replied Kelly. "David Arod himself called about an hour ago saying his campaign was getting pressure for another debate."

"Do you believe that?" asked Burk.

"Not in a New York minute," she replied.

"What else did he say?"

"He said they would go with whatever format you want; they just ask that it be in a warm climate and outside. He said he needs an answer today."

At that, Burk looked at Riley and both men seemed to instantly understand something.

Cassy Hilton had a campaign swing to get ready for, so she excused herself. She and Burk had a brief private conversation, and then she and her team left. Riley excused the rest of the team and that left just Burk, Kelly and himself.

"You're not going to do it, Tommy, are you?" asked Kelly.

Burk ignored her and said to Riley, "Are you thinking what I'm thinking?"

Riley nodded. "Warm and outside"

Kelly had gotten to know both men and how they instinctively communicated. They knew something from what Arod told her, that she had missed. "'Warm and outside' – is that supposed to mean something?"

Riley said, "They – that is the president and vice president – want the debate, and they are using the media to make it happen. Kearney is desperate and will do anything. He doesn't want a debate. Hell, you just handed him his lunch."

"That's another puzzle to me, handed him his lunch" said Burk. "Is that related to I'll eat your lunch?"

Riley knew Burk was playing with him, but this was about to get serious. Deadly serious, if they were correct.

Burk said, "He wants to debate me outside in a warm climate. He knows he's finished. He couldn't even beat Christie now. He has to take it to the next level, a level where he and the president are comfortable. They know we will destroy them and everything they stand for once in office, so we have left them no alternative. They want me alright. They want me outside and warm. With buildings, open windows, people, noise, traffic and a security nightmare. They want me dead.

"Kelly, what's our schedule for the next week?"

Kelly, momentarily taken aback by what Burk just said, snapped out of it and answered. "San Francisco/LA on Tuesday the 20th, Phoenix/Santa Fe the 21st, and Dallas/Baton Rouge the 22nd. Again, Kelly could see Burk and Riley make eye contact and she knew they already decided. Kelly look across the table and both men looked directly at her and mouthed "Dallas."

"Why don't we invite the vice president to join us in Dallas on the 22nd?" suggested Burk. "I believe we are scheduled for a campaign stop at the Dallas

Trade Mart. Why not set aside a couple of hours outside the mart for a little debate?"

Riley said, "It will be a security nightmare. They will love it."

"Then that settles it," said Burk. "Let's allow Vice President JFK to finally arrive where his hero president JFK never did—the Dallas Trade Mart. It's only a little over fifty years late and a month early."

CHAPTER 76

WASHINGTON, DC

White House, the Vice President's Office.

The Vice president and David Arod were discussing last night's debate between Kirsten Gillmartin and Cassy Hilton. The first and only debate between the two vice presidential candidates ended in a draw. A class act, not the cat fight the press was hoping for. The gals got their parties points and platforms across and did it in class and style. Leaving some in the audience to wonder if the party tickets wouldn't be bettered reversed.

David's cell rang. "Kelly, thank you for getting back to me so quickly." As the vice president listened, Arod nodded, said "wonderful," and gave a thumbs up to the vice president. When the call ended, Arod told him. "We got the debate for October 22nd, in Dallas. They gave us another shot."

"That's all I ask for David. Just one more shot. Did they agree to have it outside?" asked the vice president.

"Affirmative."

"Where?"

"The Dallas Trade Mart"

"Ok, set it in motion, release it to the press, and I will see you back here later this afternoon."

After Arod left his office, the vice president picked up his phone and called FBI Director Johns. Johns replaced Miller as director. When they were connected, the vice president asked for an update on their discussion yesterday. The vice president listened, nodded and said, "I will have Secretary of State Miller get right back to you" and hung up. The vice president called Miller and said, "Dallas the 22nd, outside the Dallas Trade Mart," and hung up.

CHAPTER 77

J Edgar Hoover FBI Building

Washington, DC

Agent Hoar had been cooling his heels for the last few months since his unceremonious return to Washington. Burk was right about he being the brunt of Barney Fife jokes, and why not? He would do the same thing to another agent, if the shoe were on the other foot. His face healed, but his finger never would. At least not in appearance. Agent Hoar was assigned, as a minor do nothing staff assistant, to FBI Director Johns and had plenty of time on his hands. He was embarrassed, mad, disgusted. But he was also vindictive and somehow, somewhere, sometime, he would get Riley and Burk – aka "the Grave Diggers," as he and the Bureau were now calling Riley and Burk – and make them pay.

Hoar was also a former Marine and combat vet. He was a corporal and scout-sniper with 3ʳᵈ BN Recon, around the same time the Grave Diggers were in Viet Nam. And as Marines say, "Payback is a mother fucker." Hoar had been a legend of sorts among the North Vietnamese Army and his fellow Marines. He had forty three confirmed kills and another twenty probable. To which the NVA placed a $10,000 bounty on his head.

Hoar was also not liked by his teammates and many teams would not insert with him. He had an argument with one well-liked and respected team leader, regarding the verifiability of several confirmed kills and that generated into a real quarrel. It all came to head one day during an ambush. The team leader was shot in the back at a fairly close range. The bullet passed right through so there was no proof, only speculation by the surviving team members that Hoar 'Fragged' the team leader. Hoar denied the accusation but without proof, no formal charges were brought up. 3rd BN Recon added $5,000 to the NVA bounty. Unfortunately no one collected. Hoar asked for and received an immediate transfer to the rear and was assigned to a unit of the 1st Military Police Battalion. He spent the next three months dodging assassination attempts by former team members and the Viet Cong. One nearly succeeded, when Hoar was literally 'Fragged' while asleep in his bunk. Someone tossed a grenade into his hooch. It exploded but Hoar had taking to sleeping with his flack jacked on, which took most of the serious shrapnel. He ended up with some metal in his legs and a mild concussion. No Purple Heart was written up for him. Hoar enjoyed his stint as a military police officer, busting up bar fights and locking up whores. Unless they became Hoar's Whores, then they were protected. Life in the rear was good for Hoar and he was becoming the poster boy for the REMF's. Real Echelon Mother Fuckers.

But yesterday things changed when Director Johns called Hoar into his office. Would he be willing to accept an assignment so secret, so black that he could never disclose it to anyone? Would he be willing to settle an old score with the person who took his reputation and his finger?

Hoar answered "yes" to both and was told to sit tight but go to the rifle range and continue snapping in.

He had been keeping his sniper skills sharp by spending a couple days a week snapping-in at the FBI range at Quantico. He was aware he was being followed by other agents and knew, they knew, what he was doing. Unlike his old USMC issued M-40 Viet Nam sniper rifle, he now used an FBI issued Remington XM2010 Enhanced Sniper Rifle, chambered in .300-7.62 Winchester Magnum. It had a Leupold Mark 4 E/RT 6.5-20x with H58 Horus reticle and an Advanced Armament Corp TiTan sound suppressor with 5-round detachable magazine. An effective range of close to a mile. He also snapped-in, using green and silver-tipped explosive rounds.

Hoar's cell rang, and he was told he would be met outside the range in one hour. A white van parked in the rest stop a half mile from the range entrance. He would then receive his orders.

CHAPTER 78

Burk for President Headquarters

October 18th

Burk and Sullivan were getting ready for the campaign swing from San Francisco through Baton Rouge while Riley and his team organized security. Riley's NYPD assistant Captain Bounty and his former driver, Sergeant Tanner, had both resigned from the NYPD and joined Burk's team and had been read in on the current developments. With plenty of on-board assets and contract personnel, Riley and Burk had put together a plan for the Dallas debate, and Riley was now implementing it.

Both Riley and Burk knew what was going to happen, and they took a chance on who the vice president would call upon to deliver the message. Hoar was first on their list, and Riley's and Bounty's asset in the Washington locked onto Hoar and set up a surveillance team. No sooner had they started their surveillance when they noticed the bureau had its own team, admittedly trainees, already trailing Hoar. This was going to get interesting.

On a secure line, Bill Dell, a former Miami Police Department detective, reported back to his contact, Captain Bounty, that Hoar had been at the Quantico range snapping in for several weeks previous to their contract, and he was there today. Before entering today, however, he had a liaison with a white van outside the gate, and they were able to record the conversation. Bounty had Dell send the recording to his secure smart phone and told Dell to continue mission. They had their man.

Burk was a major presidential candidate, and as such, was entitled to full Secret Service protection, which Riley and Bounty would use cautiously. The vice president also has Secret Service protection, and the Secret Service all trained and played together – and they all reported to the Secret Service director who served at the pleasure of the president.

Bounty had his advance team already down in Dallas securing rooms and coordinating security.

This was all heading exactly where Riley and Burk thought it would. Vice President Kearney and the Democrats were in trouble. If they lose this election, seats in the House and Senate will also be lost. If that happens they will never survive. This was becoming a death match and Kearney was about to strike that match.

CHAPTER 79

DALLAS, TEXAS

October 19th

The Dallas Trade Mart, the second Dallas Market Center building, opened its doors in 1958. The Trade Mart was the destination of President Kennedy's motorcade in 1963 when he was assassinated in Dealey Plaza. President Kennedy was scheduled to give a speech to 2,600 people at a sold-out luncheon in the Grand Courtyard. In 1964, English sculptor Elisabeth Frink created the bronze sculpture "The Eagle" which sits outside the main entrance today. It features a William Blake quote and a plaque which reads, "Placed in memorial by the friends of President John Fitzgerald Kennedy who awaited his arrival at the Dallas Trade Mart Nov. 22, 1963."

The Dallas Trade Mart, part of a four-building campus, is in a much more open area than the city of Dallas. It is, as the crow flies, two miles from where Kennedy was shot on Elm Street on November 22, 1963.

There were several hotels in the Mart's vicinity including a Holiday Inn 250 yards away, a Renaissance hotel 340 yards away, and a huge Hilton complex across Stemmons Freeway at 516 yards away. There were overpasses, underpasses, train tracks, and a lot of warehouses. In other words, plenty of opportunities for a sniper's nest. All Captain Bounty had to do was follow the sniper and find his nest. He already knew the snipers weapon of choice and his preferred ammo.

Bounty's Dallas front man was Heminio Dias Garcia, aka Angel, out of Miami. He along with his associate Eladio Del Valle, aka Leopold, were both Cuban exiles with former CIA affiliation. They did not like the FBI. Bounty had sent them to Dallas to work with the Dallas Police and the Trade Mart to plan what was being called, by Angel and Leopold, 'The Big Event II.'

Dallas Southwest Patrol Division Deputy Chief Jim Leavelle Jr., Angel and Leopold met at the Dallas Trade Mart with Herman Green, head of the Mart's security, and Sandy Summer, the Mart's special events planner. Their task was to agree on a site plan for the debate including where the podiums are situated, seating, a/v, traffic control, security, etc.

As soon as the basic logistics were settled, Angel sent a thumb-nail sketch plan, through his secure smart phone to Bounty and the rest of the "Big Event II" team. After it was approved by Riley, Kelly immediately forwarded it to David Arod.

Hoar left Reagan Airport aboard an FBI Lear jet. He was accompanied by FBI Assistant director George Veniz. Hoar's FBI tail was no longer necessary, as Veniz would be his onsite handler. Over Richmond, Assistant Director Veniz's phone beeped. He looked at the screen, and the plan layout for the Dallas Trade Mart debate opened. By the time they were over Nashville, the FBI techs in Washington had several possible sniper nests located along with yardage, wind, best elevation suggestions, etc. The final decision, however, would be Hoar's alone.

On the Lear's LED screen, Veniz opened Goggle Earth Pro, and within seconds they were in virtual Dallas just outside the Trade Mart entrance. They were able to walk through the entire area in 3D. Hoar immediately saw the perfect nest, for the perfect shot.

Hoar and Veniz landed at Dallas Love Field and were met by an agent from the Dallas field office. Within minutes they were at the Dallas Trade Mart. Veniz was not impressed with the Mart and its surroundings. The building, the exhibits, the outside – it looked tired, appeared as though time stood still from the 1960s. Hoar could not have cared less. He was looking across the freeway toward what would be the perfect sniper nest; The Hilton Anatole. Hoar eyeballed the shot at 525 yards. He would nail that down once he was in place. It would be a very easy shot. From the stage and podium plan that Veniz received, Hoar located the exact spot Burk would be. Of course, there was no stage and podium yet, but they would be set up soon. They got back in their car and were driven across the street to the Hilton.

The Washington office had already put several Mart facing rooms, at different locations and floors on hold. Hoar could sample them before deciding which room presented the best shot.

Bill Dell, aka Bernardo De Torres, arrived at Love Field only minutes after Hoar and Veniz. Dell, along with Angel, now had Hoar and Veniz in their sights and followed them from the Mart into the Hilton parking lot. They watched as Hoar went to the reception desk while Veniz stayed in the car. After Hoar went in to check out the rooms, Dell and Angel slipped in the side entrance. They headed to the registration desk and asked to see the manager.

Dell, flashing fake Secret Service credentials, got Assistant Hotel Manager, Susan Weeks' attention. Weeks, invited Dell and Angel into her office. She had just heard yesterday about the Dallas presidential debate but until this minute, didn't realize exactly how it would affect her and the Hilton. Of course, she would give whatever assistance they required, and yes she understood the need for stealth and confidentiality.

Hoar, meanwhile, checked into a north facing room on the 15th floor, under the name of Oscar H. Lima. The 30-floor hotel tower was built in 1980 and therefore the room windows opened, but Hoar had no intention of opening any windows. At least not for the shot.

Immediately after Hoar aka Lima checked in, Dell received a phone call from Weeks. She told Dell the man whose picture he showed her, checked into Room 1508 on the 15th floor, under the name of Oscar H. Lema, and that the instructions Dell gave her earlier, have been followed. She also mentioned that the two rooms on either side of Mr. Lima's were also reserved but under different names. Since these reservations occurred almost simultaneously to Lima reserving 1508, she thought this not a coincidence.

All this information was forwarded back to Bounty and on to Riley and Burk. Now they knew the sniper, his weapon, the nest, and possible alternate nests.

Dell had policed Hoar's brass from the Quantico range, so they knew what ammo Hoar would use. They knew the time and location because that was something they controlled. They would, of course, continue to watch Hoar in case he decided to change rooms or move to another location. They were hesitant about bugging the room because they knew Hoar and Veniz had the wherewithal to sweep the room, and they didn't want the hunters to know they were now the hunted.

Veniz stayed in a different hotel as he didn't want to be seen in the Hilton with Hoar. They did, however, have dinner that evening at Pappas Brothers Steakhouse just north of Love Field and just 15 minutes from the hotel.

During dinner, Veniz gave Hoar his marching orders. He was to snap in at least once at a private ranch that had been previously arranged. There were no local outdoor shooting clubs with the range and privacy he needed.

The next day Veniz picked Hoar up at the Hilton. Veniz had been keeping the Remington XM2010 sniper rifle at the Dallas FBI field office in case a nosy hotel house keeper stumbled on it. They drove 50 minutes northwest, to a private 800-acre ranch. As scheduled, no one was home so they had the land to themselves. Hoar found a hill at the right elevation and walked off the 525 yards down and set out a three watermelons. Back up the hill now, with his smartphone GPS, Hoar verified the yardage. Hoar opened the case, disguised to look like a small roll-on suitcase, assembled the rifle, and inserted the five round magazine loaded with the green- and silver-tip explosive ammo.

Hoar began the snap-in and dope adjustment for a 30 degree, 525 yard shot. With Veniz acting as his spotter, Hoar squeezed off the first shot. His shot was not at the watermelon but a tree stump. The report was suppressed, and the hit was slightly off but quite visible if not impressive. He performed a slight adjustment and fired again at the same stump. His second shot was perfect. With the dope set, he proceeded to aim at the watermelons, where the hits would closely simulate what would happen if it were a man's head. At each shot, each watermelon exploded into tiny green chunks and pink mist and then like magic, vanish. Exactly as expected. Hoar noted the dope into his notebook for future reference. They didn't bother to go back down to check the damage as there was nothing left to check. Veniz policed the brass, while Hoar dissembled the rifle and replaced it gently into the case.

CHAPTER 80

DALLAS, TEXAS

October 22nd

The second and final debate was set for 12 noon. Dallas time at the Dallas Trade Mart. The moderator would be Candy Caley, *CNN's* chief political correspondent. The debate would be two hours and focus on domestic and foreign affairs. The stage, podiums and TV camera pool were in place as well as media and VIP seating. Market Center Boulevard was closed to traffic to allow the thousand anticipated spectators room to see and hear the debate. Behind and above the stage, affixed to the Marts façade was a huge LED screen so the assembled would not miss a trick.

Hoar had room service brought in for breakfast, and after the service was removed, he placed a 'Do Not Disturb' sign on his door. He had taken off his latex gloves to administer the tip and replaced them when the cart was removed. He had spent the last couple of days watching the stage be set up and selecting a default and alternate egress for when his business was complete. He decided there was nothing to obstruct his shot from his room thus making the need for the adjacent rooms redundant. Hoar called Veniz, who promptly cancelled the two adjacent rooms.

This information was immediately forwarded to Dell by Susan Weeks.

After breakfast Hoar placed the room coffee table back from the window and half closed the sheer curtains. He turned the AC off and slightly cracked the window.

Hoar collected his breakfast tray and placed it on the floor outside his door. He made sure the 'Do Not Disturb' sign was still attached to the door lever, then checked to make sure the door was locked and set his 'tell tail'. He then took the elevator to the lobby and left the hotel. With a straw hat and sunglasses to offer a passing disguise, he took the hotel shuttle across Stemmons Freeway to stand near the stage in front of the Mart. His mission was to look back at his room to see what the other rooms look liked. Did they have their sheer curtain and sleep curtains closed or open?

He immediately saw what must be hotel policy. The hotel was almost completely full, mostly with media types, yet most of the rooms had their sheer curtains closed. His room looked, aside from the half closed sheers, exactly like every other room. There was no indication that his window was slightly opened. But he knew the Secret Service would be using binoculars to scan each Mart facing window.

He waited for the hotel shuttle to take him back to the hotel. Towards the elevator he again donned his latex gloves, selected the 15th. floor and walked to his room. He checked the 'Do Not Disturb' sign and noticed the 'tell tail,' fine thread on the door handle, put his key in and entered. Ten minutes later, a call from the front desk announced a visitor and Hoar asked them to let him up. Hoar went to his window and closed the shears completely. A knock on the door announced the visitor had arrived, and Hoar, getting the correct pass word, opened the door and accepted the suitcase. Hoar thanked the man, double checked to make sure the 'Do Not Disturb' sign remained in place, closed the door, and double locked it.

It was about thirty minutes to noon and Hoar went to the window and peeked through the curtains down into the now assembled crowd. It was wall-to-wall people, media and security. He saw SWAT teams on roofs and helicopters in the sky, some belonging to the media, and some to the DPD and Secret Service.

Hoar began his preparation. He began by assembling the rifle and inserting the explosive rounds into the magazine. He check the bolt action, checked the firing pin, extended the stock, let down the bipods and attached the suppressor. The scope was never removed. He checked the dope with his notes, and everything checked. He inserted the magazine and was now ready chamber a round. But that could wait.

Also in the suitcase was a fully charged electric drill with a 4-inch-diameter carbide tip glass cutting saw. The saw was modified with a built in suction cup to grab and retain the glass once the hole was cut.

The first thing Hoar inspected, when he first checked in, was the glass thickness. Since the hotel was older, the glass was single light, non-thermal glass; in other words, pretty much what you have in an old house. He had previously measured the hole location and had it centered 6 inches from the sill and 6 inches from the right jamb. With the AC off and the window cracked a little, the inside/outside temperature and air pressure was consistent. The room was hot. He duplicitously applied a clear 6x6 film over the intended hole area and soaked the round carbide saw with oil. He then pressed the drill against the glass and quietly and slowly began to grind it. When about half way through, he applied more oil and engaged the suction cup. He finished the cut. Removed the saw with the glass and then removed the film. Nothing happened. The drapes didn't move or flutter and that was a good thing.

He closed the window and placed a chair behind the low coffee table and set the rifle on the table. He folded the lower right sheer curtain into itself only enough to provide a sight line through the hole.

He then went behind the rifle and snapped in. The suppressor end was just through the hole, and Hoar was back from the window about four feet. Proxies for both Burk and Kearney were at the podiums giving the TV cameras, lighting and a/v cues. Hoar snapped in on Burk's proxies head and visualized the shot.

He released the curtain fold and waited. His room phone rang with last minute instructions. He was told exactly when to take the shot.

Dell and Angel were in Susan Weeks' office when that call came and were able to tap in.

CHAPTER 81

DALLAS, TEXAS

October 22ⁿᵈ

Texas Governor Rick Perry had stopped by, as had Senator Ted Cruz and Mayor Mike Rawings. Andy Midas friend and Burk's Texas campaign manager, Pinky Friedman was there most of the morning making sure everything went like clockwork. In fact, just about every Texan who's who had stopped by. Burk, Riley, Sullivan and Friedman were in one of two VIP lounges in the Trade Mart's office area. Kearney, David Arod, and his entourage were in the other. The other Secret Service agents were all over the Mart, inside and out. On roofs, in cars, and in the audience. They were checking all the high-rise buildings for open windows, and if found, an agent was dispatched to check it out.

At fifteen minutes 'til show time, Burk was cool as a cucumber. Riley could never get over how Burk managed to keep it together so well – or hide it so well. Many times in moments of sheer terror during combat, he and Burk, as leaders, would try and remain cool and steady under fire, especially while on the radio. Riley had to work at it, but to Burk it came naturally. Once Riley had broached the subject with Burk, who just shrugged and said, "I'll know when I going to die. And when that time comes I'll let you know. Until then, I'll fake it."

Riley had pulled out all the stops for the "Big Event II," but if things went south they would go so very quickly with no turning back. It was all about timing and luck. Smoke and mirrors.

Burk, Riley, Bounty, Dell and his team knew what was about to happen. And, of course, so did the vice president's and his assassins.

Both camps received the five minute warning and started to get up and get moving. Following the assigned Secret Service detail, Burk, Riley and Sullivan moved down the corridor but were halted for a few seconds while the vice president's detail took the lead.

Outside, Mayor Rawlings was wrapping up his introduction speech and finally said. "Ladies and Gentlemen, distinguished guests, fellow Texans and Americans, please welcome to Dallas for their second and final debate, Vice President John Fitzhugh Kearney and Mr. Thomas Dean Burk. Ms. Candy Caley of *CNN*, is today's moderator."

With that, Burk and Kearney entered the stage from different sides to a standing ovation.

Burk and Kearney headed directly toward one another and shook hands. There were no smiles or back pats just cold hard stares. Kearney was looking directly into the eyes of a dead man and Burk was looking into the eyes of his killer.

The vice president leaned into Burk and said, "There is nothing between us now Burk, but air and fear."

Burk had no idea why Kearney would choose a Marine Corps challenge; a squid had no right, but Burk would oblige. Burk puckered his lips and sucked in a deep breath the air and said, "Now it's just your fear, Kearney."

The two men parted and moved to their respective podiums.

CALEY: Good evening from the Dallas Trade Mart, in beautiful, warm and sunny Dallas, Texas. I'm Candy Caley, *CNN* Chief Political Correspondent, and I welcome you to the second and final presidential debates between Vice President John Fitzhugh Kearney, the Democratic nominee, and New York bombing hero Thomas Dean Burk, the Independent nominee.

This debate is sponsored by the Commission on Presidential Debates. Today's 60 minutes will be about domestic and foreign issues and will follow a format designed by the commission. There will be six segments with two-minute answers for the first question, then open discussion for the remainder of each segment.

The segments, as I announced in advance, will be three on the economy and one each on health care, the role of government and governing, with an emphasis throughout on differences, specifics and choices. Both candidates will also have two-minute closing statements.

The audience here has promised to remain silent – no cheers, applause, boos, hisses, among other noisy distracting things – so we may all concentrate on what the candidates have to say. There is a noise exception right now, though, as we welcome Vice President Kearney and Mr. Thomas Burk.

(APPLAUSE)

Gentlemen, welcome to you both. Let's start with health care, segment one, and let's begin with The Affordable Health Care Act. Why is it still not working, and how would you go about fixing it? Each of you have two minutes to start. A coin toss has determined, Mr. Vice President, you go first.

KEARNEY: Well, thank you very much, Candy, for this opportunity. I want to thank Mr. Burk for joining me and Dallas for its hospitality.

You know, eight years ago we went through the worst financial crisis since the Great Depression...

Burk's mind was now in slow motion mode as he block out the vice president's gobblygook. He looked directly across Stemmons Freeway at the Hilton Towers and at the approximate 15th Floor location.

Burk knew from the intercepted phone message that Hoar would take the shot when it was his turn to speak to guarantee the cameras would be focused directly on him. Burk slowly raised his left hand, and placed two fingers across his lips. Sort of the victory sign. Slowly he curled his index finger down to resemble a stump, leaving only his middle finger extended. To the public, it appeared as though he was contemplating his next thought. He smiled at Hoar whom he knew would have his remaining right index finger on the trigger and his focus on him. Little did Burk know that this taunt would become the basis for multiple conspiracies theories for the next fifty years.

Across the freeway in Room 1508 Hoar watched as Burk appeared to be taunt him. *But how could that be possible? He couldn't possibly know I am here and about to blow his fucken head off. If he did know, then he would an idiot, oblivious or both.*

At exactly 12:30 p.m., just as the vice president was finishing blaming Bush for the current health care disaster, Hoar, chambered a round, slowed his breathing and placed the cross hairs directly between Burk's eyes. From the TV by the window, Hoar heard Caley ask the same question of Burk, and Burk's face filled the TV screen. He gently squeezed the trigger and took up the slack. *BOOM.* The head exploded in a shower of red, white and pink mist above the stage. His body remained upright for a second then dropped behind the podium. Everyone was ducking and screaming as Secret Service agents rushed forward in an attempt to prevent further carnage and to cover the body. Everyone and everything was in complete and utter confusion and chaos. As in a fog, Hoar sat behind the rifle watching the events unfurl as if in slow motion.

Loud footsteps from the room above and the slamming of a door brought Hoar back to the moment. He got up, put his straw hat and sunglasses on, and quickly left the room. Nothing in the room could be tied to him. He called for the elevator, got in and pushed the lobby button. He then removed his latex gloves.

The loud footsteps Hoar had heard above him were those of Angel. The *Boom* he heard was Leopold taking the shot that exploded the vice president's head.

Leopold did not bother cutting a hole in the glass for his shot; he simply opened the window a crack and took the shot. He had the exact same rifle and ammunition as Hoar. Leopold disassemble the rifle and closed the window. He then removed a co2 canister and shot a whiff of freshener to eliminate any trace of cordite smell. He and his suitcase left the room. While this was happening, Angel walked down one flight of fire stairs and when Hoar disappeared into the elevator for his escape, Angel entered room 1508. Weeks had given Dell an extra room key. Angel tossed a spent cartridge, taken from Hoar's Quantico range snap-in, onto the floor next to the rifle. He then removed a co2 canister and shot a whiff of cordite into the air and onto the glass window around the hole. He exited, got in the elevator, and pushed the garage level button. He removed his latex gloves and rendezvoused with Leopold who was already in the Secret Service Suburban.

When the elevator doors opened, Hoar quickly walked through the lobby and out the hotel entrance. Across the porte-cochere, he could see Agent Veniz sitting shotgun and looking at him.

The hotel lobby appeared bizarre with everyone watching live on *CNN* what was happening live directly across the freeway. Ten minutes before the shooting, at 12:20 p.m., Susan Weeks had followed her orders from Agent Dell and called the number he had given her and relayed the message she was told to deliver. Just moments after the shot was fired, Dallas Southwest Patrol Division Deputy Chief, Jim Leavelle Jr., ran into the lobby and was directed to Susan Weeks. While Weeks was giving Chief Leavelle some additional information about the suspicious man in 1508, she stopped cold. Chief Leavelle followed her gaze and knew instinctively that that was the man. He followed Hoar out the door.

Hoar was about to cross the drive to Veniz and his getaway car. Since the shot, he had been playing out different scenarios, but so far all he could conclude was that he was either doubled crossed or set up. Either way it was not good.

Agent Veniz, sitting in his car and listening to the radio, was having similar confused thoughts. Did he misunderstand that the vice president and not Burk was the target? Did they make the switch without reading him in? Impossible. Did Hoar go rogue and take out the vice president? Probable! As their eyes locked on each other, Veniz was not going to wait and see. He told the driver to step on it. Veniz looked over his shoulder as they sped away and saw two lasting impressions. The first was the look of resignation on Hoar's face and the other was that of a Dallas police officer's service pistol pointing at the back of Hoar's head.

"I am a Dallas police officer. Hands over your head, and down on your knees," said Chief Leavelle.

Hoar turned and seemed to be looking for options when Chief Leavelle struck him with his pistol just above his left eye. As Hoar was now unwillingly complying to Chief Leavelle's previous request, two DPD patrol cars pulled right in front. Chief Leavelle directed the first two officers to search and secure the suspect and had the detective and another officer go with Susan Weeks up to Room 1508.

Hoar was placed in the back of the patrol car while a crowd started to gather. Everything being aired from across the street was now old news. Here they were witnessing live action.

When Detective Lew Roberts, Susan Weeks and Officer Bosh got up to 1508, Roberts put latex gloves on and took the door key from Weeks. He opened the door and told them to stay outside and touch nothing and let no one in. The first thing he noticed was a strong smell of gunpowder. He drew his service pistol and entered the room. He saw the rifle but checked the bathroom, closet and under the bed first. When he was certain no one else was in the room, he looked at the rifle and where it was pointed. He pulled out his cell and called down to Chief Leavelle. One word was all it took: "Positive."

Roberts used his cell to take a few quick pictures of the room, rifle, spent shell, and window. He then backed out of the room. He asked officer Bosh and Ms. Weeks to look in the room. Detective Roberts wanted corroboration. He then closed and locked the door and gave the door key to Patrol Officer Bosh with instructions to let no one in without his direct approval, or he would personally shoot Bosh. Detective Roberts then called homicide and forensics to get them to the crime scene for prints, photos and DNA. He went down to the lobby to fill in the chief and to wait for the cavalry. Chief Leavelle got in the back of the patrol car next to Hoar, who was thought to be a man named Oscar H. Lima. The chief addressed him as Mr. Lima, but Hoar said that was an alias and his real name was Michael Hoar. They would find out soon enough, and besides he didn't do anything wrong. He didn't shoot anybody. With that information now transmitted down the line, Chief Leavelle with Hoar secured next to him in the back seat, headed, with lights and sirens chirping, back to police headquarters. Secret Service Suburban's were now pulling in behind Leavelle as he pulled away from the hotel. He saw the agents jumping out of the SUV's and start running into the hotel. He hoped Roberts could hold on until reinforcements arrived. He didn't want the Secret Service screwing up the crime scene.

At the hotel and across the freeway from the hotel, at the site of the assassination, Secret Service and Dallas Police were just hearing of the arrest. The Dallas Police had released the suspected assassin's name as Michael Hoar.

When Burk heard the shot, he immediately fell flat behind the podium. He was then whisked back into the Trade Mart by the Secret Service, but they were relieved by Riley and his security team. Despite objections by the Secret Service, Burk, Riley, Bounty and Sullivan were escorted back to Love Field, by the DPD and departed Dallas immediately for New York City aboard one of Mayor Bloomfield's jets.

Still a murder scene, Dallas Police demanded custody of the vice president's body. Again the Secret Service objected, but DPD, in one of the Emergency Response vehicles, took the vice president's body and rushed to Parkland Hospital, only minutes away. Although there was no question the vice president was dead, the Dallas Police intended to follow procedure and have him officially pronounced dead and have an autopsy performed. John Fitzhugh Kearney was officially pronounced dead at Parkland Hospitals Trauma 1 Emergency Room at 1 p.m. Dallas time.

By the time Chief Leavelle arrived at police headquarters, the place was packed with reporters. Leavelle had the patrol car enter through the basement entrance where the transfer from the patrol car to the interrogation room could be more easily controlled.

As Chief Leavelle and several officers were leading Hoar down the corridor several reporters began yelling questions. "Mr. Hoar, how did you hurt your eye?"

Hoar replied, "A policeman hit me."

Another yelled, "Did you shoot the vice president?"

Hoar responded, "I didn't shoot anybody. No Sir! I am just a patsy."

While all this was happening, Leavelle remembered the stories his father had told him about the day they captured Lee Harvey Oswald. His father escorted Oswald in a similar fashion just over 50 years ago, and it was all now starting to feel like déjà vu.

The cut over the left eye, he was just a patsy, the Dallas Trade Mart, headshot, Parkland Hospital. The vice president's initials are JFK? Official time of death 1 p.m. Way too many coincidences, and Jim Leavelle didn't believe in coincidences. At least not this many. He would look into them more carefully later. But for now he was on the lookout for one more coincidence which he had no intention of allowing. "Clear everyone out of the building now! No one but DPD is to have access."

There would be no Jacob Rubinstein, aka Jack Ruby, on his watch.

Epilogue

Washington, DC
White House
Monday, January 23rd

The presidential inauguration of Thomas Dean Burk was held in Washington D.C. on Friday, January 20th. A week of festivities included the presidential swearing-in ceremony, inaugural address, inaugural parade, and numerous inaugural balls and galas honoring the elected President of the United States. The president was accompanied at these galas, by Kelly Sullivan, which gave way to interesting speculation.

The Burk-Hilton ticket won by the highest popular vote in American history. Christie-Rubio, bogged down by the interest of the far right, tea tarty, religious right, women and gay issues, and voters who were just plain fed up with business as usual, managed a weak second. There was no third.

President Burk, wanting to head off suspicion or speculation regarding the vice president's murder, convened a commission to investigate the assassination. He asked former President Hilton to head the commission, and she graciously accepted. It would be known as the Hilton Commission. The FBI would be the investigative agency.

The time was 6 a.m. when President Burk finished stretching, sit-ups, and push-ups and was ready for his 10k run. Riley would join him for the run. It would take about 48 minutes, as they were both 8-minute milers. They could run faster, but why? Later that morning, President Burk would put forward to the Senate for confirmation his good friend Riley as FBI director.

They had previously requested and received resignations from Secretary of State Miller, FBI Director Johns, and FBI New York Field Office Assistant Director Veniz. Riley would be confirmed as director, no doubt. When Riley arrived, they said nothing to each other, which was normal among very close male friends and they just started to run. After running alone all his life and running in every city he visited during his years as a consultant, Burk would now run with an entourage, two Secret Service agents in front and two behind. The agents were carrying weapons in their backpacks and Secret Service chase cars were off on the flanks. The protection and route would change daily, but for today, it would be their first and favorite run. They headed south through the many trails leading out of the White House to Constitution Avenue then right past the garden pond, past the Vietnam Veterans Memorial to 23thSt South again to the Rock Creek Park trails and east along the waterfront. North past the basin to the mall. East along the mall to the Capitol than north to Madison Drive and back to the White House. Riley at 66 and Burk at 64 worked up a sweat even though the temperature was in the teens, but their breathing was smooth and controlled. During their run, they discussed a few things but mostly just remained quiet, took in the sights and smells, and kept their thoughts to themselves.

They would meet later for dinner, but for now Burk headed upstairs for a shower and shave. He had an important meeting with the House and Senate leaders at 7 a.m.

Downstairs in the Cabinet Room sat four of the most powerful yet obstructive people in the world: Speaker of the House John Bonner, Minority House Leader Nancy Melosi, Majority Senate Leader Harry Tweed, and Minority Senate Leader Mitch McDonnell.

The president walked into the Cabinet Room at exactly 7 a.m., and all four stood in unison and said, "Good morning, Mr. President." To say they would prefer not to be there would be an understatement. They knew that this would be a severe dressing down at best and sat when the president did.

President Burk began, "You know why I asked you here this morning. You all started out, I am sure, as idealist with good intentions. But somewhere along the way you lost your way. For the last sixteen years – but primarily the last eight with you four as leaders – you prevented Congress from functioning as intended. The American people have paid the price. Instead of consensus, we got confrontation. Instead of teamwork, we got no work.

"Pork barrel bills, special interest lobbyist and term limits rejection have corrupted you and Congress, and I intend to end it all today. I have been promising the American people that I would get our dysfunctional Congress functioning. The only way I know how to that is to remove all four of you from leadership rolls.

"I expect your resignations as Congressional leaders on my desk by noon today."

They did not expect this. Melosi's lips began to quiver, Tweed grabbed his chest, and Bonner began to weep. Only McDonnell sat there stoic, and resigned.

The president continued, "In short, the rules of the U.S. House of Representative and the Senate for the 110th Congress provides for the removal of a seated Speaker or Leader during session, for the purposes of preserving the dignity, and the integrity of its proceedings under the constitutional prerogative of its function with respect to impeachment. Any member of the House or the Senate can bring forth a resolution presenting a question of privilege to declare the Speakership vacant based on this provision.

"You may remain in Congress, but you will not chair or sit on any important committees. Or you can resign your seat. I have already met with your replacements and said resolution has already been presented and accepted unanimously by your peers. But most importantly, they have the full support of the American people and their president. I wish I could say that it has been a pleasure, but it hasn't."

The president stood and as he was walking out he turned back and said, "Do it. Do it by noon and don't fuck with me."

At 7:15 a.m., President Burk was at his desk and his secretary, Noreen Ward. She gave him a copy of his schedule and together they reviewed his week's appointments.

At 7:30 a.m., the director of National Intelligence gave the president his daily update on key international developments and U.S. intelligence operations unfolding overseas.

At 7:50 a.m., Mayor Bloomfield, whose name was previously submitted to Congress and approved for Treasury Secretary, came in and had a seat at the couch. A second later, Kelly Sullivan joined them and President Burk poured each a cup of coffee, while he himself had a can of Diet Coke. The first of four he would have before noon.

The main reason for this meeting was to set in motion the dismantling of the IRS and creating a Fair Tax. The Fair Tax, as proposed by Burk and Bloomfield, would replace all federal income taxes (including the alternative minimum tax, corporate income taxes, and capital gains taxes), payroll taxes (including Social Security and Medicare taxes), gift taxes, and estate taxes with a single broad national consumption tax on retail sales. The *Fair Tax Act* (H.R. 25/S. 122) would apply a tax, once, at the point of purchase on all new goods and services for personal consumption. The proposal also called for a monthly payment to all family households of lawful U.S. residents as an advance rebate, or "prebate," of tax on purchases up to the poverty level. Charity and mortgage deductions would stay in effect. As supporters of the plan, Burk and Bloomfield believed that a consumption tax would have a positive effect on savings and investment, that it would ease tax compliance, and that the tax would result in increased economic growth, incentives for international business to locate in the U.S., and increased U.S. competitiveness in international trade. The plan was intended to increase cost transparency for funding the federal government, and they believed it would have positive effects on civil liberties, the environment, and advantages with taxing illegal activity and undocumented immigrants.

At 8:27 a.m., Noreen Ward knocked on the door and came in. She informed the president that his 8:30 a.m. phone call was standing by.

The president finished up with Treasury Secretary Bloomfield and went to his desk to take the call.

Back in New York Bernie McSorley got the signal from Bigfoot that their secret guest was on the line. Bernie and Midas have been teasing the audience and his regulars about a special guest since they went live this morning at 6:05 a.m. At exactly 8:30 a.m., Andy Midas said, "Please welcome to the program the President of the United States, Thomas Burk. Welcome Mr. President."

"Good morning, Mr. Midas, how are you?"

"Well you know, I have cancer, my shoulder is killing me, and I can't hear. But other than that I am fine."

"That's great to hear," said the president, not taking the bait. "Is Bernie there?"

"I am here, Chief," said Bernie.

"Wait a minute, Bernie, I thought I was chief," said Midas.

"You're the Boss. The president's the Chief," said Bernie.

Knowing the entire team pushed for him and it would mean a lot to them Burk said, "Is the A team there, Midas? Good morning; Connell, Dagen, Tony, Rob. Who won the game last night, Warner?" Before Warner could answer he continued, "Lou, Guns, Bigfoot, Carly, Diane, Bo, is he treating you guys OK? You know I have some openings here in Washington if he isn't."

Midas played along and said exactly what the president and everyone including his audience expected. "You know, Mr. President, this is my show, and I think we ought to be talking about me. Speaking about me and jobs in Washington, I am waiting to see what big cabinet post you are going to offer me for getting you elected?"

"You know we have an opening for the Secretary of Health and Human Services. Kathleen Cibelius has submitted her resignation, and I accepted."

"What ub? You know I can't hear," said Midas "Did you say Secretary of Health and Human Services? Is that because no one else would want it or because I know a lot about being sick?"

The show went on like this for the next five minutes, but the president did take time to thank Midas, Bernie, the team and the audience for launching his presidential bid, and for helping him get elected.

Midas said, "How did you sleep last night, Mr. President?"

"I started out restless but then the Secret Service knocked on my bedroom door and said a package came from you with a note. The note said, 'Take two before bedtime.' I opened the package and two large Mr. Pillows popped out. Thanks, Andy"

"You're welcome Mr. President, but why haven't I been invited down to the Lincoln bedroom yet?

"You, Dede and Cody were invited to the inauguration and didn't come? I had the bedroom all set for you."

"I was busy that night," said Midas. "I had to meet someone. I forget who. You know, you're a pretty good guest and a lot of fun. We like you. Connell, do we like him?"

Connell replied in the affirmative.

"Listen Mr. President, we're glad you won, but don't make me come down there and have to straighten you out."

"You won't have to, Andy. Thank you, Bernie, and the team and all your listeners and viewers for getting me here, and I won't let you down. And Andy, you threaten me again, and the Secret Service will pay you a visit.

The line went dead and Midas said, "The President of the United States calls me in the morning. Ah man, it doesn't get any better than that.

WASHINGTON, DC

White House,
Late evening.

President Burk and FBI Director Riley were sitting in the two side chairs in the seating area of the Oval Office. They were winding down after their first day as President and FBI Director.

"Hungry captain?" Burk asked.

"Sure. What do you feel like?

"Let's see if we can get the kitchen to make us up something." suggested Burk.

Burk got up, went to the desk and pressed the buzzer for the steward who immediately entered into the office.

"Would it be possible Mr. Grimes to have something made up for the director and I to eat?

"Of course, Mr. President." said Tim Grimes the president's steward.

"How about some pasta shells with a meat marinara sauce. Can you ask the chef if he can make it hot? You know, like Vincent's Hot Sauce with some Cheyanne pepper and Cholula Hot Sauce, all mixed in?" asked the president.

"I'm sure *she* can and we will get right on it Mr. President. Will you and director be dinning in the President's Dining Room?" asked Steward Grimes.

"Yes," replied the President. "By the way Mr. Grimes, can you tell us where the President's Dining room is? I am sure our FBI director here could find it but our hot pasta might be cold pasta by then.

"The President's Dining Room is located in the northwest corner of the second floor, Mr. President, and I will be happy to escort you, when dinner is served." Said Steward Grimes.

About twenty minutes later Burk and Riley were seated at the President's Dining Room oval table. It could seat eight but tonight only two would be seated.

Burk, set at the head of the oval table and Riley sat at its opposite end.

Burk was trying to cut down on his champagne consumption so they both had iced tea instead.

The pasta arrived very hot and very spicy hot. After the servers left, Burk asked. "Is the President's Dining Room recorded?"

Riley pulled out his cell and speed dialed the Secret Service duty officer and asked if the room was recorded and the answer was no.

"Since we're on the subject, I want to you to put Bounty in charge of the Secret Service. You good with that Tommy?"

"I'm good," said the Burk. "The previous Secret Service director didn't do such good a job protecting the vice president or both vice presidents for that matter. Yea. I'm good with that.

"What's up for you tomorrow? " Burk asked.

"I have to really get into our domestic terrorist problems. How all our agencies missed the bomb threats and fires? How sleepers got imbedded in the FBI and possibly other agencies? How the FBI was able to import terrorist to hit our convoy? It's a mess and I need to get on top of it and fast."

"When you meet with the agency heads, I would like your recommendation on who we should keep, who we shit-can and who to replace them with," said Burk.

"You got it. You had a busy day today Mr. President. What's on your plate for tomorrow?"

"Money! That's what's on my plate. And throwing good money after bad. You know Captain, we give out over $40 Billion each year in foreign aid. Our wars in Iraq, Afghanistan and Pakistan have cost over $3.5 Trillion.

We have over 300,000 troops based in countries around the world, including 40,000 in Germany and 50,000 in Japan. Why the fuck do we need to protect Germany and Japan? Do we think they are going to attack us again?

And that doesn't even include eleven naval carrier battle groups we have all over the world oceans.

Unless you are a really, really a good ally, you're not going to get shit. And if you want our army and navy protecting your interests, you're going to have pay us for that service. I mean, armies used to make their money by raping and pillaging. And if we can't do that anymore then we have to make money somehow."

Riley knew Burk was putting him on but took the bait anyway. "As Midas would say if he were here, 'that's way too much information.'"

Small talk continued during their quick meal but when the pasta bowls were cleared and tea and coffee served, Riley broached a touchy subject that had been brewing but now needed to be addressed.

"Something's come up with our Dallas friends," said Riley.

"After what happened a few months ago I didn't think we had any friends in Dallas," replied Burk.

It seems this DPD Chief Leavelle along with the Dallas district attorney are going to seek a grand jury indictment against our friend Hoar for the murder of the vice president. You know Hoar has been sitting down there in Dallas in a cell for almost three months," said Riley.

"Are you starting to feel sorry for Hoar? Is that what this is about? Didn't he try to kill me?" asked Burk.

Riley, shaking his head, said "We forgave the former president for trying to kill you. We didn't prosecute Miller for trying to kill you. Hell, they tried to kill me once for Christ sake. Hoar was just following Miller's orders. Both with the evidence planting and the assassination attempt. He hasn't spilled his guts yet. He just sits down there proclaiming his innocence. Actually I think Hoar is 'Hard Core'. A real trooper."

"So why don't we ask President Hilton to subpoena him back here to Washington as part of her Hilton Commission. When he gets here, she can clear him and since you feel so highly about him, you can put him to work for you. Make him your assistant director. That should raise his stature in the agency somewhat and forgive all past sins," suggested Burk.

"You may be right, Tommy. I got a heads-up this afternoon from our Secret Service liaison that Leavelle called the personnel department looking for Dell."

"What did they tell him?" Burk asked.

"Pretty standard response. They asked Leavelle to make the request on DPD stationary and fax it through. They said if it all checks out they will reply to the request," said Riley.

"Jesus Riley! If they find Dell is not with the Secret Service and they find him and he talks, it will come back to Bounty, then you and me."

Riley started laughing and almost chocked. He looked at Burk and stopped laughing. When Burk didn't respond Riley said. "You don't know do you? You really don't know Burk, do you?

"Know what? What's so funny? Fill me in."

"We don't have to worry about Dell and his crew ever talking. Dell, aka Bernardo De Torres, is really Carlos. Carlos along with Leopold, Angle and Leon, aka Lee Harvey Oswald were the three shooters and the patsy who Killed Kennedy in Dealey Plaza in '63, during the original 'Big Event.' They didn't talk then and they ain't gonna talk now. Hell they ain't never gonna be found unless they want to be." said Riley.

"Wow! That's a bit more information than I needed just now but this Chief Leavelle ain't gonna give up. Why did you bring him into the Dallas thing in the first place?" Burk asked.

"We didn't. We needed DPD coverage and he assigned himself. You know his father's relationship to the original 'Big Event' and I guess he didn't want to see another assassination in Dallas."

"Get President Hilton moving on the subpoena, we have other fish to fry.

"You got that right Mr. President and only four years to do it," said Riley.

"Captain, when were alone like this call me Tommy or Burk or Sargent. Ok!"

"I don't like your tone Sargent," said Riley and they both had a good laugh.

When their laughing stopped, Burk said "You're right Captain, four years may not enough."

"You can't go back on our promise not to run for a second term, if that's what you're thinking Tommy," said Riley

"I have no intention of running for a second term."

"Then what do you mean?" Riley asked.

"Remember what I said during the campaign?

"If our form of democracy is to survive, it must first die, be cleansed, and then be reborn.

Do you remember me saying that? Did you think I was kidding?

No Captain. If I can't get this country back on track within my first term, I am not going to run for a second term. I am just going to take it and you're going to help me.

"Today I removed a cancer that has been eating our country from within.

We are now in remission, but we can have a recurrence at any time.

"This country may need a dictator, a benevolent dictator for sure but a dictator never the less. Even with the changes we have made and are about to make, there are those who will fight us.

"The privilege of the writ of habeas corpus shall not be suspended, unless when in cases of rebellion or invasion the public safety may require it.

"I intend to be your president for four years or for however long it takes to get this fucking country back on track."

Riley looked at Burk started laughing. "You're a pistol Tommy, you're really funny."

"What do you mean I'm funny?"

"It's funny, you know. You're a funny guy."

Burk now had Riley where he wanted him. In the middle of another movie scene. This time it was "GoodFellas" and he was playing Tommy DeVito and Riley would play along for awhile, anyway, as Henry Hill.

"What do you mean, you mean the way I talk? What?"

"It's just, you know. You're just funny, it's... funny, the way you say you're going to be a dictator."

"Funny how? What's funny about it?"

"Just... ya know... you're funny."

"You mean, let me understand this cause, ya know maybe it's me, I'm a little fucked up maybe, but I'm funny how, I mean funny like I'm a clown, I amuse you? I make you laugh, I'm here to fuckin' amuse you? What do you mean funny, funny how? How am I funny?"

"Just... you know, how you tell the story, what?"

"No, no, I don't know, you said it. How do I know? You said I'm funny. How the fuck am I funny, what the fuck is so funny about me? Tell me, tell me what's funny!"

"Get the fuck out of here, Tommy!"

"Ya motherfucker! I almost had him, I almost had him. Ya stuttering prick ya. Frankie, was he shaking? I wonder about you sometimes, Henry. You may fold under questioning"

They were both now almost in tears, laughing so hard but Riley was not so sure it was all a joke. He knew Tommy and what he was saying was different than what Riley was seeing in Tommy's eyes. Tommy might have tried to turn everything into a big joke but his eyes told a different story. They were the eyes of Kipling's "The Man who would be King."

Burk seemed to sense Riley's apprehension and seemed to read his mind and said.

"Don't worry Captain, I am not 'The Man Who Would Be King,' besides, 'for what good are treasures and the kingdom if you're a king without a queen'"

Washington, DC

White House
James S. Brady Press Briefing Room
The next day.

The Press Briefing Room is just down the hall from the Oval Office. The president gave his press secretary some last minute updates then she was off to the briefing. Kelly Sullivan stood, for the first time, in front of the entire White House Press Corps as press secretary. After a minute of applause from her peers, they settled down in their seats, and Kelly began to bring them up to date.

"Good morning, ladies and gentlemen," she said. "Thank you for being here this morning. The president has asked me to give you a run down on what he has been up to and then I will open it up for questions. The president had a very busy first day in office, so bear with me.

"Yesterday morning the president asked for and received the resignations of Secretary of State Miller, and FBI Director Johns. The president has put forward respectively to Congress for immediately approval, Colin Powers and Raymond Riley.

"The president has authorized a commission to investigate the murder of the vice president in Dallas, and the commission will be headed by former President Hilton.

"A Fair Tax Act eliminating the current Federal income tax and dismantling the IRS will be voted on this afternoon by the House and sent to the Senate today for approval. It will be approved later today, and the president will sign it into law tonight.

"Additional bills will be voted on by the house today instituting term limits, eliminating professional lobbyists and removing all pork from legitimate bills.

These bills will be approved and submitted by the House today and approved by the Senate tomorrow. The president will sign them into law tomorrow afternoon.

"The president is determined to fix The Affordable Health Care Act and to that end he has asked for and has received the resignation of Secretary of Health and Human Services Kathleen Cibelius. A successor will be named this afternoon by the president in his first Rose Garden address.

"And finally, the president has asked for and received the resignations of Speaker of the House John Bonner, Minority Leader Nancy Melosi, Majority Leader Harry Tweed, and Minority Leader Mitch McDonnell as leaders of Congress. Both the House and Senate have approved and accepted their resignations and have selected and approved their replacements. The new speakers and leaders will be announced this afternoon by the president during his Rose Garden address."

With that the hands went up and questions started flying. Never had so much happened in so little time in the first day of any presidency. Press Secretary Kelly Sullivan looked as though she was going to call on the first reporter but instead she held up her hand to quiet the room. When quiet, she said, right out of Steve Job's playbook, "There is one more thing."

Everyone got very quiet.

"The president has asked me to marry him, and I said yes. Any questions?"